# STEPHEN J. C. ANDES

APOTHEOSIS PRESS



JADE, DAUGHTER OF THE WASTELAND



ISBN: 978-1-953366-60-3

Edited by Stacey Glemboski

Cover Designed by Deranged Doctor Design

www.derangeddoctordesign.com

# AUTHOR'S NOTE

I have it on good authority, from none other than Stephen King himself, that when you write a story and set it in a particular place—say Baton Rouge, LA—you, as the writer, can do whatever you jolly well please with the place, so long as it suits your fiction and doesn't absolutely piss off your readers.

I hope, therefore, that my speculative vision of Baton Rouge, should hordes of virally pitiful human beings invade it, should bands of feral children populate it, should white supremacists vie for control of it, and should a Librarian and her two wards seek to remake it better and more free, strikes the right balance between the above considerations.

~ Stephen J. C. Andes

PART I

*15 Years After The Event*

# CHAPTER 1

# JADE

I OPEN MY EYES. Whispers buzz and hiss outside in the dark.

*They've come for us...a pack of Ferals.*

The wild children must've picked up the scent of our dinner in their nightly search for food. *Dammit.* I should've been more careful. They're definitely an annoyance. But we can deal with Ferals. I thought they'd just pass over a house that appears charred from the street side. There's plenty of easier places to score a meal. *What am I missing? Maybe someone knew we were here...*

But at least it's not the Antis—thank God, Buddha, or whatever Spaghetti Monster in the Sky we're supposed to thank for such things. We wouldn't have been ready for gun-toting wackos who like to wear freaky plague masks for kicks. We saw a detachment of them yesterday. The Antis seem to be building a new camp outside of what was once Baton Rouge City Park. Samuel and I had to find shelter. Sleeping outdoors is no good with Anti guard patrols in the area. We found this abandoned home not far from where they're organizing.

*More whispers outside. Creaks and thumps on the porch.*

Definitely Ferals. They don't have the heavy footfalls of

virally-deranged Twitchers. Infected people moan and groan like wounded animals. Pretty easy to hear them coming. Sneaking and stealth is not really something you have to worry about with Twitchers.

*Formulate a plan, Jade. How is this gonna play out?*

My mind rehashes the last twelve hours. The house we found yesterday seemed like a good place to hide. The wooden structure leaned oddly, I thought, as though constructed from a child's building blocks, once straight and upright, all right-angles, simple triangles on top of rectangles, but now long-forgotten and teetering on the brink of collapse. But it would have to do. All the other options on the block were even worse. Rain or fire or encroaching nature are the only elements left to play with these houses now, edging them with mischievous fingers ever closer to collapse.

We have a set way of entering a new house. We do a loop around the perimeter. If all is quiet, we throw a little rock at one of the windows. We wait. If nothing moves, the backdoor is often the easiest entrance. It was actually locked this time. I had to wrap my hand in my sweatshirt and bust a windowpane to get in.

Inside, we found the house abandoned, moldering under a layer of dust—plates and cups still on the kitchen nook. Some canned stuff had bloated with botulism, but a couple cans of olives seemed ok. Upstairs we found an office. Whoever lived in this house must've been some sort of history buff. Old pictures on the wall—like, undeniably old pictures.

That's where we found the prize. A mounted saber in a glass case. I looked at Samuel. He shook his head. I smiled and took the sword down from the wall. I expected it to be dull, an ornamental oddity, but apparently whoever kept this sword had it restored in the craziness of the virus and after. Still sharp as hell. He probably thought he'd use it, whoever he was. And now, he's probably dead.

The grip was heavy, the blade adorned with flowers at the hilt.

My father's voice rang in my ears. *"Hold the sword like you would a small bird--not so tight as to crush it, but not so loose as to let it fly away..."*

I slashed the air, stretching my wrist, letting the blade speak with a *whiffle* and a *whoosh.* I tested it out on a piece of furniture in the small, dusty room. The office chair. My feet shuffled forward in a quick Balestra lunge, blade arced in a moulinet. A chunk of pleather and stuffing sloughed off the chair, sending it wheeling on a squeaky glide across the hardwood floor.

*"Well done, Jadey,"* I heard Dad's voice coaching me. *"Now try that again, remembering to keep your wrist motionless—it's the blade's pivot point."*

The memory of fencing with my dad sprang involuntarily, as though holding the sword had unlocked precious keepsakes I'd concealed and forgotten. It started with his research for a book he wrote on this old superhero called Zorro. Dad geeked out on Zorro, even going as far as learning to fence with a saber. And also, teaching me. He said he felt his daughter should learn how to handle a sword. We spent hours on footwork and sparring.

*"Again,"* he'd say after countless drills. I'd start the succession of moves over: double-advance, double-retreat, advance, half inverse advance, press. *"Ok, good, Jade. Now, let's do it weighted."*

I'd roll my eyes. *"Really, Dad?"*

*"Yes, really,"* he'd say with a cheesy grin, a faux-maniacal laugh would follow. He loved to torture me with drills. I hated it. He'd start loading a backpack with stones for me to wear

while I trained. *"If you want to be light on your feet, you have to develop strength and endurance..."*

The scene, so palpable for an instant, faded and Samuel shook his head again. I rushed across the room, using my new saber to stab a framed picture hanging on the wall. Glass shattered and scattered like ice cubes across the floor of the office. Samuel told me in his own way—in his silent way—that I'm crazy.

Yeah, I might be a little nuts. But I've been without a weapon too long. Finally, once again, a part of me has been restored. I'm a woman with a sword.

---

## *THAT* WAS YESTERDAY.

Now, we've been sleeping, Samuel and I, or trying to, on twin couches in the living room. It gives me the creeps to sleep in people's beds. When I can, and when possible, I go for the couch. Samuel doesn't talk, a result of the trauma of seeing our parents murdered in front of him, but my brother snores. I'd nodded off. Dreams of buzzsaws woke me up.

My eyes are open, now, staring blankly into the dark.

*Whispers, yet again.*

The thing about Ferals is each group—packs of eight to ten, usually—all have their own way of communicating. Some use grunts. Some are more sophisticated and can incorporate whistles or clicks. All of it gets mixed in with a few words or hand gestures they've picked up from other groups, or from people like me...

Ferals call people like me, the Olders. Some Olders—most, in my opinion—get off on using force, violence, and extortion to control Ferals. Sorta like in that book *Oliver Twist*. An old crafty character named Fagin manipulates a band of child-thieves, the Artful Dodger and the lot, for his own benefit.

It works sometimes. But only if the Olders find the right balance between fear and incentives like food, shelter, or clothing. Ferals have no real loyalty except to their packs. When food and shelter, or fun, can be had elsewhere, they usually leave.

*Pitter-patters.* Hushed voices on the deck outside the front door. It would be easy to mistake them for some stray dog or maybe a raccoon. I pull my hoodie up to cover most of my face as I peer over the couch. I want to spot them before they find me. A set of eyes in the window leading off the side of the house sends shivers down my spine.

I gesture at Samuel lying on the other couch, his eyes are already open. He puts a finger to his mouth. *Quiet.* Apparently, he hears it—or them—too. Samuel might not talk, and he also snores like crazy, but my brother's hearing is pretty damn sharp.

My sword lays ready on the floor and I glance at Samuel. He shakes his head and positions one arm slightly above his stomach, swaying the hand of his other arm back and forth in a slow wave.

*Sing. He wants me to sing.*

Shit. It would be so much easier to wound one of them. Scare them off. Samuel, I know, doesn't like that idea. Ever since our time with the Sisters of the Way of Absolute Hospitality, Samuel has been on a distinctly non-violent track.

It bothers me. The Sisters' non-violent crap is gonna get Samuel killed one day. Get me killed one day. What do I care about some abandoned Ferals?

*Sing.* He signs it to me again.

The thing about singing to Ferals, which I've done before, is that it only works *sometimes*. Ferals are, at root, kids. Even if their little non-animal brain parts have shriveled—or simply not developed—they're still kids. If you sing, with confidence, if you provide some rhythm, a beat, you can make them docile. That is if they're not too hungry...

The front door creaks open. It's the oldest of the Ferals, I'm pretty sure, who enters first. She stands silhouetted in the moonlight.

She—the oldest—is probably around nine or so, gangly arms, a little girl in a body stretching awkwardly toward adolescence from a recent growth spurt. She sniffs the air. Most likely she's tracking the remains of our dinner. Canned olives and a bag of Nestle Chocolate chips that had turned white with age.

I consider the sword one last time. Samuel shakes his head.

*Fine*, I think. Here it goes...

"Stir it up"—I start to sing Bob Marley. My dad loved him and played his music for us all the time. Samuel nods and gives me a brief smile. It was one of Dad's favorite songs. My brother starts a slow beat. He begins on his chest first, switching after a moment to the dusty coffee table.

*Boom bah Boom Boom Boom bah...Boom bah Boom Boom Boom bah...*

Samuel taps the wood table in the dark and it reminds me of how Dad sang to us in the middle of the night in the days after The Event. We were hiding from Twitchers. Mom would make up the sheets and blankets on the floor in their room. Dad would sing the melody and Mom would harmonize, their voices surrounding us, filling us, driving away gloom and fear.

I shake out of the memory as the younger Ferals come in first, unafraid of the dark. The oldest makes a brief click with her tongue and the younger ones stop, hesitate, but slowly keep coming. Whatever we are doing is interesting to them. The younger ones can't help themselves, four or five of them. Samuel keeps the beat and I sing on.

I arrive at the chorus again, and even the oldest inches toward the little circle that forms around us. The youngest is probably two or three. He reminds me of my youngest brother Mason at this age. All curls—ruddy-cheeks on pink, sunburnt skin—and wild smiles. Eyes full of mischief. I inherited my mother's olive complexion. My brothers got Dad's sun-starved pallor.

The little boy climbs up on my lap. He's hesitant. Shy. Ready to scamper off at the first sign of a threat. And then curiosity gets the best of him. He reaches toward me with a tentative hand. He touches my lips, my hair, my eyes, my cheek, before finally snuggling close to my chest, his ear on my breast feeling the vibrations.

The rhythm stays strong from Samuel: *Boom bah Boom Boom Boom bah...Boom bah Boom Boom Boom bah...*

Samuel has a few older kids next to him. He teaches them to hit the couch cushions. I laugh thinking that Samuel is basically running a Feral drum circle. The oldest hums, trying to vocalize words she doesn't know.

She closes her eyes and sways with the music, lost in a song from The Time Before.

# CHAPTER 2

# JADE

WHEN THE LIGHT of morning comes through the windows I wake with a start. All eight of the Ferals slept next to us for most of the night. Many of them hugged my chest as I hummed, letting the breath of my body move them up and down.

They're gone now but they left a present. A dead rabbit and a loaf of bread. That could indicate they are owned or controlled by an Older. We're already closer than I'd like to be to the Anti camp. Perhaps we're also close to some other threat—someone who can supply Ferals with meat and bread.

I flop back down on the couch and rest my hand on my chest. The littlest Feral had lain there listening to my heart, like Mason once did. Mason has to be out there. He'd be seventeen by now...

Staring at the ceiling, white paint and plaster peeling above me, I smile wryly and say to myself: *Don't Panic*, the phrase everyone remembers from The Time Before. It's become something of a joke. At least for those of us who are old enough to remember. To those of us who are still alive.

Digging through the garbage for food—*Don't Panic!*

Riding up to another burned-out set of homes, bodies white bone and dust—*Don't Panic!*

Hiding in the bush from a group of Antis, those plague-masked, heavily armed, white supremacist assholes. *Don't panic!*

Or taking cover from a horde of Feral children, because who likes to deal with those ankle-biters? Yup. *Don't panic!*

And you breathe a sigh of relief. You study your brother hiding with you. You detect the fear on his face, a mirror, probably of your own. You try to lighten the moment. *Don't panic!* you mouth to your no-longer-little brother. He smiles at you. He gives a silent laugh. Silent, because he hasn't spoken in ten years, three months, and eleven days.

*Don't Panic!* was from The Time Before. Before the whole world actually did panic. Before the Twitch and before most of the adult population died. *Don't Panic!* was a comfort for those who lived before the world ended.

Now, for those of us who *do* live, and want to keep on living, for those who, like my brother and I, want to find the remnants of our families we know have got to still be out there, *Don't Panic!* is a joke. The memory of it—its comfort, its ease, its stupidity—is what keeps us alive.

"This is the way the world ends, not with a bang but a whimper..."

I found that quote in my father's notebooks. After he and my mom were murdered—ten years, three months, and eleven days ago.

Apparently, according to my dad's notes, it was a line from the poetry of an author named T.S. Eliot. I started to comb through the ruins of as many libraries that were still left. After our old life completely crumbled. After my dad died. After Samuel and I buried our mom and dad. And after our seven-year-old brother, Mason, was stolen by a horde of white supremacist Antis. I tried to find names of books or authors that I remembered my dad talking about.

I salvaged a few T.S. Eliot books. They're basically crap, in my opinion. Eliot has one called *The Waste Land*, which is ironic since that's what everyone calls the city that once was Baton Rouge, where I live. Another poem, the one about the *bang and the whimper*, that one's called "The Hollow Men." It's written for boys; apparently, he never mentions women.

I wish I could tell that guy off. *You know what, Eliot? I'd say. I have hope. Hope to find my little brother in my very own Wasteland. And, Eliot? I'm not even a man at all. I'm my father's* daughter. *The eldest sister of my brothers. My father and mother named me Jade—a stone born to weather the elements, hard and vibrant and...precious.*

My father always ended his description of my name with precious. But that's only for me, now. It's something for my memories. I sit up on the couch finally. It's February 14th. Happy Valentine's Day, Daddy.

Another song comes to me, one my mom would sing in the mornings, as we woke up on the floor of their room.

Bob Marley reminds me not to worry.

Samuel's awake, too. "Let's eat and let's get out of here," I say.

He nods, his mouth already full of a hunk of bread.

T.S. ELIOT DID GET the *whimper* part right.

He may be full of it in many other ways—April is actually not so cruel after all, not when you have to live outside under the stars. Usually, January is the cruelest—the coldest, anyway—at least in Louisiana. *And hell, August sucks hard!*

But the *whimper* part was fairly spot-on. The world ended with a big, collective whimper. So many people rolled over, wheezing, and died. That is before the virus mutated and the Twitch started.

My dad was a historian. After The Event he took to writing constantly about how it all went down. When I was eight, I remember overhearing him talking to my mom—fighting really—in hushed whispers. He said writing 'focused his anxiety.' It was his way to unleash a bunch of internal anguish—using a blank page.

Dad even had me start writing at the time; said that by keeping a journal I would be helping record and preserve history. I had no idea what he was talking about. I usually drew pictures instead.

The last memory I have before the fear set in is of my eighth birthday party. It was High Tea with all my little girlfriends. We wore dresses and drank lemonade out of teapots. Not long after came The Event and the multitude of *Don't Panics!* from adults and authorities.

"*This is serious,*" I overheard Dad telling Mom. "*We have to take this seriously.*"

"*You're overreacting,*" Mom replied. "*This will pass...*"

But it didn't.

I've been able to piece together a bit of how the end began. My dad's notebooks helped, as well as the stories you learn on the road in and around The Wasteland. It's comforting to me to read my dad's attempts at preserving his sanity. I decided to start copying them in my own set of notebooks. It makes me feel like he's still talking, writing, believing. Maybe it's keeping me sane, too. I read a few paragraphs.

"*I believe no one will read this. I'm sure the publishing industry will crumble—is crumbling. Books, already nearly artifacts, will now become relics. The remains of a once-alive civilization, venerated for their powers, but ultimately, fuel to heat campfires and wipe asses.*

*But still, somehow, I have to write. I have to remind myself that I can still have words. That the words still matter, the writing still matters.*

*Some people said that we should've seen it coming. It was another virus from China, they said. Like SARS. Like MERS. Like the novel coronavirus, COVID-19. Like a seasonal flu, but perhaps a little more communicable, a little more deadly to those already predisposed to die.*

*Except it wasn't.*

*Everyone said it was from China. Turned out it was actually from some military lab in North Dakota. Experiments with germ warfare gone haywire. But the narrative had already been scripted.*

*It hit older folks hard. The mortality rate for people over eighty was scary. But the younger the infected person, the greater likelihood that the patient would recover. It lulled us into inaction. Into ease. The people dying were somehow disposable, not worth taking the drastic actions public health officials suggested and later begged for. It was like every pandemic movie you've ever seen...*

Hearing Dad's voice in his words comforts me. But whenever I read them, I can hear—I can feel—how hard he's trying to keep it together.

I put Dad's notebook down and finish cooking the rabbit left by the Ferals—some of these old houses still have working gas lines and we lucked out with this one. I find plates and cups, even silverware, and I make Samuel sit down at the table. We don't have tons of time to waste on supper—life in The Wasteland teaches you quickly that it's no good pretending the world out there isn't completely screwed.

*But, we still gotta eat, right?*

I can't resist the temptation of taking the opportunity to sit down at a normal table. Remembering the inventory of a disappeared life: normal plates, chairs, forks. Almost normal.

I sit down across from Samuel, who's found a bottle of wine somewhere in the back pantry. Bread and rabbit and wine and some canned green beans—it's a veritable feast. We dig in. The rabbit is overdone. The bread is mostly hard. The green beans...well, they taste like green beans. Canned green beans last, seriously, forever.

During supper, because I want to read to Samuel from it, I notice Dad's other notebook is missing—some poetry he'd copied from Pablo Neruda that my mom always loved. It's not there. I was reading one of his journals a second ago, but where's the green, spiral notebook? Not in my backpack. My breath catches and my chest tightens. Samuel gives me an *It-wasn't-me face.* It must have been one of the Ferals. I'd had to slap one of their hands away from my backpack last night.

"We have to go after them," I say to Samuel while rooting around in vain in my backpack.

Samuel stares at me while chewing his rabbit.

"Yes, we do, Samuel," I snap at him. "I have to get Dad's book." He sighs. He takes a long pull from the wine bottle.

"I know, Samuel. I understand that singing a song won't work this time."

Samuel touches his shoulders and head.

"Yeah, we might be able to find some protective gear in the house. Possibly the kid's room upstairs has some sports equipment. I don't know."

The Ferals will be going back to whoever is controlling them. An Older that keeps them. We're inviting trouble we don't need. But I won't let that notebook go.

Dad's advice buzzes in my ears. *"Don't do anything stupid, Jade. Stay alive."* The advice he used to give me every day.

Sorry, Dad. I'm not listening this time.

# CHAPTER 4

# JADE

**BEFORE WE LEAVE THE HOUSE,** we pack up the extra canned food and cobble together some supplies. I find two long belts and criss-cross them over my shoulders into a harness so I can wear my sword on my back. I want to be mobile and don't want a sword jangling at my hips. Samuel discovers an old pair of shoulder pads that I think they used to wear for baseball or basketball...one of the ball sports. They are clearly ridiculous on me and I decide it's better to go light.

I return to the office, where I first found the sword mounted on the wall, and find a beautiful hat on a stand nearby where the sword had been hung. I hadn't noticed it the first time. A Civil War hat. Blue. Cavalry. I know that much because Dad made me suffer through a multi-part documentary on the Civil War, back when we were still under quarantine before the power stopped working.

I veto the shoulder pads but keep the hat and the sword.

Finding a pack of Ferals can be hard, but we have a few leads. They have to be somewhere close. They had food. They were surprisingly clean. And they'd found us quicker than I would've thought.

When night falls, we leave out the back, our packs full of new supplies. A working flashlight. A box of matches. An empty notebook and some pens. Most travelers don't have guns anymore. Only the Antis have weapons in any substantial quantity. A girl carrying a sword can be, let's say, a basic deterrent for any unwanted attention. And for those who think it's a bluff, well, I'll let them find out if I can use the sword or not.

We hop fences through the neighborhood, trying to keep off the road. Full of decrepit houses, I remember how Dad used to say this area of Baton Rouge was pretty at one point. The live oaks are still standing. Still growing. The arching, woody limbs of winter honeysuckle give off the crisp aroma of lemon as we make our way past an overgrown garden. Branches twist wherever they will. Massive tree roots have shattered the cement sidewalks like tentacles of some deep-sea creature breaking the surface of dark waters.

We silently cross Wisteria Avenue and come to what was once called Government Street. Samuel sizes up the street sign from our cover in the darkening shadows of a magnolia tree. He shrugs. I get the joke. *Yeah, what government?*

While I think briefly about the unraveling of our lives Before, Samuel spots what might be a light coming from a building diagonal to our position. The words *Yvette Marie* are barely visible on the clapboard side of the structure. He glances at me. I nod. We don't cross directly toward the building but traverse the street to our left which will put us directly opposite the back door.

We go one at a time, Samuel first. Once he's across, I wait for a minute. No movement from inside. I join Samuel on the other side of the street from *Yvette Marie*. We take cover among the low-hung branches of a particularly big and spreading live oak.

A wrought iron fence skirts part of the property where we

see the light, and from what we can make out in the moonglow, piles and piles of junk are kept enclosed by that iron fence. It's some sort of courtyard. There's an old rusted-out bus. Mangled farm equipment. A few machines busted and stripped for parts. The best approach is to go over the fence and hope no watchers wait on the other side.

Samuel gives me his, *Are-you-sure-about-this?* look.

"Yes, Samuel," I say in a whisper. "We are getting that notebook back."

Samuel doesn't wait for an argument. He takes off across Government Street toward the building. I love my brother. He might be some sort of Way-of-Absolute-Hospitality freak now, but he's bold. In fact, he's the bravest person I've ever known. He shelters in a shadow for a moment and sprints toward the fence. In one fluid motion, he grips the wrought iron bars, his legs cantilever up and over, and he lands on the other side without any effort at all.

My brother disappears for a few minutes into the oblivion of the courtyard. When he reappears, I breathe a sigh of relief. He gives a brief, hushed whistle—my signal to cross to the fence. The fleet seconds of crossing an open road gets my blood pumping. I crouch in the corner of the building, where the wood clapboard siding meets the wrought iron fence. Samuel drops silently from an overhanging awning right next to me. He points to deep shadows farther down the length of the fence. He signs that, apparently, he's found a way into the courtyard.

"What, do you think I can't climb as well as you, dumbass?" I hiss.

He smiles and immediately crouch-walks the fence length toward an opening. Once inside, I get a better view of the back door to the property. A line of small windows reveals faint light coming from within. If there are several Olders in the building, we might have to make a new plan. We make our way past the rusted metal in the courtyard and hide under the row of windows.

Through grimy glass panes, we recognize what was once some sort of restaurant—tables, a counter, a kitchen in the back. I can make out someone in the kitchen. No doubt, an Older. Around the interior walls of the restaurant dining room, there are about fifteen The oldest one comes into view. The girl who'd led the pack to our house the night before. She brings plates of what appears to be food out to the younger ones.

Samuel nudges me and points at what I missed on first inspection. Chains. The younger Ferals all have shackles on their ankles that are anchored to hefty cement blocks arranged around the perimeter of the room.

"The hell?" I whisper under my breath. Samuel ducks to hide beneath the windows. I follow.

A voice inside squawks, "It's all you get, you little freaks!" It's a voice of practiced cruelty, petulant and whiny. "If you bring home shit, well, shit is what you eat for dinner." Whimpers swell in protest. "What?" the voice says exasperated, then answers. "It's not actually *shit*, you little shits. It's moldy-ass sausage. But, you should be grateful for that. All you brought back was an open bag of chocolate chips!"

I poke my head up to peer through a tiny corner of the window. The Feral girl stands in front of the Older, trying to communicate. He's a man, probably no older than thirty although he appears twice that age. He's skinny. The pallid skin on his face is pockmarked with craters of acne scars. His nasally twang cuts through the evening. "And you...you think because you're the oldest you get a bigger share? Hell no."

The Older slaps the girl. She puts her hand to her face and glares daggers at him, as another small cry comes from one of the littles.

I duck below the window again and whisper to Samuel.

"We've got to do something." I reach for the sword handle jutting up over my right shoulder. Samuel's eyes tell me no. "I'll try, Samuel. No promises."

We crouch-walk back to the door we'd spotted on the way in. I test the handle. Locked. *Damn.* I softly bang my head against the door in frustration and sense it give. *Sweet!* The handle was locked but the latch was broken.

We duck inside. A long narrow space stretches out ahead of us leading to the Feral dungeon. More old junk. *Antiques,* Mom used to call them. Moving through the junk room silently is surprisingly difficult. Perhaps that's what Fagin, as I've begun to think of him (Dad made me read Dickens, too), was going for. His own brand of an early detection warning system.

We hop-scotch our way through piles of books, music players, desks, broken chairs, and freaky-as-hell disfigured dolls that crowd the corridor room. The building turns a corner at the end of the passageway, and we wait in the dark.

"Shut up and eat!" The man bellows at the Ferals. "And stop crying!"

A few whines come from some of the Ferals. It sounds like the Older storms back into the kitchen, moaning about the ungratefulness of the Ferals. Dishes clang as they are thrown into the sink. We pause for two beats. Hearts pounding, we enter the dining area, which reeks of rotten old food. The pungent tang of urine hits us. The Ferals instantly freeze, fear on their faces. It's a panic that was absent the night before.

The oldest Feral hesitates. She glances at the kitchen and back at us. She nods. Samuel darts toward where the Feral closest to him is shackled. He turns back to me and signs with two fingers of both hands latticed on top of each other. *"It's locked."*

The oldest Feral turns her hand counterclockwise and points to the kitchen. *The keys. The man has the keys.*

As I try to work out a plan, the Older suddenly returns from the kitchen. The Ferals clutch one another and back up toward the cement blocks that hold them in bondage.

"What. The. Hell. Is. This?" he says, shock and rage registering on his face as he stands in the doorway to the kitchen. His eyes dart between Samuel, me, and the oldest Feral. His gaze finally settles on me and his expression contorts into a leering grin. Licking his lips, he croons, "Well, look-y what we have here."

Samuel glances at me and retreats to the far side of the room, clearing a path between me and Fagin.

"A pair of street rats, huh?" He moves a few steps toward me and watches me put my hand on the hilt of my sword. He stops.

"You know how to use that, little darlin'?"

"If you come any closer, you'll find out."

"You sure are pretty." He adjusts the crotch of his pants. "What's a pretty gal like you doing with a sword?"

"Let the kids go," I say.

He laughs, dismissing me. "Nah, I ain't lettin' these worms go, but I sure could use a sexy little minx around here. It's been a long time since I've seen anyone pretty as you." The Older reaches for something behind the counter. I stand my ground. If he moves any closer, I know my next move. Samuel, I can see from the corner of my eye, is crouched and ready to assist. I honestly tried, Samuel.

"It sure is a pity to have to use something like this on such a dollface." He lifts a bat, twined with barbed wire. He takes a quick step toward me and swings. I duck and draw my sword. His swing goes wide and his momentum carries him farther across the room. As he flies past, I spring and pivot from my crouch and slice his hamstrings. He goes down hard. The Ferals bang their chains as the Older cries out in pain, contorting his body to clutch his lacerated legs.

"It's just a flesh wound," I tell him. I roll him over on his back with my foot. Samuel's eyes plead, No. "You get off on beating little kids, motherfucker?" I say through clenched teeth. Blood is pounding in my brain as I grip the hilt of my sword. I want so badly to end this guy. I'm standing over him now. I take my sword and bring it down on his face, but at the last second, I hit him with the flat of the blade.

Swaaaack.

The sound is sickening and leaves a white welt that quickly turns crimson. The Older curses at the pain, spittle comes from his mouth as he sputters with rage. The Ferals clatter their chains louder, now. I turn to face them. I walk in a tight circle pumping my sword, power and exultation driving me, then point the blade back to the Older on the floor. I study the sharp edge of the weapon in my hand.

Swaaaack.

I hit him on the other side of his face with the flat of the blade. More curses. More spittle. I straddle both sides of the Older and bend down until his rank breath and his fear wash over my face.

"You will never hurt these children again." I grip his oily chin, squeezing his cheeks together. "You understand?"

"No," the Older gasps desperately and I release my hold on his face. "I never touched them."

I reflexively wipe my hand on the top of my thigh, removing whatever scum I may've touched. "Something tells me you're lying, and I frankly don't believe you can be trusted with little kids." I lift the sword and bring the pommel down on his head with a swift crack. He's out cold and a little stream of blood winds down the man's pockmarked face.

The Ferals, who had breathlessly watched this last interchange, erupt into a frenzy of whoops and shouts, beating their chains even louder, pulling against their shackles. The oldest

Feral reaches in the man's pockets and pulls out a string of keys. She begins to unlock their ankles from the steel tethers.

Ten minutes later we leave the man chained to one of the cement blocks in the dining room of the defunct, dingy restaurant. The oldest Feral runs into the darkness of the junk hallway and returns with Dad's notebook. She presents it to me with both hands, silently gazing into my face. She reaches for my chest and keeps her hand there until she finds my heartbeat. She turns back to the roomful of newly freed Ferals. The Older groans pitifully as he begins to come to.

Samuel and I leave the old restaurant with its junk, and as the building recedes behind us, we hear the clanking of chains and the cries of a man left to face the vengeance of untamed children.

# CHAPTER 5

# JADE

IT TAKES the better part of an hour for my heart to stop pounding in my chest after we leave 'Fagin' to his fate with the Feral children.

I've forgotten—almost forgotten—what that kind of combat feels like. I can't stop shaking. Adrenaline. Like I'm flying.

I trained constantly when Samuel and I lived with the Sisters. That was eighteen months ago. We left the cloister and have been on the road ever since. The Sisters kept my technique sharp. I sparred. Learned to breathe properly. Gained experience fighting opponents who used weapons other than swords. Knives. Bo staffs. Bamboo sticks. I even practiced mixing Capoeira and Kendo footwork with Sabre Fencing.

Long before that, I drilled for hours and hours with Dad. It feels like a lifetime ago. Training is nothing like what I experienced in the antique shop just now. I've fought Twitchers since we've been traveling. But not uninfected, fully alive people. I thought that kind of combat was behind me. It's hard to describe. This...this feeling. *Power*. Having *my* will done, like some goddess of death. Facing an opponent who means you harm...or worse...and showing him he's nothing—that's a complete and total rush. It's a high I don't think a drug can mimic.

My hands are still clenched into fists and I want to start sprinting. The badass woman who can beat the shit out of a creep—I love that woman. She's strong. Not a victim. My mind didn't have to tell my body how to move. I did it all—with power and grace. It was like someone else in control. Automatic. Exhilarating. The Older was completely, totally under my power. I could've snuffed out his life with a half-turn of my wrist. But I didn't kill him, and I'm having a hard time figuring out why not.

My adrenaline high soars and crashes suddenly. The shaking worsens and it makes me nauseous. I hug my arms as we walk and a central, driving question begins to nag at me. *Isn't my power supposed to be for something more?*

It's always been about protecting my brothers. Not delighting in the humiliation of some sicko in a junk shop. I start to feel shame. I've had to be a warrior to survive. *I must rescue my brother Mason who was kidnapped a decade ago.* It's been like a mantra for me. My power is *for* someone.

Keeping Samuel and I together is part of that, but also getting our brother back. Mason is still out there and I know he was stolen by Antis. It's why the Anti camp being built not far from here is so important.

My stomach does a flip, and I almost vomit. The person I was back there in that antique shop both empowers me and terrifies me. My fear in combat is gone and yet I fear something else—losing my ability to care. Forgetting my purpose. It's the only thing that binds me to my parents. To my past. Honoring their memory by being there for my brothers. *"We exist for others, Jadey,"* I remember Dad always told me.

Accusations start. Blame. A tightening in my chest. It's hard to breathe. I'm failing my parents. My brothers. There's a facet of that woman in the junk shop that likes holding someone's life or death in her hands and gets off on it. The memory of standing over the Older, finally able to vent my rage on someone who deserves it. I love the wash of chemicals it gives me. And it scares me. I hate myself for it.

That's a line I don't want to cross, can't cross, because it could make me forget who I am. It's not supposed to be about my own selfish high. I wanted to end him. That doesn't sound like me. It sounds like someone else. Some other force I'm trying to keep at bay. How far is too far across the line? Would I even know?

I quick check over my shoulder and make sure Samuel is following. He would know.

I need to walk. To think.

After about half an hour walking down Government Street toward downtown, I finally start to slow my pace. Sections of the road are not easy to pass. Deep potholes in the asphalt sprout thick, wild grasses. Weedy undergrowth bulges inward from the street's edge. Creeping vines coil upward like serpents lying in wait around teetering power poles.

My mind, too, feels choked—with anger and doubt, and if I'm being honest, with fear. Samuel won't make me talk when I'm like this. Samuel knows me. I'd like to think I know him.

We shelter in an old graveyard. The busted above-ground tombs tilt at odd angles like sinking ships caught in a frozen sea. They can be dangerous, graveyards. So many places to hide. Twitchers can amble, in their half-crazed delirium, into places like this. Their minds are full of insane hallucinations. Illusions. Seeing things that aren't there. Eyes fluttering like trapped moths. In an instant, they'll try to kill anyone, or anything, in their path. I've seen them up close...so many of them.

But Samuel and I have already crossed into the Librarian's territory, so we'll probably be safe. The Twitcher Hunters usually keep this area swept clean. I should know, as I used to be one. A Twitcher Hunter. Don't dwell on that, I try to tell myself. *That's the past.*

A tall stone mausoleum offers cover and I take off my pack, put my back against the cold rock and slide down into a crouch and, finally, sit down to rest. I take several deep breaths and try to focus the way Sister Lola taught me. Breathe in...hold...breathe out...hold.

Samuel is beside me. He's breathing, too. The moonlight gently glows off the white tombs.

After a few minutes, I break the silence. "Samuel, I get it." Samuel takes a breath in and lets it out. "I know that was not in the plan." I can make out my brother's face as he turns toward me. "It was impulsive, Samuel, I understand."

And? Samuel spins his hand in a rolling motion, asking for more. I can't tell but he's probably lifting his eyebrows in that super annoying way.

"*And*, it was impulsive, Samuel, *I know.*"

*And?* Again with the hand, this time accompanied by a patronizing head nod.

"OK! *And*, I'm sorry," I say.

Samuel reaches for my shoulder and gives it a brief squeeze, before returning his hand to his lap. He starts to breathe in and out again, wanting me to follow suit.

"But here's the thing," I say, breaking his concentration. I can't *not* say what's on my mind. My thoughts churn on the sizable Anti camp that's forming. There hasn't been a camp like that in a decade. Not this close to The Wasteland and not since our parents were murdered and Mason was kidnapped by a group of Antis. Something is up. "We've got to figure out what's happening in that Anti camp." A sigh comes from Samuel. And it's not part of the breathing meditation. "There hasn't been a big Anti camp like that in Baton Rouge, in The Wasteland, in years." Samuel pivots away. He doesn't like where I'm going with this. "We have to be sure, Samuel. We have to investigate..."

We've been through this sort of conversation before when we were traveling outside of New Orleans. My brother knows what I'm thinking. *This might be the piece of the puzzle that leads us to Mason.* And I know what he's thinking. Samuel's probably thinking that I need to let it go. To let Mason go.

I grab for my pack and take out Dad's notebook, the one we rescued from the Ferals. I open the pages, run my hand across the brittle paper, across the words, the sentences, that are there but are obscured in the darkness.

Memories. My parents. My brothers. Life Before. I take out the flashlight from my pack and flick the button on. I read what Dad wrote about the Antis.

*But people travel. A lot. Planes. Cruise ships. International students. Mardi Gras. There was no stopping it. It popped up in Italy. In France. The pope died—he was old, and he only had one lung to work with anyway. No one worried too much. When the virus came to the US or was identified as such, schools shut down. Bars and restaurants stayed open a while longer. People wanted it to be like a friggin' snow day. But the cases mounted. 700 presumptive positives to 5,000 in about a week.*

*Everyone freaked out. You couldn't buy toilet paper. One enterprising capitalist motherfucker decided to buy up all the hand sanitizer in the state of Louisiana and sell it on Amazon for $15 bucks a pop. I remember Jayla telling me at a Walmart: "You know, this doesn't freak me out because as a Black woman I am used to insecurity, not feeling safe, in America."*

*Reports of white supremacists began. It was easier for them to blame 'foreign influences' for the disease than our own government. Or, the real truth, to have no one to blame. To have so many people to blame that blame no longer matters. People always need scapegoats and the white supremacists had an old script to play from.*

*The prof. whose office is down the hall from me went on a tirade about his TA—an international student from China—endangering his life by being Chinese. As if the TA's nationality was enough to transmit the virus. Groups of white assholes started terrorizing foreign nationals resident in the United States. GO HOME FOREIGN DISEASE! was one note that was left on the doorstep of a family from China in our neighborhood.*

*Discrete, pre-existing groups of white supremacists certainly pushed a radical, violent ideology that came to be associated with the Antis. But white supremacy was a latent force in our society, always had been. To say the Antis started solely from the fringe is a denial of our history. White supremacy was the air we breathed, the water we swam in. The pandemic catalyzed white supremacy in America.*

*The pandemic wooed people—white people—to the familiar, soothing comfort of blame-shifting. The evolution of the Antis didn't start with racial terrorists. It began with the racial virus that America had been born with, passed on in its genetic code generation after generation. The Antis' evolution, like the Twitch itself, is the product of a more severe mutation of previous disease.*

I click the flashlight off. "Look, Samuel, I get that you left the Sisters' cloister with me because you think I need you. Which I do. I do need you. But...I made a promise, to Dad, to Mom, that I would take care of you and Mason. That I would keep our family together."

Samuel sighs again. He turns and faces me. Dim light illumines his lambent eyes.

"We need information." I close the notebook. "I've been thinking—and you're not gonna like this, but hear me out—we need to go to the Librarian. She knows things..."

Samuel's gaze angles away from me to some point in the dark.

"Maybe she and the Hunters can tell us what's going on with the Anti camp," I say. "If the camp might have someone fitting Mason's description."

No. Samuel shakes his head. He doesn't get along with the Librarian or approve of the methods used by the Hunters to kill Twitchers. My time with the Hunters is not among his list of 'Jade's Greatest Hits.' But that was before I left and went with him to the Sisters of Absolute Hospitality.

"I know I didn't leave under the best circumstances," I continue. "But I was respected there, Samuel. I've done plenty of favors. I can call in a few."

Samuel stands up. I follow, grabbing his arm.

"We need to do this." Samuel stops because he registers my tone. Stubborn. "I'm going to the Librarian and...well...you have to go with me."

Samuel turns to me. He puts his hand on his chest and then holds out his pinky. He wants me to swear.

"Yes, Samuel. I swear. I won't work for the Hunters again. I won't go back to that." Samuel's pinky is still extended. I wrap my little finger around his. We've been doing this since we were kids. The pinky swear. While definitely laughable to anyone else, it's basically sacred to us. I've never broken a pinky swear to my brother.

He nods.

"Ok, let's take five minutes," I say. We both put our backs against the cold stone again. "Let's just be silent. And after...we'll go see the Librarian."

We sink down the side of the tomb and sit and breathe and try not to think.

WE LEAVE the cemetery and start for North Boulevard, which leads straight downtown. A patrol of Hunters is out for a nightly sweep. If you act confident, pretend like you know what you're doing, and keep walking, the Hunters usually ignore you. They've got bigger jobs to do than harass a pair of randoms. These Hunters aren't on horseback, which means they are probably new recruits. Sometimes new recruits are a little extra itchy for action. We see them before they spot us. We duck into an ally and let them pass.

And soon after, we arrive. The undergrowth thins. Nature's progress recedes. The Wasteland—Old Baton Rouge, technically—but everyone calls this place The Wasteland. Its borders are always fuzzy, but it's basically everything from the Magnolia Cemetery west to the river. It was once the capital of the State of Louisiana. Now, it belongs to the Librarian. The Hunters are her personal army of a sort. They keep the peace...or, at least whatever the Librarian says is the peace.

From the darkness of the surrounding ruins of the old city, light spills out before us. The Librarian runs the old Exxon-Mobil refinery north of town. Almost every one of the five hundred souls who live here are somehow connected to oil production. Some work the refinery, others transport it, still others distribute it. The credit system is tied to oil. Buying, selling, trading—power over oil is power over people. She provides electricity. 'A Light in the Dark,' is one of her famous lines.

And also, business—of a kind. There's gambling and prostitution, of course, but also small artisan shops, some food distribution centers and the like. There's plenty of trade in liquor from sugar cane production, as well as a free school subsidized by the merchants. There are places to drink, places to forget, and places to buy whatever pleasure is your deal.

Most of the "adult" population is in their twenties. A few people are in their forties and fifties, those immune to the

Twitch. And there are lots of little kids, as the "adults" have been nothing if not expert at seeding the next generation—literally. All of us live with uncertainty. Every year over the age of eighteen brings with it the threat of catching the virus. So people in The Wasteland like to party. To dance. To eat. To drink. To love—or its equivalents. And, hopefully, you wake up the next day, which is a gift, and do it all over again.

There's also an amazing...well...library.

The Librarian was actually, in The Time Before, a *Librarian*. And the downtown library was one of the only libraries in the area that miraculously survived viral panic, looting, Twitchers, death, and general chaos. It is four floors of floor-to-ceiling books, tiered upward and out in a kind of uneven pile. It has always reminded me of a small, half-finished tower of Jenga tiles—a game I used to play with Dad in The Time Before. Its walls are covered almost completely in glass.

The Library is a kind of sanctuary, really—the one place that remains much as it once was. The Library balcony hangs over a central plaza, which has become The Wasteland's primary meeting zone. The plaza hosts hawkers, food sellers, and plenty of music on most nights. And this night is no different.

You can hear the buzz of gas-powered generators running DJ turntables. A four-on-the-floor house beat thrums through the plaza, as people get food, dance, drink, do business, and live while they can. Several sleazes are trying to lure people over to the Old State Capitol, next door to the Library. It's a white-washed castle with turrets and all, but inside you can find the gambling operation and a brothel. From what I've read in Dad's notebooks, nothing much has changed.

I have to pull Samuel away from the smell of cooking food—we have no money, anyway—and push him toward the entrance to the Library. Outside the main doors a beefy guy stands guard.

Shaved head, a huge lion tattoo on one forearm, and a generally sour disposition. I take a breath and we weave our way through a throng of sweaty dancers high on one of the many drugs on offer and ask to be let inside.

"Weapons," says Beefy Guy at the door.

"I don't leave my sword with anyone. Sorry." I try to sidestep him, and he moves his bovine frame in front of me. Samuel shrugs and turns longingly back toward the food vendors. I turn to Beefy Guy. "I didn't hear you say please." I flash a weak, though not unpleasant smile. The mouth-breather isn't fazed but humors me anyway.

"Please," he says in mock subservience to my request.

"Ok. Well, since you said please, I suppose I can make an exception." Without smiling, I unbuckle the belt holding my sword and hand it to him. He signals for someone to take it.

"It'll be returned when you leave," he says.

"Yeah, I know it will." I grab Samuel's arm and brush pass the guard.

---

INSIDE THROUGH THE GLASS DOORS, an upscale menagerie of people engages in more or less the same activities as outside: eating, dancing, drinking, doing business, and politics. I keep my head down and hope I won't be recognized by anyone I know. We exit the party in the front lobby and cross into what was once called the Welcome Center. A long circulation desk—smooth and white—sits on one side of the interior room. A few people mill around, but no one is actually reading anything.

At the circulation desk sits a sole attendant. It's Bea. Shit.

She peers at us over the top of her book when she senses our approach. I know Bea. *Of course, it would be Bea at the desk.*

She's wearing one of her usual print dresses—she likes to call them vintage—and her hair is pulled back in a tight bun. Perched on the bridge of her nose is a pair of glasses connected to a long chain around her neck. Except for her cat-eye makeup, red lipstick, and arm tatts, she's playing the role of a circulation-desk librarian quite well.

"May I help you?" She says it matter-of-factly. No hint of recognition. Classic Bea. The perfect picture of a prim librarian...but the bitchy attitude, that's all her own.

I sigh, swallowing the snarky comment I'd like to make. I'm here for a purpose, not to inflame whatever bad blood Bea and I may have.

"I'd like to checkout El Quijote," I say. The thought occurs to me that Don Quijote was one of Dad's favorite novels. It's also the code you have to use in order to speak with the Librarian.

Bea takes off her glasses, lets them dangle from the chain. "I'm sorry," she says through pursed lips. "We checked out our last copy. And, I believe your lending privileges have expired." She clasps her hands together, lays them on the desk, cat eyes narrowing in condescension.

Silence.

I don't react. Instead, I lock eyes with her. "I think you need to check again." I place my hand on the circulation desk, leaning in close. "And lending privileges—my lending privileges—are most definitely active." Bea breaks the gaze first. Samuel lets out a small chuckle. She tells us to wait as she disappears into the back room. She's communicating upstairs. They keep a handheld transceiver in the back. Protocol.

A few minutes click by and Bea comes back to the desk. She isn't in a hurry, carefully sits down, puts her glasses back on the bridge of her nose, and finally says that someone will meet us at the elevators. She points out the direction like this is my first time in the Library.

"Thanks," is all I say. I bare all my teeth in a smile that hopefully cuts daggers and Samuel and I head to the lift upstairs. She'll be on the fourth floor, waiting, I'm sure. I'm second-guessing coming here, to this place. Confronting the Librarian means also facing my own time here, and the bridges I'm sure I've burned, in The Wasteland.

# CHAPTER 6

# JADE

THE ELEVATOR DOOR slips open before we reach it and out steps a man—tall, strong, attractive, though for the record I should add completely irritating and self-centered, but also mesmerizing and, well, sexy as hell...

*Ok, Jade, keep your head on straight. Don't lose focus.*

His name is Ty, the Librarian's nephew.

We trained together. We were friends at first, but also fierce competitors, both vying for the Librarian's attention—both a little obsessed with being the best. So of course, he was the first boy I ever kissed. Hell, we lost our virginity to one another. But it was always a struggle with Ty. No one else has ever made me more exhilarated, more punch-drunk with infatuation.

Or more furious. He never understood my need to find my little brother Mason. Instead, he told me he loved me, wanted to marry me and start a family.

It was too much for me. I cared about him, but I just couldn't. Not then. My brother was still lost. How could I forget that fact and start a family of my own? He grew cold toward me before I left The Wasteland and started hanging out with other girls. I suppose it was his way of trying to punish me for my inability to tell him what we both knew—I've always been madly in love with him.

*Why'd it have to be Ty?*

"I'll escort you to find *El Quijote*," is all he says. One hand rests on the hilt of his sword; with the other, he motions us inside the elevator. Samuel takes the left side of the compartment and I take the right. Ty settles in the middle, slightly in front of us. He hovers a key card over a sensor and pushes "4."

It's stiflingly quiet as we ascend and, between floors three and four, Ty says "Hello, Jade," without looking at me. He doesn't break his stare at the lights of the floor selection buttons.

"Hi, Ty," is all I manage, my eyes also fixed on the floor indicators.

"Samuel," Ty says flatly without glancing over his shoulder. "Loquacious as always, I see."

Samuel gives me a look behind Ty's back, he tells me with a lift of an eyebrow what I already know. *Awkward.*

The elevator mercifully pings that we've arrived at the fourth floor. When the doors open, Ty exits and again extends his hand. "This way, please."

Protocol. If the Librarian cares about anything, she cares about protocol.

Ty escorts us down the hallway toward what was once called a "Conference Room"—a spacious room with vaulted ceilings, halo lights, and a terrace view of The Wasteland. The Librarian's office.

At the far end, she sits by the windows at a tidy mahogany desk, head bowed over an open book. A long, scarlet strip of carpet runs from the entrance to the Librarian's desk, bisecting the room. Ty leads us down the path made by the carpet and I take a moment to glance at the tall shelves packed with books that line the office. She always liked to say that if a book entered her office, she had read it.

The Librarian's name is Jayla.

When we're almost at the end of the red carpet, I can see her black locs slung over her right shoulder, fingers absentmindedly fidgeting with one of her favorite wooden dread beads. I remember the first time I saw her do that. It was from The Time Before. She was a friend of my mom's and she'd come over and they'd talk about books. One time, my mom made a joke about Octavia Butler's book. "You know," Mom said offhandedly, "the one that has all the tentacle sex."

"Sarah," Jayla told her, fidgeting with a loc bead, "I'm gonna have to explain a few things about interstellar sexuality and gender dynamics in Octavia Butler before you can say that again." They both laughed and I had no idea what they were talking about.

Much later, when I first came to The Wasteland, not long after my parents died, I was fascinated by watching her read. I was thirteen. I'd stare at her eyes scanning the pages. They were like two silent apertures moving rapidly down the rows of words, imprinting the letters and symbols, the ideas and imagined worlds, deep within her soul. I used to imagine she was on a secret mission for hidden knowledge that I knew nothing about. She'd finally notice me, her dark brown eyes registering my attentive stare with a light smile that would crease three lines above her cheeks.

"Haven't you ever seen a Black woman read, Jade?" she'd say and laugh.

I'd look down blushing. "Sorry, ma'am," I would reply.

"It's alright, Jade, just read your own book. The book in your hand is way more interesting than I am." I would return to my book, sneaking glances at this woman who took Samuel and me in. She taught me to lose myself, and my sorrow, in books.

Ty motions us to stand in front of the desk, where several chairs sit unoccupied, and takes up a position on one side of the

Librarian, rigidly at attention. Without looking up at us, the Librarian reads aloud:

*Here rests the fair Dulcinea;*

*once rosy-fleshed and plump.*

The Librarian's eyes dart from the page to me and for a silent moment, I'm thirteen again and enthralled by this woman who commands the whole world known to me.

And who I always felt was out of reach. How many hours did I read, devouring all the books she loved, hoping that if I finished another one, she'd find me interesting enough to give me her attention? And the training. Becoming who I thought she wanted me to become. Was it good enough? Why was I so rarely granted the honor of seeing behind the mask of the Librarian? Why was I never good enough—just as I was—to always know her simply as Jayla? There are so many things I'd like to tell her, questions I need to be answered.

"End of Part One," I say instead. "It's the end of Part One of the Ingenious Gentleman Don Quijote of La Mancha."

"Indeed." The Librarian, or Jayla—I don't know which one she'll present to me in the moment—closes the book. "I apologize for the formality of your reception, Jade." She turns to my brother. "Samuel," she says simply. He nods, holding her gaze. "But," she regards me again, "you know me. Protocol." She leans back in her high-backed leather chair. "What, dare I ask, brings you here?"

"Look, Jayla, I'm..."

The Librarian flashes disapproval when I say her name. I guess she evidently does want to keep this formal. I settle myself, pause, and start again. "We've come for information, Ma'am."

"And what information might that be, Jade?" The Librarian busies herself with some papers on her desk. Ty has not moved from attention on the other side of the desk.

"I'm sure you know about the new Anti camp...being built in City Park?"

"Yes, Jade. We know. Captain Tyrese and the Hunters have it well in hand." She pauses her paper shuffling. "Certainly, after all this time, you haven't come simply to tell me what I already know."

Jayla has always been good at unnerving me. She also anticipates everything I say, almost like she can read my mind. "No." I wait for a beat, collecting my thoughts. "I want to know if...I think maybe Mason...Mason might be among the Antis." Samuel has settled in one of the chairs around the desk. He's curled sideways, arms hugging his knees.

The Librarian motions toward Ty, her gaze trailing behind. "Captain Tyrese, please brief Jade on what we know."

Ty breaks his stiff position and says matter-of-factly: "The Anti camp is led by a man calling himself Anton the Great. He's a disgraced zealot who was run out of Houston about six months ago. His forces are meager. Nothing we can't handle."

"And..." the Librarian prompts Ty to continue.

Ty shoots her a questioning glance and clears his throat. "And, Anton has a son named Valerian. Probably seventeen or eighteen years old. He has a crescent birthmark on his neck."

Ty's words drop in my stomach like a stone and the room spins. *Mason. It's got to be him.* I step forward and Ty motions me to be still.

"It's ok, Tyrese. Let her come." She stands up from her desk and beckons me to walk with her. I glance at Samuel and he shrugs. I follow the Librarian out to the terrace.

A warm, damp, blanket of late-February Louisiana air greets us as we walk out on the balcony. The music still pulses in the plaza beneath us. Light from the Library fails to penetrate very far into the old city. Light, however much of it you can find, never seems to be enough in The Wasteland. The Librarian moves to the edge of the terrace and rests her hands on the rail. I stand a few feet behind and wait for what I know is coming.

"Jade, you know what the critics almost always miss about Don Quijote?"

I sigh to myself...a lecture...I knew she wouldn't be able to resist giving me a lecture. And a book talk, no less! Once a librarian, always a librarian. I wait without saying anything.

The Librarian turns to me, the hazy half-light silhouettes her. "Dulcinea," she says. "Dulcinea is who no one ever talks about. She's the crux of the tale, actually, yet she's never truly in the story."

I can't handle this lecture right now. "Ma'am, I need to know...is this kid, Valerian or whatever his name is, do you think he could be Mason?"

"Why is Dulcinea in the story at all?" continues Jayla, ignoring my question. She proceeds with her lecture without missing a beat. "She's Quijote's fantasy—and she suffers for it— but we, the reader, know she will not, can never be Quijote's real salvation. The only one who can save Quijote is...Quijote." She pauses for effect. "Dulcinea is a convenient signal to the reader of how batshit crazy Quijote honestly is. Dulcinea is merely trying to survive the affections of a crazy, ill-fated hero."

"Ok. Fine," I say with petulance reserved only for the woman who is functionally my mother, whether or not she actually cared for me in that way. "I get it. You're saying I'm Dulcinea..."

"No, Jade. That is not what I'm saying," corrects Jayla, sharply. "You still don't understand." Her eyes are less intense now, and she passes a hand over them in weariness.

Looking up at me again, sadness reflects back at me. She only shows me those eyes when she's Jayla, and the sudden appearance of Jayla's tenderness after the Librarian's aloofness fills me with remorse.

"Jayla, I'm sorry," I gulp, all protest gone from my voice. "I'm sorry I left this place...I'm sorry I left you. Samuel was drifting from me. I didn't like who I was becoming. I couldn't be here anymore. I had to see, for myself, because..." my voice trails off.

Jayla turns away from me to face the dark city. I stand beside her—our hands on the rail.

"Because..." she begins bitterly, but hesitates. "Because you were becoming like me."

"I didn't say that."

"Jade, you didn't have to," she says more gently, with a quiet, rueful laugh. Jayla moves her hand, opens it in an invitation, and I place my hand on hers. "Jade, all of this, right here, this is All. There. Is, honey. It's all there will ever be." She turns toward me, takes my other hand in hers, and locks her eyes on mine. "I loved your parents, Jade, in The Time Before." I don't avert my face like I did when I was thirteen. "That's why you came to live with me. We rescued you and Samuel after that Anti attack."

"I know, Jayla, you've told me."

"Jade, your parents...they would want you to live, not follow a ghost."

"But If Mason is alive..." I protest.

"Jade, Mason is dead," Jayla cuts me off. "He died the night your parents were murdered. There's nothing there for you in that Anti camp, or in any other."

My eyes burn with unshed tears, and my chest tightens. I try to pull my hands away from hers but she holds them fast.

"Hope can be as dangerous as it is life-giving," she says.

"How do you know he's dead?" I almost shout. "Did you see...his body? If he's dead, where is he?"

Jayla's voice remains calm, patient as though she's talking to a very young child. "No, Jade, I didn't see his body. But...Mason is dead. Whoever Valerian may or may not be. *Your* Mason is dead." I close my eyes and shake my head no, but Jayla continues. "This, here, today, is all there is, Jade. You. Me. This dark city. The moment you realize that—that's when your real life begins."

"I can't. I won't accept that. Valerian—whoever this guy is—he has a crescent birthmark. Like Mason..." I can't help pleading.

"It's a fool's errand, Jade." An edge returns to her voice. Not yet sharp but prepared to cut if it needs to.

"You have to help me, Jayla. We have to go to that camp..."

"And what?" Jayla snaps. "Blow it to pieces? Bring war back to The Wasteland? We lost too many last time, Jade. Too many died ten years ago driving the Antis out of this area."

Blood starts to beat in my temples and I can't think. Jayla becomes the Librarian again. She faces the half-light glowing in the distant sky, signaling the coming morning with a few streaks of amber dawn.

"There's no we, Jade," she says. "You left and went to the Sisters of Absolute Hospitality. And, you left them, too. I've already mourned Mason's death, your parents' death. Your death." My breath catches in my throat like I've been smashed in the chest. "I've already given you information—that much you were owed. But—violence, war, lives—these I do not owe you. I only concern myself with the people who work for me. And you...you do not work for me, anymore."

"Jayla..." She glares disapprovingly at my breach of protocol. Our moment has passed. I steady my breath and adjust my approach. "Ma'am, if there is a chance that Mason is in that camp, I have to go..."

"And get yourself killed along with your silent little brother." She raises a hand to silence me. The conversation is over. "The only brother you genuinely have. Off on a foolish quest."

"I owe it to my parents...to my family."

The Librarian tilts her head at me and narrows her eyes

when I say the word family. My words cut, too. "Jade," she says while starting to walk inside, "you can stay here, get some sleep, something to eat, but I want you gone by nightfall tomorrow."

And she's left, back inside. That's it. She sits down at her desk, picks up another book, and without looking up, motions for Ty to escort us out. Why did I expect this to go any other way? Fuming, I gaze out at the brightening sky beginning to break the gloom of the city. *Well, that approach definitely failed.*

As I walk back inside, past the Librarian, striding down the scarlet carpet leading to the exit, I think about how Samuel is not gonna like the new plan I'm even now concocting in my head.

# CHAPTER 7

# JADE

BACK IN THE elevator after meeting with the Librarian, we take our former positions: Samuel on the left, me on the right, and Ty in the middle.

Smugness radiates from Ty—he's no doubt gloating internally over how colossally bad that went. But keeping Ty on my side, if that's even possible, might be the key to getting help with investigating the Anti camp. Apparently, it was he who got the Intel on the camp in the first place. *If I can get Ty to help, would Jayla even have to know at all?*

Ty's pride might be wounded, but he's never been a complete jerk; at least, not always and not when we were close. He's also a sucker for a damsel in distress. This much I know.

"Captain Tyrese, huh?" *Maybe simple ego stroking will do the trick?*

"Lot's changed, Jade." Ty's eyes remain fixed on the numbered lights counting down our descent.

"I can see that." I pause for a beat. *If flattery gets you nowhere, you're not laying it on thick enough.* "But I always knew you'd be *captain* one day." Even before the words are out of my mouth it sounds fake.

Ty casts a sidelong glance over his shoulder and catches my eye. He cocks an eyebrow at me and tilts his head. I give him a weak smile. In no time at all, though, it's genuine, my smile. It's actually true that I always thought he'd be captain one day—of course, *after* I made captain. Ty holds my gaze for a moment and suddenly we're sixteen again and in training, late nights talking, dreaming...

The ping of the elevator jolts me out of my memory and Ty leads us back through the lower floor of the Library. Bea is still at the circulation desk. She smiles coyly at Ty as we pass, and Ty nods back. He still clenches his jaw when he wants to look tough.

Ok. So, that's a thing. That's probably why Bea was so, well, extra-Bea with me when we entered the Library. Bea always had an eye for Ty, even when we were serious. I guess it makes sense she would sink her cat claws into him once I'm gone. *Whatever.* They probably deserve each other—the one needy, insecure; the other, needy and selfish. A match made in heaven.

Ty walks with Samuel and me across the plaza. The music and partying have wound down and a hush has fallen with the coming of the new day. Many have crawled off to their beds or wherever they can find some sleep. The morning erases the night's carefree vibe. But people are safe. The Librarian's leadership may not be perfect, far from it from my perspective, but Jayla has built something here. Space for people to live. Black or white, queer or straight—there's freedom to live in The Wasteland. And that is precious and it's not so common outside this community.

Deference and respect greet Ty in the eyes of the few we pass. Captain Tyrese is a big man in The Wasteland. It doesn't hurt that he's got a sword on his belt and arms that seem to be made of steel. *Calm down. Don't lose focus.*

We arrive at the old Watermark building across the street

from the Library. It was a hotel once. It's all marbled floors and chandeliers and, like the Library, a showcase of the "Civilization" the Librarian has brought back to The Wasteland. It still houses people, but it's become one of the prominent living quarters for Twitcher Hunters, as well as for other important people in the city.

As we enter, we pass twin portraits that face each other across a central foyer. One portrait is of a man on horseback, wearing a funny hat; the other, a man with a high collar and shaggy hair. Jayla told me their names once: Napoleon and Jefferson. Emblems of a history lost to The Time Before.

"There's running water and power for most of the day," Ty tells us. We pass a small dining room with plush chairs. A long bar stretches to our left. "The Bar's stocked, too." Ty smiles, the first real smile he's given me. He clears his throat before asking. "If you...want a nightcap?" He's trying, and failing, to sound nonchalant.

"Oh! Ah, that'd be great, but..." Trying to keep things light, I search for some easy excuse. I glance at Samuel. "Um, Samuel and I are totally tired." Before I can stop myself, I let spite speak for me. "Maybe you could ask Bea?" my voice gushes out, equal parts saccharine and sour, "I'm sure she's coming off her shift soon at the Library." Samuel shoves my shoulder as Ty rolls his eyes, his smile gone. *Oh Jade, what was that? I'm losing him. Keep talking.* "Hungry, too. We're hungry. Especially Samuel." *That's so lame, Jade.* "But, yes, let's get that drink before I leave."

"Ok. Yes. That would be good." Ty's gaze slams into me, snatching my breath. *Goddamn. He does have undeniably nice eyes,* I have to admit to myself in that moment. I was always a sucker for his deep, infectious laugh, his beautiful dark brown skin, the way his presence always filled a room. His competitive streak always made me want to chase him—or, him to chase me. A long silence rises between us. The tension in his jaw increases as he surveys me. It's like hope is too damn tired of sitting and is finally standing up with one long, luxurious stretch.

Samuel breaks the spell. He hits Ty's substantial shoulder and Ty's eyes dart from me to Samuel and for a moment he resumes the role of Captain Tyrese—proud, invincible—but softens into the Ty we've always known.

"Yeah, Samuel, ok," Ty says, a little annoyed. "We get it. You're hungry. For a guy that doesn't talk, you sure know how to shout someone down." Ty laughs. Samuel gives me side-eyes.

"Come on," I say, "let's see if the Cap'n can get us something decent to eat."

"I'll have ya'll's food brought up to your room. Let's head upstairs, second floor." Ty lets a little Louisiana slip into his voice and it's warm and familiar. Like home.

The room is small but it's got two beds, clean sheets, and, as promised, running water in the bathroom. Ty lingers in the door. For a moment the figure he cuts strikes me as funny—like he's an overgrown kid playing dress-up with a sword on his belt. But Ty stops joking with Samuel and gives me a stare that obliterates everything else in the room. *Noooooo, he's definitely not a kid anymore.* There's too much history—and too much chemistry—between us to pretend like we could ever be *just* friends.

He starts to say something but hesitates. "Jade, you can...come back, you know. The Librarian, Aunt Jayla...she would accept you back. And...I would, too." He realizes what that could mean, and to save face adds, in a rush: "For the Hunters, I mean."

"I know, Ty." I can't think of anything else to say. What do you say when there's so *much* that needs to be said, and it feels so big that any words you *do* say might backfire and end up widening the gulf you're trying to bridge?

Samuel clears his throat loudly from the bed he's stretched out on.

"Ty," I murmur, "I made a promise to Samuel. To myself." I look down at the pattern of the carpet and then back into his eyes again. "I made a promise that I wouldn't come back."

"Was it so bad, Jade? I mean, we had so much." Ty gives me a hopeful smile, like an attempt to suss out whether my memories match his. "We could have had everything together, right?"

"Not everything." I turn away.

"Jade, Jayla is right. Mason..." Ty sighs in frustration. "I know you. I know what drives you. I know you're already planning to go and find out for yourself." He holds up a hand as I open my mouth in protest. "Hear me out, ok? If Valerian is who you hope he is, if he's Mason, the kid is gonna be messed up. But, if you come back, if you work with us—with Aunt Jayla and with me—I swear I will help you find out."

His vulnerability throws me off balance. I want to believe him. I want to accept his offer. What I actually want is to melt into his beefy chest, wrap my legs around him, and have him carry me to the bed—tell Samuel to get lost, he can sleep somewhere else...but, Samuel. I pinky promised Samuel.

And I left for a reason. I didn't like the feeling of killing Twitchers. Of intimidating people for Jayla. She always said it was for a greater good. *You have to be harder than the world to survive, Jade,* she'd always tell me. *We're building society from the ashes. It's difficult work, and sometimes you have to make difficult decisions.* Eventually, it got to the point where I felt like I was losing myself. Losing Samuel. But what if the only way to find Mason is by coming back? *Is that worth it?*

"I can't talk about this right now, Ty." Samuel has left the bed now and is walking toward us at the door. I change the subject as fast as I can and raise my voice a little. "And, can you get the food sent? Samuel's gonna go Feral in a minute."

"Alright, alright," Ty says, and locks eyes with me. "But let's get that drink."

"Ok, yes...maybe," I fight the laugh bubbling up inside of me as I playfully shove him out the door, shut it in his grinning face, and lean my back against the closed door, unable to stop grinning myself.

C'mon, Jade, focus. I made a promise to Samuel. Breaking that promise might break my relationship with him. But what if coming back, *on my own terms*, gets us closer to that Anti camp? Closer to finding out if Valerian is who I hope he is, but fear he isn't. Samuel walks back to his bed. I'm not sure how to even begin to have that conversation with my brother.

---

THE FOOD COMES and we eat—gorge, really—on bread, cheese, bacon and eggs. And milk. I'd forgotten how good fresh food can be. I write in my journal, make some notes, while Samuel is already conked out, breathing hard. Asleep.

Stretching out on the bed, my sore muscles relax. I slip Dad's notebook out and start to read.

*As the pandemic worsened, Anti groups grew in power and in membership. It wasn't the beady-eyed racists. It was your aunt, your cousin, your friend. People flocked to the Anti call because they offered protection and a narrative for how to persevere in crisis. And they did it by manipulating that most basic quality of American life—racial superiority. They stockpile guns and ammunition in preparation for civil war against their neighbors. "Defending their way of life," they call it. They wear plague masks or gas masks. There are rumors I'm not sure I believe that they kidnap kids to help fill their ranks...*

And sleep takes me. I dream we are eating. Waffles. With my whole family, from The Time Before. Dad and Mom. Samuel and Mason. And me. Mason still has his curls and he comes and sits up on my lap. Powdered sugar and syrup are everywhere, and he starts to try to feed me broken pieces of now soggy waffle. Dad and Mom are laughing. Samuel is talking about one of his maps of the United States he is obsessed with studying.

Everyone disappears. The light fades and it's night. Mason still sits at the table but faces away from me. The crescent birthmark on his neck glows scarlet. He's older, but it's still recognizably him. As he turns to toward me, his eyes start to flutter and...*twitch...twitch...twitch...*

I wake up to the sound of screaming.

It's somewhere distant. Outside. Samuel is already up and putting his shoes on. It's late afternoon. Samuel and I slept for most of the day. I realize I haven't gotten my saber back from the Library. I put my hat on and tell Samuel to get moving. I glimpse the plaza through the window. People running. As we walk to the door, someone starts pounding.

"It's Ty, Jade. Let me in!" Ty's voice had lost all of the tender yearnings from earlier. I run to open the door and zip my hoodie. "We have a situation," he says, every inch the military captain.

"What's happening?" I sit on the corner of the bed and put my boots on.

"Twitchers," Ty says. "Somehow they got through the perimeter. Around 20 of them. Maybe more. I've assembled a group of Hunters to stop them."

"Ok, so why are you here, Ty?" I finish lacing my boots and stand.

"I want you to come with us." He holds my sword in one hand. "We have an extra mount for you to ride."

My heart starts racing. I can't confront Samuel, but I turn back toward him. I haven't even had this conversation, but I have to go. Something tells me I can't miss this chance. Samuel glares at me—he can see what I'm about to do. "This is not me joining the Hunters, Samuel," I say, knowing he knows. Samuel's angry. He holds up a pinky and signs that I'm breaking my promise.

"I know it feels like that, but it isn't, I swear." Samuel doesn't back down. "I have to do this."

"Are you coming?" Ty says impatiently. I send one last imploring look at Samuel. And without waiting another moment, without trying to explain to Samuel, I take the sword from Ty and we're halfway down the hall toward the exit. Samuel follows and I can feel his eyes burning holes in the back of my neck.

Once we're out on the street we head to the plaza. Stores are shuttering. Littles are being hustled inside. There are six horses ready, only four of them have riders. My hands tingle and adrenaline shoots through my arms and legs. Somewhere, and it feels far away, I'm thinking about Samuel. He catches my arm, turns me around, and mouths the word, *No.* Ty is shouting that we have to go. Samuel's eyes smolder. He's had enough. He signals that he's leaving.

"No, Samuel. Wait. Just wait!" I shout at him as he backs away, as he fades into the crowd, and he's gone. "Samuel!" I call one last time and as Ty shouts my name.

"Jade, we have to go. We have line of sight on several Twitchers."

I mount the horse, a sturdy dappled white, flecked with grey and black. On the Library terrace, Jayla surveys the scene. She gives me a slight nod. I nod back and wheel my horse around to see if I can glimpse Samuel. Nothing. I spin my horse in place and then I stop hesitating and head off at a trot and gallop to catch up with Ty and the Hunters. Once again, to kill Twitchers in The Wasteland.

*15 Years After The Event*

I BACK INTO the crowd forming on the plaza outside the Library as my sister, Jade, mounts a horse. Jade wheels it several times in place, frantically looking for me. She can't find me, but I see her as she stops the horse. She gazes up to the Library's balcony and nods at the Librarian looking down on the plaza from her high vantage point. Ty yells for Jade to hurry and she kicks the horse into a trot and then gallops to join the Twitcher Hunters.

She's gone, riding into setting sun, and I watch her leave. I watch her break her promise to me and it hurts.

*You gotta be kidding me.*

Resentment swells as I turn and walk toward the old Water-mark Hotel. I have to get our stuff. As much as Jade might believe she is the only one who cares—about Mom and Dad's memory, about finding out what happened to Mason—I care just as much. In *my* way. In a way that actually thinks and plans and tries to prioritize. Not just rides off into the fucking sunset...

I climb the stairs and find my way back to the room where just minutes before I had been sleeping. I finish packing Jade's backpack, collect Dad's notebooks, and take a seat on the floor by the bed. I need a moment to center.

*I am here and Jade has left. I cannot change that fact. I love my sister. And I am angry. The only thing I can do is breathe. I am the master of my next move.*

As I sit with my eyes closed, as I take another long breath, something swirls in my gut, which descends rapidly and I tilt the right side of my body slightly upward and let out a very long, very loud, fart.

*There. That's better.* With my eyes still closed, a thought brings a broad smile to my face and I start to giggle: *Samuel speaks!*

*Ahh, Jade,* I think as I return to the reality of an empty room, my sister out riding with Twitcher Hunters, and the sobering realization that I will probably have to save her dumb ass in the near future. The joys of brotherhood.

I get it...sort of. Jade is working off impulse at the moment.

Note to self: I gotta talk to Jade about boundaries...

I smile again and take another breath. *Talk to Jade?* Well, at least talk to her in the way we talk. I sign to her. She learned to sign a bit. But somehow we always manage to understand one another. When we lived with Jayla—from the time I was 11 to the time I was 17—I tried to teach myself ASL. I did adequately, considering I was the only one who knew anything about it. Jade learned some, but it was always hard to practice with her because she'd get frustrated and fall back on speaking.

It wasn't until we left Jayla and The Wasteland and went to the Sisters that signing truly clicked for me. And that was because of Zion, my best friend and the guy who I fell in love with, who is deaf, and legitimately *does* know how to sign. I guess it's ironic that the person who finally taught me to sign is the one with whom words have always been superfluous.

I suppose I should be coming up with a plan. I can't go to

Jayla, at least not yet. Jayla was always kind to us. I know she loves us, in her way. But the whole reason we left—Jade and I refusing to enforce her hold on power—all that shit has yet to be dealt with.

When we first came to Jayla, Jade continued training with the sword and I was taught the bo staff. Jayla wanted us to lead the Twitcher Hunters, which we started to do. Jade was geared up to be Captain. Jade and Ty quickly became friends in spite of their competitiveness. No one was surprised when Ty and Jade started snogging all the time. *Whatever.*

The real problem started when a group of merchants began to challenge Jayla—or should I say, challenge The Librarian—with the idea of free elections. Jayla is a pragmatic sort. Democracy, freedom, liberty—that's all wonderful in theory, but maybe not so great in the middle of the fucking apocalypse. We were rebuilding, she said. We had the refinery. We had an almost functioning society. Twitchers rampaged less and less.

The Antis had been run out of town around the same time as, well, when my parents died. Peace had come, in other words, and people in The Wasteland started to call The Librarian power-hungry. She was great in times of conflict, they said; not so great at peace. People have an incredibly short memory and they generally talk more than they listen. I might not talk, but I see things.

Pretty soon, Jayla started using the Twitcher Hunters as her personal guard. Her enforcers. Early on I said, "Fuck that"—well, not in so many words—but at any rate, I quit. Jade, on the other hand, took a bit longer. And it required more painful experiences to finally see the truth: we had to leave.

A tip came that a group of merchants had secretly been hiding the fact that several people had gotten sick. This was against the laws of The Wasteland. Transparency in sickness was one of the basic rules of the city. Jayla assembled the

Hunters and Jade led half-a-dozen of them to see if it was true. The merchants fought back. It got bloody. Two of them were killed—one of them by Jade.

In reality, no one was sick. Somebody had used the Transparency Law as a pretext for coming down hard on the merchants. Jade thought she knew who that was, and she was sure Jayla was behind it all.

Jade confronted Jayla, accused The Librarian of lying about the potential virals to settle her own political scores. It didn't go well, the conversation. That's a bit of an understatement. Jade pulled her blade and Jayla lost her shit right there in the stately office of The Librarian.

"Have you always been a liar, Jayla? Or just lately?" Jade yelled at the woman who had basically been our mother for the previous six years.

As per usual, I stayed quiet. It's one of the fringe benefits of not speaking, like, ever. You kinda get a pass during uncomfortable domestic moments.

Jayla responded with your standard *Don't take that tone with me, young lady* retort. "There are things you absolutely don't understand, Jade." But Jade did take that sort of tone and she didn't want to understand. We left the next day and we didn't return until last night. Four years passed between the leaving and the return. Honestly, all intrigue aside, the real issue was always our relationship with Jayla. Jade wanted a mother, not an aloof boss. I wanted to be seen. I'd like to think that if Jayla had only taken us into her confidence more, things wouldn't have gone down as they did.

So, *no*, Jayla's not the best person to go to right now.

I finally come to a decision as I sit on the floor of the old hotel room. *The Sisters. I'm going to the Sisters.*

After we left The Wasteland, we took refuge with the Sisters of the Way of Absolute Hospitality. We made a new start. A new direction. Some peace. I met Zion there and his twin sister Camila, along with Santiago—Santi, we always called him. Sister Lola taught us the Way of Absolute Hospitality, how to embrace a world that was and is scary as fucking hell. And Jade connected with Santi, a guy absolutely as strong as Ty but, in my estimation, larger souled, kinder, more whole.

Going to the Sisters will be a place to start—to figure out how to reach Jade, how to approach the distance between us.

I stand up and shake the stiffness from my legs. Time to leave. I know what I have to do, so best get on with it. I grab the backpack and quickly make my way out of the room, down the hall, the stairs, through the fancy lobby, and I'm out on the street. I don't take the direction Jade and the Twitcher Hunters rode off in, instead, I head west toward the river, then south along the River Road, which takes me past the ruins of the Old World. An ancient warship founders on the banks of the Mississippi. A huge arena gutted by fire has become home to squirrels, raccoons, wild hogs, and stray dogs. There's a return to nature in many places once you leave the heart of The Wasteland. Buildings, long since captured in a net of green, have become hostages to a leafy menace come to snuff out any trace of civilization's improvement on Nature's original design.

I start jogging at a decent clip. This stretch of road used to be dangerous to travelers. After you pass under the old Interstate, Nicholson Drive leads you straight toward the rubble of the university, which was bombed to shit in the early days of The Event. The virus hit what was then called the United States harder and faster than most of the rest of the world.

Dad's notebooks describe that it was during the chaos of the initial wave of dying that the Sisters of the Way of Absolute Hospitality first came to Baton Rouge. The United States quickly devolved into a series of battling jurisdictions—all for the lack of a clear national policy to the crisis. When fear and panic set in, thousands of people started to run, to migrate across the border with Mexico and Canada.

Dad's notebooks are full of ironic humor. Where once apparently the United States had tried to close its borders to Mexico and to the rest of Latin America—the "immigration problem," Dad said many had called it—now Mexico, the Caribbean, and much of South America had closed its borders to the United States.

Thousands tried to escape Baton Rouge, New Orleans, Houston, as well as scores of other cities and towns in the southwestern United States. But the borders were closed. A robust business in human smuggling developed—you could hire a guide to lead you and your family into Mexico. Dad got a kick out of that in his notebooks. Said the world power dynamic had flipped and U.S. citizens had finally figured out that migrants were simply people, like them, had always been people like them—regular people put in a bad situation outside of their control. Issues that had once driven migration to the United States were now driving it in the opposite direction. Poverty, violence, and economic insecurity aren't respecters of people. Apparently, Dad wrote one time, the world had realized that no country held a monopoly on freedom, security, or hope.

And that's why the Sisters came.

Sister Lola led a group of missionaries from Mexico, Cuba, Haiti, and Puerto Rico to set up a project to help displaced people in Baton Rouge. They came despite the risk of infection, violence, and the growing anti-foreign sentiment in the United States. The Sisters of Absolute Hospitality, they called themselves. They were Catholics, in the main. Sister Lola had a history of working with the poor in Mexico. But the coalition was actually quite broad—Pentecostals, other Christian denominations, and eventually other faith traditions, such as Buddhists, Jews, and Muslims. Sister Lola always used to say that the end of the world seemed as good a reason as any to give up on petty theological fights.

In addition to the diversity of faiths, the Sisters became a model multiracial community. A parish of predominantly Black Catholics moved from New Orleans to Baton Rouge. Several AME congregations joined, as well as a couple dozen Black Baptists from the city. Building a diverse community of faith in Baton Rouge was no small project, considering the white supremacist resurgence in the city and around the American South. But, they persisted.

Sister Lola chose a particularly odious place to rebuild her haven for the dispossessed. She picked an old slave plantation called Magnolia Mound. It was once a forced labor camp that imprisoned African Americans for life. A white family owned everything and somehow convinced themselves that other human beings could be property. I remember thinking after I had first read about American slavery in some books kept in the Library that it sounded like a huge joke. I mean, *really?* From what I read the United States constantly viewed itself as this, like, beacon of freedom. And yet, even decades after slavery ended, Black Americans weren't treated equally.

At any rate, Sister Lola decided both to make Magnolia Mound into a true monument to the atrocities done there and to also re-consecrate it as a place of complete solidarity with the oppressed. She began by utterly destroying the old plantation home on the site. In its place, she rebuilt a chapel to all faiths, united by the common bond of Hospitality.

She also decided, on the advice of several members of the community, to cut down several of the enormous live oak trees on the property. They'd once been used to subjugate and murder enslaved African Americans—people had been chained to the trees and whipped, some had even been hanged from the trees' limbs. She used the wood to construct several shrines dedicated to the memory of those unjustly killed.

My silence doesn't mean I can't think or don't think. Sometimes people mistake being mute for being, well, dumb. *Their loss.* Silence has given me a chance to learn, to read, to remember.

---

IN THE DISTANCE, the lights of the Sisters' cloister tell me I'm home. There should be a few guards, armed with bo staffs. Absolute Hospitality for the Living and Dead doesn't mean pacifism, as Jade always thinks. It means, simply, the aim to act not out of anger or fear, but from love. Ending a life—or ending a waking death in the case of the Twitchers—must only be done if it can't be avoided. If it's an act of kindness. A radical acceptance. An embrace. In that context, there is no violence. Only love. In other words, the Sisters still teach physical combat and training. They can still kick ass, but the said ass-kicking must be a protection of the mission of Hospitality.

As I'm jogging toward the lights, I start to imagine Zion's face when he sees me. I am so eager to see his bright smile and dark eyes. But will he be angry? Hurt that I left so quickly over a year ago, without so much as a word of departure? I'm thinking about what to say instead of watching my surroundings. I'm nervous to see Sister Lola, Zion, Camila, and Santi. The community.

From the shadow of a tree by the road, a figure rushes toward me. The force of the charge knocks me down and it takes more than a beat to get my bearings. There's a sharp pain on the side of my head where I hit the road hard.

And then it's on me—he's on me. It's definitely a man. Breathing hard. Scratching at my face. I shift my body to counter his weight and manage to flip him off me and I roll to my right. I'm up on my feet and spin. I start toward the lights of the cloister, probably 200 yards in the distance, but I run straight into another figure, who's raving with rage.

Two Twitchers? *How did I miss them?* I was so lost in thought I was blind to my surroundings. *Stupid.* Both Twitchers begin to run at me. I have no weapons, no time to think about my next move. I crouch in the road and brace for impact. I close my eyes and hear it—*Thwack-Thwack.* Two swift sounds of wood cracking heads.

A woman in a red robe appears, a phantom pulling her bo staff back to its ready position after delivering the two lighting quick blows to the Twitchers. Her first swings only stunned the Twitchers. One is on its knees howling. The other walks punch drunk shaking its head in pain.

The woman wheels the staff once, twice, and on the third revolution takes a stutter step and brings the staff level as she pirouettes in the air. Her robe ripples and flutters in flight, and her staff makes contact with the first Twitcher's head and continues on to greet the second Twitcher's face. *Thwack-Thwack.* Bone crunches. *Swack-Swack.* She delivers the final hits and the two Twitchers lie on the ground motionless.

Sister Lola stands backlit over me now, her staff at rest, her robe seemingly unruffled.

"Samuel. Welcome, *mijito.* I had a feeling it would be you." She reaches her hand out. I take it. "Before I give you a year's worth of hugs, we must pray for those I've embraced."

I kneel with Sister Lola as we pray.

"*Remember, O most gracious Virgin of Guadalupe, that in your apparitions on Mount Tepeyac you promised to show pity and compassion to all who, loving and trusting you, seek your help and protection.*"

*"En Ti ponemos toda nuestra esperanza. Tú eres nuestra vida y consuelo..."*

As we pray now together, in Spanish, I smile. It's good to be home.

Then: the hug from Sister Lola. She brings my head to her chest and her arms envelop me. I feel lost, once again and not for the last time, in the arms of Dolores. Until that is, she squeezes too tight and I feel lightheaded. A throbbing pain follows, I grunt discomfort, and she pushes me away while still holding on to my shoulders.

"Child, you're hurt."

All I can see are stars and a big dark blot where my head had been on her robe. Sister Lola studies my eyes.

"And, you have a concussion."

I wince at her touch and before I can let her know I am gonna be sick, I lean forward into her embrace and proceed to barf all down the front of Sister Lola's robe.

"Bienvenidos a casa," she says under her breath and laughs.

WE RIDE into the setting sun, leaving Samuel and my broken promise. To keep myself and the other Hunters safe, I need to put that out of my mind. Twenty Twitchers come into view.

"Hunters," yells Ty riding in the lead position, "swords out!"

Each Hunter reaches for a sword at their side—mine's on my back. Two riders flank Ty on his right and left. I ride directly behind, in the sweeper position.

Fifty yards out, my body clicks into automatic. We practiced and then executed this maneuver dozens of times. When facing one or two Twitchers, you can surround the target and eliminate it without too much danger to any particular person on your team. A horde of Twitchers is different—small as this one might be.

Twitchers have all the faculties that non-infected people have. And, when they're alone, they often amble around, led by some crazy hallucination going on in their brain. Sure, they're still dangerous, but not like when several or more band together. Then it's like they feed off one another's hysteria. They go into overdrive. They're activated, and whatever cocktail of brain chemicals may be firing, it's a potent mix. They don't stop.

Wound them, and they keep coming. They shout crazy things—things from their past lives, or whatever their brain is telling them is there but not actually there. It's unnerving, to say the least.

Forty yards out Ty yells, "Look alive, keep your heads up. They're carrying."

The Twitchers have weapons—bats, others brandish iron pipes, one has a long chain, another has what appears to be an ax.

Twenty yards out Ty lifts his sword. The Twitchers sprint toward us. Ty's sword sweeps downward, and we gallop at them.

Five yards out, Ty and the front-line brace for impact. The key is to keep speed, to break their line and their momentum on the first charge. After that, you can isolate sections of their force. It's like a super violent, and dangerous, game of Red Rover—a game I used to play with my cousins in The Time Before. If any Twitchers make it through that first charge, those will be left to me to sweep up.

Ty lets out a yell as his horse splits the two lead Twitchers. The one on his right loses its head while its body runs a few more yards before crumpling to the street.

And then several things happen all at once.

To Ty's left flank, two Hunters I know—Trina and Caleb—flawlessly execute the charge and quickly dispatch the lead Twitchers. They manage to separate the remaining Twitchers on their side—two each—and begin to pursue them.

But in the middle of the charge line, the Twitcher to Ty's left flank ducks the initial onslaught and cuts Ty's horse. Ty's momentum carries him forward, as his horse bucks him off. I don't see Ty land, because the Twitcher who cut his horse is barreling straight at me. I don't let up on the reigns of my speckled white but take my sword and backhand the blade through the top of the Twitcher's skull.

I glance at where Ty had been and realize he's on his feet and he's withdrawing his sword from a Twitcher's body. He sees me.

"Jade! Right flank." He turns and engages another Twitcher whose swinging chain almost head swats Ty before he ducks, sidesteps, and thrusts.

I check right. I don't know either Hunter, but one is down-- on the ground--and four Twitchers are on him. I kick my horse toward the circle of pounding, cutting, and dying. With my fore-hand, I slash one Twitcher whose ax is raised ready to strike the downed Hunter. But I can see the Hunter is already dead. He's gone. One Hunter gone. Shit.

Ty is yelling. I snap out of my thoughts about the dead Hunter and realize Ty is shouting about the other Hunter, surrounded by Twitchers, about to do to him what they did to the other. He has drifted incredibly far away from the fight, far to the right flank.

I'm flying—floating—on my ride toward him, and with three paces left I sweep my legs over the saddle to my right and launch feet first, sword in a crescent lift, and sever the head of the first Twitcher I meet. My speed and momentum carry me past the remaining Twitchers and I roll, making sure the point of my blade is down as I hit the ground. The street feels like sandpaper on my forearms.

I pop up to a crouch and see Ty running toward the still-surrounded Hunter. I start to sprint toward him, too, and the Hunter falls to the ground—above him, a Twitcher with a bat. It feels like slow motion as I'm almost there—the bat goes to full extension; the prone Hunter braces for pain, I ready my sword, I jump when I'm four feet away, and my blade hits somewhere between the forearms and elbows of the Twitcher's extended arms. The metal bat clangs loudly to the street, followed by a sickening *thud-thud* of two half-arms.

Ty is busy with two of the Twitchers, and I dispatch another. While Ty's focus is on his task, the now-armless Twitcher runs at him. He's almost on Ty's back, but I quickstep and jab my blade through the Twitcher's fluttering eye and out the back of its head. I withdraw in a clean movement and Ty turns in time to see the poor creature slump to the ground. I ready myself for more Twitchers, but it's done.

Trina and Caleb join Ty and I, and the Hunter on the ground finally gets up, mostly unharmed. I hear a moan come from one of the not-yet-dead Twitchers and walk over to her. She sees me, and it's almost as if the pain of the wound in her gut has made her sane again.

"Plea, please," she sputters. "My so, son..."

I take my sword in both hands, blade down. There's no coming back from where this Twitcher is. And while I know this, my stomach drops and I start to feel cold.

"Please..." the Twitcher reaches out a bloodied hand.

And there's silence after I bring down my sword on her and on her misery. But mine has only begun. I can feel the pain of that woman—so human, so normal. This business of killing the pitiful is why I wanted to leave The Wasteland in the first place. That, and the knowledge of the dead Hunter who Trina and Caleb are now saddling, belly down, on one of their horses. The other Hunter I don't know, the one who lived--the one I saved--starts to cry. Over his dead friend. Over his own failure to act. Over living...

Ty inspects his horse's haunches and sees the gash left by that first Twitcher. I wipe my blade on the dead woman's tattered clothes.

"Horse is fine," Ty says. "Should heal up. Probably can't run for a while, though."

I just glare at him, put my sword in its sheath, and squat to close the now unfluttering eyes of the dead woman.

"You were good...as always," Ty says. He puts a hand on my shoulder. I shake it off.

"Not good enough." I stand and meet Ty's eyes. "Not good enough to prevent painful, shitty tears tonight for whoever loved that Hunter." I point toward the limp body hanging off Trina's horse. "What was his name, anyway?"

"Carlos," Ty says. "He was new. He's...not our best."

"Then why did you let him come?"

"We needed him," Trina says, giving me a scowl. "And Hunters know the risk. You have to be tested..."

"Test?" I wheel back to Ty. "He's fucking dead!" I want to hit him. I want to scream at him. The memory of Samuel floods back. Oh my God, I've got to find him. My broken promise.

"Jade, you're right," Ty says. "I know. But you need to remember. This...right here." He points at Carlos. "This is why we have peace in The Wasteland. We kill so they can rest. It's the way things are. Have you forgotten?"

"No. I haven't forgotten, but maybe I just don't believe in that anymore. I don't want to live like that anymore."

Ty opens his arms wide and gestures to the battlefield. "But you were born for this, Jade. Look. Holy Shit. You...you're one badass Hunter. I've never seen anyone like you." Ty steadies my horse after it comes to nudge my arm. "And we're good together." The horse paws the ground. Ty holds the reins out to me. He lifts my hand to take them.

And then I know. I can't. I can't take the horse, can't go back with him, can't...face Jayla.

"No." I shoot daggers at Ty and his eyes flinch slightly as though I've wounded him. He lets go of my hand. "I'm not going back, Ty. Not now. Not like this. I have to find Mason." My throat starts to tighten. "I have to find Samuel." I turn from Ty and take a breath. "I need you to go."

Ty doesn't say anything. He turns to his own horse, busying

himself with the bridle. He mounts and, though the horse can walk, it's clearly in pain. Trina and Caleb and the other Hunter are on their horses. Trina has the dead Hunter—Carlos—face down over the horn of her saddle. Ty joins them and I lead my horse to Trina.

"Here, you can put our friend on this."

"I'm good," Trina says.

Ty speaks up. "The horse is fine empty and mine will be ok once it stretches its legs a bit." He starts his horse at a slow walk. The speckled white's reins are in one of Ty's hands. He turns back. "When you get your shit together, the horse will be waiting. Me too." He pauses. "But not forever."

I stand there in silence and watch the four riders turn back toward The Wasteland, letting Ty's wounded horse set the pace. The street is almost totally dark now and I crumble into a crouch with my arms around my knees. Ty and the riders are far enough away. And for the first time since I was 13, when I had just moved to The Wasteland after the death of Mom and Dad, I begin to cry.

I'm alone. *I need to find Samuel.*

I stand up and turn away from the city where the only light appears to come from the distant Library. I wipe the snot off my face with the sleeve of my hoodie. *Not now. There's no time for that.*

I will find Samuel. But first I know I have to go to the Anti camp. I must see for myself.

Alone.

THIS IS the view from the balcony of my Library. I have been tasked with it. To govern it. To protect it. I do what I must.

Jade rides a white horse. It spins in place with nervous energy and from where I stand above it all—above the plaza below—Samuel backs into the assembled crowd. Jade searches frantically for her brother, but then steadies her horse and gazes up at me on the balcony. I nod my head to her. She nods back, she spurs the animal's flanks and gallops after Captain Tyrese.

This is what it feels like to send your nephew and the child you raised into danger. It feels like power. Awful and terrible. And necessary. They must fight an enemy you knew was coming...*Ah, Jayla dispense with the safety and the justification of detachment*...an enemy I knew was coming. There, that's better. Truer. An enemy, in fact, that I have had a hand in creating—an enemy I have allowed to exist in order to draw out and annihilate those who would threaten the world I have built.

It is part of a larger plan--not without risk, mind—but a plan meant to finally end a scourge that The Event and the Twitch could not.

I TURN AWAY from the blue and pink knitted dusk that overshadows my city and walk back through the glass doors into my office. I glance at the book on my desk. Alejo Carpentier's masterpiece will have to wait. I have an appointment to keep.

A man—a boy, really—stands half-shadowed by the bookcase adjacent to my desk. I've left him waiting while I oversaw the emergency response to a horde of Twitchers within our borders.

It is this man, incidentally, who released the Twitchers.

As he moves from the shadow into the glow of twilight, his face comes into view. Lean and unsmiling, but confident and self-assured. His face reminds me of the sepia portraits of brown-shirted German youths from the 1930s. A hard mask of indoctrination that hasn't quite erased the child completely. His temples are shaved and one side of his head is tattooed with a snake eating its own tail—the ouroboros. His hair is long on top; dark curls drape his shoulders and upper back. He wears all black, but not the typical robe worn by the Antis. A red, blotchy scar—a burn, possibly or, a birthmark—creeps out of his shirt and spreads like splatter paint on the right side of his neck. He calls himself Valerian.

"I gather the Hunters have been sent out to meet the Twitchers?" he says. He stands six feet from me with hands clasped in front of his body.

"Indeed. I do not appreciate sending my men and women— not to mention, Jade—into harm's way for your carelessness."

"It's unfortunate, yes," Valerian says and takes a step forward, "but necessary. It couldn't be helped. A growing suspicion of my actions--of my loyalty--has increased among my father's—among Anton's—inner circle."

"I see." I avoid his scrutiny and sit down at my desk. Valerian takes another step forward, while I busy myself writing in a notebook to make him wait. Without looking up, I ask: "How do you intend to deal with the problem?"

"I know the man on whom I can lay blame—a loyalist; one who would present particular difficulties for our plans down the road."

"Hmm. It appears you are solving two problems at once, then. Eliminating a potential rival, as well as covering for your mistakes."

Valerian bridles a bit when I use the word mistakes but keeps his composure. "We all have our weaknesses," he says as a slight smile extends his lips, almost as though an imaginary cord tied to his mouth goes taught, "The reappearance of the siblings does present a weak point in the plan, but what matters is whether we have the resolve to carry through with our promises to the end—whatever the cost."

I pivot in my high-backed leather chair to face him. He fidgets under my direct gaze, while I pause to remind him who is in charge of my office. "I must not have *heard* you correctly. I know you did not just question *my* resolve," I say and leave it at that. He breaks eye contact and I continue. "What is sure is that Jade, no doubt, will try to see you. Perhaps even tonight after she helps to neutralize the Twitchers you released into my borders." I don't raise my voice. I don't need to. I learned long ago that my words can shout or whisper all on their own.

Valerian's brief attempt to spar with me has passed. He returns to rigid attention and the imaginary cord stretching his lips into a smile has gone slack.

"I will post extra security for tonight's burnt offering," he says, "which—no doubt—will see the elimination of my rival."

"As for Samuel," I say, "he will most likely return to The Sisters." I turn back to my desk and shuffle some books from one pile to another. "You might consider sending a team there, to the

Sisters, in order to keep up appearances with Anton—if, in fact, you do manage to capture Jade at your borders."

"It will be done," Valerian says without hesitating.

I study his face for a moment. He carries himself like a man, but I remember he's only seventeen. "Jade—especially Jade—believes you to be..."

"As you've told me," Valerian stops me mid-sentence. "But it matters little, as long as you are able to manage them?"

"I have managed them before. I'll manage them now." Valerian is once again trying to undermine my confidence. I don't bristle under his condescension, which is a product and a consequence of his upbringing.

He's been taught that a Black woman is of no account, is not capable, and is not to be trusted. Unraveling the knots of his racist worldview has been slow, painstaking. One twisted thread at a time. It's something I had to do with Jade and Samuel, albeit to a lesser extent, when they first came to live with me. I did it out of love for their parents. I wouldn't do it under other circumstances. It's difficult, wearisome, and frequently pointless, work. But for Valerian, I must do it. Whatever tightly knitted vision of his own superiority he's speaking out of, it won't work, even where Jade and Samuel are concerned.

"I must go," he says all at once. "The offering will be tonight." He pauses a beat. "But I must reiterate the terms of our arrangement." For an instant, fear distorts his face, like a statue of wax that begins to melt and then manages to arrest and reverse the process. "Anton will die" he continues, "and I will be confirmed as the new Grand Dragon. For this, our Southern friends will leave me to rule in my own way."

I clasp my hands in front of me, on top of my copy of Carpentier. "Yes," I assure Valerian. "Give us Anton and you'll be free to rule as whatever sort of mythical creature suits your fancy." I smile slightly.

Valerian doesn't return the expression. He considers a reply, thinks better of it, and then turns to go, exiting behind the book-shelf—an exit I had built for my own egress, but which has facil-itated Valerian's diplomacy and, perhaps, his own education over the past several months.

---

AFTER I'M sure Valerian has safely exited the Library, I consciously relax the muscles keeping my neck and shoulders rigid. I stretch my head to the right and to the left. It's difficult to manage so many emotions emanating from others. From Jade and Samuel. From Valerian. Their feelings cling to me like wet clothes. It's almost as if I know their thoughts before they speak, like whispered secrets meant only for me. Octavia Butler called Lauren Oya Olamina an *empath* in her book. I suppose that's as good a word as any for the power I have—an empath.

The emotional mask I wear protects me from being too vulnerable, from feeling too much. I let the mask drop now and let out a deep sigh. I rearrange my long locs and take a moment to study my favorite bead, running my fingers over it, remem-bering what it signifies: my love for Her, and Lolita's love for me. A gift from the woman the rest of the world knows as Sister Lola.

Scandalous! I think. The Mexican Nun, who runs religion, and the Black Librarian, who runs, well, everything else. We used to joke, Lola and I, about how the trashy romance novel blurb of our relationship would read. *When the love of learning and the love of God is not enough...the Librarian and the Nun must seek satisfaction together in the bookstacks of an ancient library touched by the sacred fire of the old gods. Ha! Yes, simply salacious...*

I allow myself, just for a moment, to go to that place in my mind that's only for Her and I.

Lolita arrived in Baton Rouge just as the world was going to Hell. She was trying to save it, of course. She established a community of committed women, and later even a few men—The Sisters of the Way of Absolute Hospitality. For my part, I was actually a librarian in this place. I'd been hired after the hurricane drove me from New Orleans to Baton Rouge. I started as a Library Tech. For the first time in years I felt like I was home, and began studying for my Master's degree in Library Science and then went on to a doctorate in history. I wrote my dissertation on the Haitian Revolution—the first and only successful slave rebellion that led to the creation of an independent republic. I wrote about Louisiana slaveholders and their fear that a similar insurrection would happen in the American South. Some even believed that the Haitians would invade and free enslaved Africans in the United States. It never happened.

But, oh, how I thought about that. What if Dessalines or Boyer had sent their troops north across the Caribbean? There was plenty of homegrown resistance to slavery by the enslaved right here on American soil. That fact should always be remembered. But a freedom army of Haitians coming to liberate enslaved people in the American South? That would've been something amazing and terrible and glorious.

It's an irony of history that the so-called Age of Reason was also an era when the most people in the history of humanity were held in bondage. Carpentier's line comes to me: "Man finds his greatness, his fullest measure, only in the Kingdom of This World." It's true, I suppose, but I do wish a man hadn't been the one to lead the Haitian Revolution. The mistake of Dessalines and Boyer was accepting peace through capitulation for the sake of economics and recognition. For security. A woman would've finished the job. At the very least, I think, as I settle back into reverie about Lolita, a woman will.

I remember the day she gave me the loc bead of course—a small token, really, but special, treasured, because it came from her. I gifted her a small silver crucifix she could wear as a neck-lace. It was December 12th, the feast day of Our Lady of Guadalupe. But what I really long to savor, like the taste of cane sugar in fresh coffee, is the day I first saw her. I had risen to head of the Library in The Time Before. The newly rebuilt Library, a symbol of hope and progress downtown. Hope. I remember being full of hope, despite the growing pandemic. I helped establish a place open to all despite the growing sickness.

I met Lolita at a community meeting for an organization called FORWARD. It was a consortium of progressive groups, churches, activists—all trying to come together to build an equally just society even while white supremacy grew bolder and more blatant. The Antis in their infancy. But the boil that the Antis became erupted only because of the systemic infection.

Lolita was charismatic. Kind. She was a force to be reck-oned with. But also gentle. It's best not to describe Lolita through contradictions, but through her virtues, exploded. A poem by Clarissa Pinkola Estes always comes to mind when I seek to describe Lola. "Mi Guadalupe"—I always switched it to Mi Lolita—"is a girl gang leader in Heaven...she is unlike the pale blue serene woman...and with Such Immaculate Love."

We talked for three hours after we met at the FORWARD gathering. Both of us, wearing our masks, walking together on the levee's path. We would begin to say goodbye, that we had to go—had to be up early—and then one of us would say something that unleashed a fresh conversation. Our connection was deeper than words. It was understanding. Although, ironically, we never agreed completely on anything—especially the role of violence in addressing hate groups—but still, there was respect and admiration for the other. The brush of her hand against my shoulder as she finally said she had to go—the only physical contact we had that night—felt like the moment you jump off a diving board. Motionless for an instant and then you feel the fall begin in your stomach as gravity takes you.

I wanted that feeling again and again and again. There were more nights of talking after community events. More walks on the levee with the sound of the river not far away, the current rolling despite the world stopping, halting, dying. But never more than an intimation of something more than deep regard, than friendship.

I told myself we had an implicit understanding that conceivably if things were different—in another life—we could investigate our connection further. But there was no room for that exploration here, or now. She was a nun. Not a Sister of Impenetrable Chastity as one might expect, but a nun, nevertheless. She was consecrated to her community and to her work. And I to mine, for that matter.

Once I tried to tell her I thought I was falling for her. I asked her to dinner. Not many restaurants were open anymore, but I made her come with me to an Italian place where you could still sit on the patio. We drank pinot grigio. We ate cambozola cheese and roasted garlic on toasted bread. On my third glass, my inhibitions sufficiently weakened, I said I thought I loved her. "Y yo tambien te quiero," she said, dashing my hopes with a laugh and a pleasant smile. She meant she loved me in a friendly, platonic way. Her expression changed. Five minutes later she said she had to return to her community. Something about duties to attend to, like a weak excuse, meant to provide a quick exit. And she was gone. Silence. Nothing. I was left in my Library, with the knowledge that I'd driven her away.

I pick up my copy of Carpentier on my desk as the vision

subsides. I intend to read. But as I open the book, my hand returns unbidden to the loc bead Lola gave me as a gift. I let myself remember more—just a bit more—of the night, so long ago now, it's as if it happened to someone else. Reports of the Twitch, as people were calling it, were all over the news. Many had thought the pandemic was behind us. The world was getting better. Then: a news item of a man in Mississippi killing his whole family after making them pancakes. Crazy reports of people going mad. It was a series of occurrences that would come to be called The Event. No turning back.

It was a night not long after I'd heard a similar report, but this time, it had happened in Louisiana. Just past midnight, I was in bed reading, some book I don't even remember now. I heard a knock at my door, and a jolt of adrenaline made me reach for my 9mm that I kept in my nightstand. My heart pounding, I went to investigate the knock. There had been rumors of murders all over the city. Parents turning on their children. Lovers found dead in their beds. I crept up close to the door. Another flurry of knocks.

"Soy yo," the voice said softly, almost in a panic. I heard crying.

"Lolita?" I said through the door, my heart still thumping. "Why are you here? What's happened?"

"Can I come in? I need to talk."

"Of course. Yes." I opened the door and Lolita fell into my arms and started to sob. She wasn't wearing her robe and simple red habit. She had on jeans, white tennis shoes, and a black T-shirt. Her black hair hung loose and wavy.

"Jayla, I can't. I can't. I can't." That's all she could say. She kept crying as we moved to my couch and I held her. She wept. With bloodshot eyes, she looked up at me from the crook of my arm and chest. Our faces inches apart.

"I'm afraid," she said, her voice almost nothing.

"Why?" I asked, lightly stroking her hair. "We will be ok. I will protect you, trust me."

"No. I'm not afraid of the murders." She paused and sat upright, turning to face me. Her eyes darted from me to the wall behind me and then back again as though resolving to go further. "I'm afraid that I will lose...*you*. There is something I must say." She took a short breath and licked her lips nervously. "I am afraid I will lose you if I do not tell you but scared to take the risk." She looked down, rubbing anxious hands along the tops of her thighs. "But I'm not sure where we fit."

"We fit, together. Always. I'm not going anywhere." I tried to calm her, comfort her.

"I have to tell you that I have been afraid. I was afraid, too much, of the pain of loss. What if I told you the truth, and lost you? It would hurt too much."

"Tell me what, Lolita?"

"That yo te amo, Jayla," she whispered, her shoulders rising slightly waiting for my response.

Her words struck me like the moment on the levee when her arm brushed my shoulder. The falling was inevitable, now. But we would fall together.

The words tumbled freely from my mouth. "I love you, too, Lolita. Whatever that is or whatever it means." I laughed.

A frown darkened her face. She began to push me away. "But, I love you, entiendes?" Lolita said. She thought I was making fun of her.

"Yes, I understand you," I laughed. "I'm happy, Lolita. I'm laughing because you make me so, so happy."

"No, Jayla. But I really love you." A blush painted her cheekbones.

Without saying anything more, Lolita kissed me. Tenderly. But I could feel her lips tighten as she tried to hold back tears-- hot tears running down her cheeks and then wetting my own.

She didn't pull away again but murmured "te amo, te amo, mi amor," as we tasted salty tears, like the tang of ocean brine on a swimmer's lips. We held each other that night and we found one another—time and again—the one becoming the other and finding on the other side that you'd found yourself. Together that night.

---

AND THAT'S all I allow myself to remember. No more. It was too much to let myself remember. I'm tired. That was then. I kiss my hair bead softly and straighten my locs. And this is now. Sister Lola and the Librarian—bound together and forced apart by the world we've tried to build. I would trade it all, I think as I turn to my book, I would trade every last molecule—my Kingdom of This World—to return to that night.

I finish reading my copy of Carpentier, which I've read so many times its pages are crumbling. It's been several hours since the Hunters went off to eliminate the Twitchers. I should hear something soon.

Moments later, Captain Tyrese comes into my office. His face is drawn tight, eyes intense.

"Ma'am, we subdued the threat. But one of our Hunters is dead." I tense with momentary concern. "Jade is fine. It wasn't her. As always, she saved our asses."

Tall, strong, smart, a little vain, but Tyrese is always honest when it comes to Jade. I know he still loves her. I hope Jade hasn't clouded my nephew's judgment. I hope his love for her doesn't get him killed.

"But, there's something else," Tyrese adds. "Jade wouldn't come back with us. She headed in the direction of the Anti camp."

"Jade is a grown woman," I say as I set my book aside. "She can take care of herself."

"Yes. Of course," Tyrese says, perhaps a little embarrassed. "But as we were coming back to The Wasteland—back to downtown, I mean—we heard the drums begin."

"There will probably be a cleansing tonight." The words come without emotion. "I wouldn't worry about her." I pick up a pen and start writing. Tyrese remains at attention. He has something to say. "Is there something else, Captain?" I ask.

"When are we going to deal with the Antis, ma'am?" His posture relaxes and his tone becomes casual. "I can't understand why we haven't done anything to stop them."

"Captain Tyrese," I say sharply, bringing him back to attention.

"Ma'am," he says standing rigid.

"Trust me. Don't question me."

Captain Tyrese nods. "I'll secure our borders, ma'am, with extra vigilance tonight."

"Thank you, Captain," I say more gently. "That will be all. And thank you for your bravery." He turns and walks down the red carpet that leads from my desk to the doorway on the far end of my office. After he leaves, I rise and stretch my legs and go to the windows that overlook the city.

I sigh as I exit through the doors onto my balcony. A momentary breeze comes in off the Mississippi, a reminder, in spite of the merciful relief it offers, of how hot the nights are growing. Jade, I think, well you're nothing if not predictable. I can always count on Jade's ability to undermine my plans. *But*, I smile to myself, *it's a good thing I saw that coming.*

# CHAPTER 11

# JADE

DARKNESS DESCENDS as I take North Boulevard up to 19th, then cut over to Government Street. I'm passing all the roads we —Samuel and I—just took less than twenty-four hours ago. The cemetery. The junk shop with "Fagin" and the Ferals we set free. (There's no light coming from the building). And then I head straight down Park Avenue past the house Samuel and I crashed in the other night. Everything remains unchanged.

But this time I'm alone.

How far is too far across the line? Would I even know?

The thought—the question—runs through my mind and it strikes me as darkly funny. *You're wondering this now, Jade?* There's no one left to tell me. I've pushed everyone away. No one left to answer the question: except me. I'm the only one left to talk sense to this woman walking toward a camp of white supremacists armed only with a sword. I'm not sure I give the best advice.

Except: Maybe come up with, like, a rough outline of a plan?

I leave the street and make my way toward City Park, cutting through skeletal ribs of burned-out houses, using my sword a few times to hack through jungled backyards, hopping fences, even breaking through a few. Weedy vines twine their branches through the chain-link, like a vice grip of long green fingers. Antis. What do I already know? I pause to get my bearings. To ground myself in something I do know.

Anger. Anger overwhelms me when I think of the Antis. I have flashes of the day when my world utterly fell apart—ten years ago. For most of the planet, the world had already gone to pieces by then. But for me, it was ten years, three months, and twelve days ago.

My family was still intact. Mom was strong. Dad, too. The Twitch and the ensuing unraveling of society toughened my parents. For five years my family survived. Dad went from being a professor with a potbelly to a swordsman, sure-footed and quick. And when Dad was away, more than once I saw Mom bloody the nose of some creepy guy who had started to bother us at one of our camps. Our family bound together, and like those weedy vines twining through the chain-link fence, we managed to hang on *together*. I was a big sister to two little brothers.

*"Jade, I'm counting on you,"* Dad always told me. *"You have to take care of your little brothers. You have to be responsible for them."* The old life of The Time Before had ended, but we had each other and had to count on each other. Dad told us the dangers. He told us about the Antis. We heard about raids. Purges. Yet we also heard about life rebuilding in Baton Rouge. Dad and Mom had been friends with Jayla, she wanted them to join her new community--it was being called The Wasteland. It was a possibility, Dad told us, but not yet.

I remember overhearing Mom and Dad talking one night. We were camped with several families. We had kids our own age to play with. We lived in tents, tried and failed to keep dry, and scavenged. We trained with what weapons we had. It was late, my brothers had fallen asleep. I heard Dad's voice from my parents' tent. The hushed tones of my parents. Their questions. Their lack of answers. Listening was entering their world of uncertainty.

"I don't have a plan, babe." Dad's voice whispered. "Leaving could be just as dangerous--more dangerous--than just staying put."

"We have to do something," Mom said, her voice urgent.

"Yeah, I know," Dad said, sighing. "But Twitchers are still out there. What if we..." His voice hesitated. "What if we get sick, too? What will happen to the kids?"

"What about Jayla?"

"I know, Sarah. But there's no guarantee there, either. The last time we talked to her...she's different. Talking about any means necessary. She had armed guards."

"But Jayla knows us. We could..."

"Is that what's left?" Dad's voice cut her off. "Stuck between crazy white supremacists and a would-be warlord?" He cursed under his breath. "I don't mean that about Jayla, I just..."

"Jayla is not a warlord. She's actually doing *something*, at least."

Dad's voice was silent. "The Hospitality Sisters might be just as bad. Peace is great, except when you're surrounded by a horde of friggin' virals. Where is it *safe?* Where can we give the kids a life worth living?"

"We are strong, Joseph." Mom's voice had certainty. Intensity. "We have to be."

"I don't know anymore." Dad started to talk slower. Deliberately. "I told Jayla, I asked her, to take the kids if anything happened to us. She owes us. I stood with her in that skirmish with the Antis last year. I helped clear downtown of Twitchers. And she agreed. She invited us to stay. Maybe..." Dad's voice trailed off.

That was the last time I heard Dad's voice when he wasn't yelling for us to take cover. The next morning, early, the Antis came.

I had just opened my eyes, as weak light filtered into the tent I shared with Samuel and Mason. I heard voices and crept up to the tent flap, unzipped it, and saw men standing at the treeline. They wore dark robes and beaked masks and looked like black vultures patiently awaiting the glut of a carrion feast. I glanced at my parents' tent. Dad was already standing outside, sword in hand, the moment suspended in a stillness that still haunts me.

And then my world shattered.

My memories blur together like I was submerged underwater. The robed men called out with garbled voices. My father yelled something back, loud and defiant. I remember one of the tents of the families who camped with us bursting into flames. Screaming. I remember the screaming. Running. Gunshots boomed from the treeline like thunder. Bodies dropped to the ground, limbs twisting unnaturally. Antis, two big shapes in dark robes, swooped in and grabbed my mother. I had the boys by the hands and began running toward my parents. Dad wheeled around, desperate, his face a mask of rage and anguish. "Go! Now!" he yelled at me. "Hide!"

We ran for the trees. From our hiding place, I watched horses enter the camp. An Anti unleashed his semi-automatic rifle and a horse crumpled to the ground, its rider flung from the saddle like a rag doll. Cries of agony came from a robed Anti as another horse, snorting with fury, trampled the life out of him. Dad's sword came down on one of the Antis who was on top of Mom. The man went limp and slumped forward, dead. Dad helped Mom up and they stood back-to-back. Dad lacerated an Anti who rushed them. Mom swept the legs of a second charging Anti, kicking him senseless while he struggled on the ground.

But there were too many of them. All I could see were robes and legs and fire. I thought Mason was right beside me, but suddenly I saw him sprinting through the chaos, rushing toward my parents who were motionless—dark stains on their clothes. I clambered out of our hiding place, telling Samuel to stay put. Before I could reach Mason, a hideous bird-man caught him, carried him off, while another slammed into me, knocking me off my feet. I coughed as thick, acrid smoke enveloped me. Powerful hands pinned my arms. I choked for breath, unable to scream, heavy, black cloth covered my face.

When I woke up, the first thing I saw was Jayla's face. She told me my parents were dead. Mason was gone. Samuel wouldn't speak.

"It's my fault," I whispered to Jayla, clutching her tight as I rode behind her on the saddle of her horse. She was taking us to the Library.

"No, child," she told me. "It's not. Put that out of your mind."

But I couldn't. I've never been able to. From that day to this, there is one truth I've lived with. *It's my fault.* It was my responsibility to protect my brothers...and I didn't. Even when everything else fell out of focus and uncertainty spun around me, the one concrete unchanging reality that I was able to cling to was that I had failed my parents, I had lost my brother, but I would find him and bring him back. So, it's not over. As long as I'm alive and breathing I can make it right...

*What do I know about the Antis?* What I know of the Antis is overwhelming pain, fear, and hatred. And none of that serves me now as I make my way to the edge of City Park where the Antis have once again started to build a camp.

I stop at an outcropping of trees about five hundred yards from the Anti camp. I breathe. I remember Sister Lola's meditation. In and out. Empty my mind of clutter. After a bit, focus returns.

So, what do I know that's actually useful?

The Antis usually have a perimeter watch. Depending on the size of the camp, that means at least two or three mobile guards. I'll need to find cover, somewhere I won't be spotted, but also close enough to actually see what's going on in the camp.

I breathe again. Slowly. *In...hold...and out...hold.*

What do I know about City Park? The North end, closest to me, has a few scattered structures. Paved sports courts long since overgrown with kudzu. An old squat building, red roof, with arched porticos in the back. Jayla told me once it used to be a place where they kept art, a gallery. If I had to guess, I'd say that would be the best place to establish headquarters. So, that's the place I need to see.

A single story is visible from the front of the building but, as the terrain drops off, it reveals a second story around back. There's an upper terrace on the backside. It overlooks a sort of grassy plaza, which feeds into more or less open grassland to the south, which ends at a lake.

I decide to approach from the East. Where once stood grand, stately homes that skirted the park and the lake to the south, skeletal cadaverous houses now molder in decay, undergrowth sprouting from bones made of wood, plaster, and brick. At least the ruins provide some cover. There are a few lines of trees between the road on the East and the old gallery building. I take one more centering breath before standing and starting for the East road.

As I walk, I hear drums beating, the loud thud-thud-thud grows stronger as I get closer to the old gallery. When I'm in line with the building, I crouch behind the wispy witches' hair of Spanish Moss hanging from the low-lying limb of a sprawling live oak. My view of the activity is blocked by another line of trees. Damn. I scan left and right, and then quickly move to the next tree line.

The beating is almost deafening now, and a huge bonfire ignites in the middle of the grassy plaza that sits below the terrace of the old gallery building. On one side is some sort of cage. Human shadows move erratically on the other side of the iron bars, I can't exactly make out how many. Probably hundreds of Antis circle the fire; most of them also carry torches. Their robes and masks trigger all the fear and hatred I've been trying to push down. I can feel my fists close and my jaw clenches. In that moment, I have an overpowering urge to run headlong into the crowd, screaming my vengeance, sword out and thirsty for blood. Suddenly, the drums stop.

All the masked faces gaze up at the terrace of the old gallery. Floodlights bathe the balcony in a harsh glow. The Antis must have a generator and gas...how did they get gas? A hooded figure wearing a hideous beaked mask appears. He's flanked by two similarly dressed torchbearers. Another hooded and masked figure, shorter, stands to the right of the man in front.

The lead figure holds his hands up to the crowd. Cheers arise from the grassy plaza and then a slow chant: An-ton, An-ton, An-ton. The figure holds his arms out again and silence descends on the crowd. For a moment crackling and sparks from the bonfire are audible. Firelight illuminates the grotesque masks of the Antis in half-shadow. Weird voices, cries, and mumblings come from the iron cage just below the terrace. I can just make out guards with weapons, trying to silence the prisoners. Anton is given what appears to be some sort of microphone.

"Beautiful, my friends. Beautiful are the feet who bring good news. And I bring good news: Purity and Health!"

The masked figure's voice is nasal, high-pitched. It's like a bad toothache—acute and constant, drilling through your skull. More cheers swell from the crowd. More chanting. Anton raises his hands and silence falls again. The figure to Anton's right stands motionless.

"Purity is fire that cleanses. Purity is fire that consumes. And, like fire, purity winnows out the chaff." Anton motions his torch-bearing guards and gives an order. Down below the terrace, a prisoner is taken from the cage. At the same time a figure is led out from the porticos on the West side of the building. The two captives are brought together directly below Anton, who observes all from his terraced perch. Screams can be heard from both of them. "Bind the unclean together," Anton says.

Cries of "No, not that," come from one of the prisoners. From the other: unintelligible raving.

"Purity is also a fire that brings health, my friends. But, tonight, we have disease in this camp."

Chants thrum from the crowd: Burn-Burn-Burn...

"The disease is not just the despicable animals within this cage, justly punished for their iniquities, judged by the Almighty with plague."

The cage is full of Twitchers, I realize. Why is he keeping the Twitchers in a cage?

"The sickness," Anton speaks again, "has even spread to our own ranks, and the smell of that iniquity rises to the Heavens!"

Burn, Burn, Burn, the crowd starts again.

"Here, we have one that has trespassed under the cloak of our kindness. Under the cloak of our civility, here we have one that has trespassed." Anton points to the man who is clearly not a Twitcher, struggling frantically, pleading for mercy. "One of our own Elders has been consorting with the vermin who infest The Wasteland. Wooed by Jezebel's promises of peace and friendship with the unclean." Anton points again at the prisoner: "Ecce homo!" New cries rise from the masked crowd.

"We, my friends, have learned from past mistakes," Anton

continues, his voice becoming more shrill. "From the mistakes of our predecessors. A decade ago our people were pushed back from this place. But here we stand! We have returned to fulfill our Promise—to go into the land." He quotes a verse from what I can only guess is the Bible from memory. "'Now go and smite Amalek and utterly destroy all that they have, and spare them not; but slay both man and woman, infant and suckling, ox and sheep, camel and ass.'"

"Tonight we will make an offering, and we will bring health to this camp, just as we intend to bring health to The Wasteland. Let all the unclean take notice! Both viral and mixed blood and everyone who pretends friendship with these—Our God is a consuming fire!"

The drums start beating again and the crowd parts for the prisoners, leaving a path all the way to the bonfire, which roars ever higher after being supplied with fresh wood.

"And there came a fire," Anton begins to shout, "out from before the Lord..."

The two chained prisoners—one, the Twitcher; one, the so-called Anti traitor—are dragged by several guards toward the fire.

"...and consumed upon the altar the burnt offering and the fat..." Anton continues amidst the growing clamor of the crowd.

The two men scream as they are held aloft. Another long chain is secured to them and brought to the other side of the bonfire. I realize I'm digging my nails into the palms of my hands and biting my lip to keep myself from screaming as I watch the Anti and the Twitcher get tossed into the bonfire and kept there by chains locked on both sides. I want to close my eyes and my ears.

Anton finishes speaking as the drums grow louder. "...which when all the people saw, they shouted, and fell on their faces."

The crowd kneels with faces to the ground. On the terrace, Anton takes his hood down, as does the young man beside him.

*Valerian? Is that him?* I think.

Both Anton and the figure beside him remove their masks as the crowd continues to keep their faces in the dirt. *Valerian's face.* It's too far away. His hair is long and it's dark, curled slightly at the ends. It resembles Samuel's hair. My father's hair. I've got to get closer.

As I move from my hiding place to get a better vantage point, I take a step and sense someone behind me. Before I can turn there's a sharp crack, a blinding light in my eyes, and a dreadful pain.

And then everything goes dark.

# CHAPTER 12

# JAYLA

MY DESK CONTAINS a vital link to the outside world—my BCH-270 dual-band two-way transceiver. Without it, I would not have been able to coordinate the plan that I am now trying to safeguard from Jade's blundering interference. Which means I have to contact Lolita.

Dammit. I'm not looking forward to having to apologize.

I enter my office from the balcony doors and sit in my dark brown leather chair. I slide open the drawer and pick up the two-way radio. Apologies are not my strong suit. Our last conversation transmitted over the BCH-270 ended in a fight.

Most experience Sister Lola as a sweet presence. Yes, she's sweet. But that nun can also be a holy terror when she wants to be. She radiates stubbornness with a smile and a prayer. Her stubbornness, her sweetness, her faith—it's everything I loved about her when we first met. But you learn after loving someone for so long that the things that attract you, in the beginning, can be extremely difficult to live with more than a decade later. Falling in love takes no effort at all, really. Actually loving some-one, now that's harder. Especially when she never wants to listen to you.

I hold the small, plastic BCH-270 transceiver in my hand for a moment before pressing the call feature. Lolita keeps her own handheld—a copy of this one—under her robe. Usually, she responds quickly. A few minutes click by and then the transceiver comes to life, clear, but with a bit of static.

"This is She," I say. "Over."

"Bueno, this is Her, mi amor."

She and Her. Our call signs for one another.

These calls are always a chore. We've never figured out how to communicate as partners *and* as the leaders of two very different communities. Polar opposites, really. I'm a realist, a pragmatist—I have no room for the faith and optimism Sister Lola exudes. At my core, I know this is the only world we'll ever be given. Sister Lola believes in worlds without end. It's really a rubbish foundation for civil communication.

I take a breath and begin. "Our contact is in play, but there are issues."

"What issues?" Lolita says.

"Two little, inconvenient issues—who are always meddling." The static hangs for more than a moment. "Are you there?" I ask, my voice rising. "Why do you do this? We need to make some decisions."

"*Sí*," Lolita replies. "But your tone. I cannot speak with you if you talk this way."

*Dammit. Tone.* I have to work on my approach. We've had this conversation before. I take a deep breath and try again.

"Yes, I know," I say, my voice softening a bit. "I am only trying to inform. I am probably unleashing my anxiety on you. You are the only one I can do this with."

"Just remember," Sister Lola says sweetly, "that you are talking to *Her,* not someone else."

I close my eyes and grip the BCH-270 tightly. "Yes, of course, my love," forcing the words out as kindly as I can.

"And, those *two little issues*, as you call them. They, along with all our people, are who we fight for, no?"

"I fight for *you*," I say. "I fight for *us*. I never asked for the additional task of raising two orphan children—even if their parents were our friends." Ten years of piled-up resentment pushes up from my belly and burns in my chest. "Grown babies, really, and one of them never acts with any sense." I unclench my hand around the transceiver. I try to relax my neck and steady my breathing.

"There, that probably feels better now, *mi amor*," Lolita says. I know she's smiling. I let out a small laugh myself—more a transfiguration of my fury than a letting go. "When you release your feelings," Lolita continues, "when you're honest about it, that's the first step. It feels better, no?"

"Maybe," I say. I still want to hold my resentment. It keeps me focused.

"The ways of Providence are sometimes mysterious, mi amor..."

Oh Jesus, I think. Not the ways of Providence...

"...And los santitos have plans for those two. Just as they have plans for you and for me."

I decide not to respond to that. It's a losing battle. She is welcome to her little saints. "Plans are what we need to discuss," I say, trying to steer the conversation back. "The boy, no doubt will be heading your direction."

"I already have him," Lolita says. "He's sleeping now. He received a fine bump to his head. A Twitcher attacked him outside our gates. He's fine."

"Beware any new visitors. I believe our contact will be sending someone to you as well."

"I have it in hand, mi amor."

"Good." I take a deep breath. A full gulp of air, which fills my lungs, and then I keep it in my cheeks before letting it out. And now it's time to talk about Jade.

"Is there anything more?" Lolita asks.

"Our eldest daughter has most likely been captured."

"Any ideas on the next steps to take?" Lolita says, not sounding concerned.

"I don't know. I believe our contact will be forced to make an example of her in order to keep up appearances."

"What?" she says, the concern now creeping in. "Does he not know who she is?"

"Yes...and no. I have not been able to truly find out what is driving our contact. I had thought I made progress, but the boy's true motivation—I am not certain with whom his loyalties lie."

"Well, you must do something. We've been given a responsibility."

"No. I am not responsible to do something." I let the words out but immediately regret them. There's silence from Lolita. Static over the BCH-270. I've got to work on my tone. "I don't know what to do," I say, softening my voice. "This is the moment. If we start things in motion too soon our Southern friends may not be ready to assist."

"Mi amor, it is an act of faith."

"But," I say, wanting to dismiss the idea of faith, "if our contact chooses to go another way, I may not be able to save her." The words feel foreign to me. Resentment is one thing—letting a girl you helped raise die is quite another. My choices are narrowing. I don't like it when my choices narrow.

"I believe," Lolita says, thinking for a moment, "I believe our contact will come through. Possibly her captivity will play in our favor—that child has Protectors we may not have counted on."

I retrieve from my mind an image of the siblings. Jade—just thirteen, and Samuel only eleven. That day when I rode my horse into the encampment and rescued them both from the Anti attack. Both parents dead. People I had known and loved for years. The children's hollow eyes, confused and shocked and empty of hope, pierced my heart.

I had seen hollow eyes like that before--my mother's eyes the day after the storm destroyed our home. No one charged in to rescue us when my family and I were stranded in the city. Instead, they charged in and accused of us looting when we were simply looking for food and water. Armed forces arrived, but not to help those of us destitute from the storm. No, the troops came to protect property, stores, buildings, and assets. I saw a woman, her clothes filthy, and she was hot, sweaty and shaking with rage—I saw this woman yell at the National Guard: "Look at me!" And no one did.

I let the thought go and Jade and Samuel appear again in my memory—just briefly—I see them clinging to me. They were afraid to leave my side for weeks. Fast forward half a dozen years and it's both of those kids accusing me of being a warlord, settling political scores with the Hunters.

What do they know? I didn't tell them about the racist Anti rhetoric that was beginning to take root in our community. They couldn't understand that. Nor did they ever realize their own latent racism at work in how they viewed me. Jayla, the Warlord--they didn't pluck the title "Warlord" out of thin air. It was nothing more than a recycled stereotype of the Angry Black Woman, the "Sapphire," an age-old mechanism of social control employed to punish Black women who challenge the status quo.

Still, emblazoned on the tablets of my memory, despite all the hardships those two have caused me, I'll always see them as two helpless kids with dead parents holding onto me for dear life. Are these the children I'm willing to abandon now if saving them means losing the world I'm trying to recreate?

"Trust and faith are in short supply," I tell Lolita on my

transceiver. All the memories fade from sight. I'm alone in my office. High ceilings. A scarlet carpet running from my desk to the door. A piece of plastic and electronics gripped tightly between my fingers. "All I'm left with is anger."

"But, mi amor, it is said that anger only serves to mask sadness."

I try to think of something to say. But nothing comes. I'm very rarely speechless. It's not that I'm afraid of sadness. But sadness is not an emotion I can afford. Tears are the costliest thing in The Wasteland. If I did let them start, those tears, I'm not sure I could make them stop.

"Send me word," I tell Lolita, "if we need to inform our Southern friends to come early. That might be the only way to make all the ends meet."

"It will be done. Yes," Lolita says, empathy clear in her voice.

"And..." I pause. "I want to apologize."

"What? You? That is one thing I do not believe," she laughs.

"I apologize for our fight." The words are slow to form. "I just think we could find a doctor for you. Someone could help."

"This is not open for discussion," she says, her voice sharper now.

"Cancer is not like the Twitch," I tell her again, as I've said so many times before. "We can fix this."

"The lump in my breast is there, mi amor. We both were saved from the Twitch--immune to the virus. So, if Diosito wants to allow cancer, who am I to argue with Providence?"

"Okay, fine," I reply, seriously annoyed with *Diosito*. "It's clear this conversation is going nowhere." I realize just how tired I feel. "We need to speak about that in person..."

Lolita cuts me off. "We may not have that chance. Let's get through this and believe our little issues, as you say, will come out ok." I imagine her face as she says it, the lines around her eyes, the half-moon parentheses around her mouth. "I have faith in the one with the bump on his head who is now fast asleep."

"True," I concede. "That one sees everything and, like Odysseus, is never at a loss."

"See, there's that faith again," Lolita says, laughing a little. "Books. I always know your head is on straight when you start quoting me books."

Static crackles to life through the BCH-270. I'm almost certain our connection is lost, but then Lolita comes back--clear, strong. "I am still here," she says. And I realize it is the woman I love—Her—with whom I am speaking. Perhaps she has faith enough for both of us.

"I will send word to you," Lolita says. "Perhaps the message will come through the one who is now sleeping with the little bump on his head."

"Ok." A long moment passes. "Te amo," I say.

"And I love you, mi amor. Her out,"

"She, out," I say as I put the transceiver down. I push my chair back from the desk. I close a few books. My neck is tense and all I want to do is close my eyes and sleep, without dreaming.

# CHAPTER 13

# JAYLA

I AM DREAMING.

I know, as I reach for my receding consciousness, that I finished speaking with Lolita on the two-way transceiver. I got up from my desk and walked to my quarters in a hidden alcove behind my office. I remember feeling the softness of cotton sheets and the spongy resistance of a memory foam pillow. And then: sleep. Falling. Relaxing my grip. I must exert every ounce of my strength to control my present. To bend it to my will. I know I am dreaming because I am no longer in control.

And I am falling, again, into dark waters. It's always the same, this dream. Every time. Falling. I am immersed in cold, murky water and sinking backward. I find myself near the bottom, looking up. Diffuse light shimmers above the surface. My back scrapes the asphalt of a road with twelve feet of water covering it. Initial shock turns to a fear that grips me. I am looking for my younger brother. My lungs burn, I want to open my mouth, to take a breath, and then I roll to my right and see an upended car. All bent metal. A twisted frame. Broken glass.

I swim to it and cut my hand on something sharp as I reach inside the car's dark interior. Nothing. There is nothing there. I have wasted time and still, I cannot find him. I can't find Jamarion. It's all I can do to keep my mouth shut, to keep the storm surge water and debris out.

I use my hands to pull myself up and over the car. A dark shape sways in the water, suspended upright. It stops me in my tracks. I don't have to force myself to understand what it is—*who* it is.

My momentum carries me to the dark, swaying shape of my brother and I grab his T-shirt. I grasp at his jeans. My hands seek purchase on his body, somehow to pull him up toward the surface. I let out a scream and dozens of air bubbles escape my lungs and filter upward. I feel down his right leg and I find that it's stuck, caught somehow and I cannot see enough to figure out how to free him. I grasp upward along his body and find his face--a gash on his forehead lets out wispy lines of brown or red, or...I can't tell. I reach my arms around him, the breath almost gone from my chest. I feel a backpack--Jamarion always wore his backpack. It's heavy with the books he was trying to salvage before he fell from our roof; before the dark waters swallowed him; before I went in after him.

In a moment, an instant, I glance at his face. Mouth gaping open. Eyes staring blankly. Jamarion's beautiful face. Lifeless, suspended in water. I turn from the cold form of my brother and push off the bottom, struggle to reach the surface and when I can no longer stand it, I take a breath...

...And I wake up.

It is still dark when I sit up in bed. My mind tries to make sense of where I am. With a groan, I check my watch. Just before 6 AM. For a moment, I feel exactly the same as I did then—after finding the body of my little brother. Cold. Numb. Ashamed. After I surfaced, I saw the small boat that had finally come for us. Too late for my brother. I heard my mother's keening. My sister, Janeesha, reached for my outstretched hands.

Two men in the boat helped lift me beside my weeping mother. All I could say, barely in a whisper, was: "He's gone. He's gone." I could not look at my mother. I failed to bring back my mother's son. I was too late.

A knock from outside my bedroom in the alcove interrupts my thoughts. "Ma'am, we have news." Tyrese's voice filters through the wooden screen that serves as a door. I can hear him shift his weight and see the light bend with his shadow.

"I am coming," I tell him. "Five minutes."

"Yes, ma'am."

I swing my legs over the side of the bed and stand up. Clothes. A clean tank top and a faded denim button-up. Black Jeans. Boots. I dress automatically as an image of Tyrese comes to me. Janeesha had him at twenty—seven years after the hurricane and the flood took Jamarion. I had already moved to Baton Rouge by then. I was studying for my doctorate, learning French so I could read primary documents about the Haitian Revolution.

Tyrese was not part of my life at first. I had left New Orleans and never wanted to go back. My mother had died, soon after we lost Jamarion. Cancer came and she was gone within eight months. I was by her side to say goodbye in a hospital in Houston. She still cried for Jamarion, and I still could not bring myself to look at her. At that moment, I decided never to be too late again.

I click on the small lamp that sits on top of my dresser. An antique mirror, oval, and rimmed with white carved flowers, hangs on the wall. I pause and consider my reflection. The woman staring back at me is not afraid to look anyone in the eye. Not anymore. I slip off my black satin bonnet, which always reminds me of my grandmother, and untie the floral print satin headscarf keeping my edges smooth. I uncinch the band keeping my locs together in a high bun and then straighten them. I flip the ends with my fingertips and feel the loose locs on my back.

Fifty-five and still alive. Somehow immune to the Twitch. Never asked why. Only for more time—more life to finish what I have started.

I turn my face to the right and trace a thin scar that runs along the ridge of my cheekbone. I remember the day in the library—in this library—when I got the scar. It was several months after Lola spent the night at my apartment. We realized soon enough that we would never be able to live together. She had her "call" to the community she was building, and I could not be part of it. We saw each other infrequently. She would stay with me overnight and by morning we were arguing. She usually left in tears—mostly because I was pushing her away. I wanted her closeness, her intimacy, but it also repulsed me. I could not be that vulnerable all the time—not like our first night together.

Baton Rouge, and the world beyond, was coming apart. There were more attacks every day. I fought to keep the library open, even after the city shut down. The coterie of homeless patrons, mostly men, who showed up at the library each day needed a place. Eventually, the violence—the Twitch—reached my library.

It began with one of the Library Techs, a woman named Sandra. She was smart, cute, single, but she lived alone with her cats and never wanted to socialize with any of the library staff. She always wore one piece of clothing that was cat-themed. One day Sandra started acting erratically. She began mumbling to herself about monsters in the tunnels below the complex of downtown buildings. She complained of her eye twitching.

Later that afternoon, I heard shouting and came out to investigate what was happening at the information desk. She grabbed a letter opener and lunged for me. The blade caught me on the ridge of my cheek. It was as if the pain—sharp and quick—unleashed all the rage I'd carried my whole life. I didn't hesitate. I was already carrying my 9mm under my cropped suit jacket. I unholstered it and backed away from Sandra, clicked off the safety with my thumb, pulled back the slide, cocked the hammer for a short trigger pull, and calmly unloaded four shots into Sandra-the-Librarian-Tech's face.

Standing over her limp body, little anime cats on her button-up shirt turning from white to pink, to dark red—that was the moment I knew that the Library was mine and no one was going to take it from me.

The crew of homeless people became my first Twitcher Hunters. When most of them eventually got the Twitch themselves and had to be put down, others came. I recruited mostly younger folks, people unaffected by the virus. My sister, Janeesha, died from the Twitch. She almost killed Tyrese, who was nine years old at the time. Tyrese never told me how she died, or how he managed to survive. I never asked. Family friends in New Orleans drove him to Baton Rouge and he came to live with me at the Library.

Affable, full of bluster even then, Tyrese gave me a reason to forget any weakness, any hesitation, I'd had before the Twitch. But Tyrese, along with Lolita, never let me stray too far from some sense of morality—even when it was damn hard to remain moral. We had to fight for every inch of downtown Baton Rouge, which most people began to call The Wasteland. Twitcher attacks. Looting. White supremacists actively attacking anyone Black or Brown. It would have been easy to become the bloodthirsty warlord everyone expected me to be. Tyrese, taking care of him, training him, forced me to see a bigger picture. Hope for the future, yes, but a future I controlled.

And now Jade floods my thoughts. What do I do about her? Will she be able to take care of herself?

The questions hang in the air, unanswered, and I turn off the light. I can barely see the reflection—my reflection—in the mirror. Despite our fighting, despite our constant disagreements, Jade, along with Samuel—they are also my family. I did not choose her, but she became mine. Always independent, ready to take on the world. I liked that about her when she first came to live at the Library.

I knew her parents and loved them. Jade's mother and I bonded over a love of books, we spent long hours reading and discussing them together. They attended meetings of FORWARD before the city descended into chaos. In many ways they were your common, garden variety "nice white people," but they were kind to a fault and utterly unsuited for what the times demanded of them. I was glad, honestly, when Jade's father took his family and left the Library's protection. They were not committed to a war with the Antis—they never quite understood it as *their* fight. They did not condone or agree with what the Antis stood for, but they never saw the existential threat the Antis posed to everyone until it was too late.

The day I saved Jade and Samuel was just blind luck. Our assault on the Antis had already been planned. The fact that we surprised them as they were raiding the camp where Jade's family was—it was fortunate timing. That was the sum of it. We managed to catch the Antis off-guard. We routed them and they left The Wasteland with their tails between their legs. Until now...

I could not abandon Jade or Samuel any more than I could abandon Tyrese. I will not abandon them now. But neither will I give up on my plan. Too much has gone into figuring out how to rid the Southern Gulf of the Antis. Giving up is not my mode of operation. I don't do failure. Not anymore. When I go into dark waters, I come back with my children.

I realize I am still staring at my reflection in the half-light. Just for a moment, I allow myself to feel, to reach out with my mind. I have always had this ability to sense other people—their feelings, sometimes even their thoughts. It is an ability I usually keep muted. It does not often serve my purpose.

But, for an instant, I allow myself to reach out for Jade and I know she is fine. Hurting, perhaps. But still alive. And then, my serenity is shattered. A picture flashes in my mind and fear greets me with lifeless eyes. I have reached too far. Jade floats upright, her hair like seagrass, eyes wide, empty, questioning why I did not find her before it was too late.

A tear slips down my cheek. *Dammit*, I scold myself. Dreams. They cloud my judgment. Dreams may lie, too. I cannot trust them.

I quickly brush the tear from my face and take my belt with my holstered 9mm off the bedside table. A shaft of light and shadow catches my eye and I know Tyrese is waiting for me. I sense he is nervous on the other side of the doorway. He's probably worried about Jade. The shadows cast from the light outside my room shift and then shift again as I make my way out of the alcoved bedroom.

# CHAPTER 14

# SAMUEL

IT'S morning or something like it. I must've blacked out because the next thing I know I am lying in a bed, in a room, staring at a crucifix on the wall, thinking how the crucified figure reminds me of someone else I know with a Messiah complex.

*Where is Jade?* I worry.

Before I can follow that line of thought any further, a creaking floorboard outside the door to my room alerts me to someone's presence. I realize I'm dressed in a long white night-shirt, care of the good Sisters no doubt. It's like one given to the novices. I pull back the sheets and put my feet on the floor. The room tilts a bit and I've got a splitting headache. Throbbing. I'm gingerly starting to put weight on my feet when I glance up and see Zion's face peeking around the door—his broad face alight with a mischievous grin.

I freeze. I've thought about him every day since Jade and I left over a year ago. I would be worried about what to do with my hands at a time like this, but I need my hands to sign. I stand somewhat unsteadily, and Zion starts across the room. His mischievous grin turns into pressed lips, a hardened chin, and eyebrows drawn together. He stops a foot away from me, furious.

I shape my hand into an "A" and rotate it clockwise twice over my chest. *"I'm sorry."*

Zion puts a strong, open hand out, and angrily closes it in front of his lips. *"Shut up!"*

My palms turn in. The index finger and thumb of both my hands connect, my other fingers on both hands spread apart, and I move my hands in syncopated motion back and forth toward my chest and then away. *"Let me explain."*

Zion shapes one of his hands into a flat palm, while the other hand becomes an L-shape and his thumb acts as a fulcrum to a forward-moving clock. *"Later."*

I handshape a combo of three fingerspelled letters, I+L+Y, into one perfect, simple gesture of commitment and deep feeling. *"I love you."*

Zion, his gaze still burning, sends his index finger to his cheek, then moves it toward the open palm of his opposite hand, taps it twice, and ends by putting his hand to his forehead. *"I know."*

He closes the distance between us and wraps me in a hug that sends me--that sends us--tumbling to the mattress behind me. I grunt in pain. Zion remembers my injury and regards me sheepishly, but with a bit of glee. He wants me to hurt as badly as my absence has made him hurt. I push him playfully, he grabs my hand, our fingers twine, he kisses me...

And then Camila walks in.

"Samuel!! Oh Good God!!" she squeals. "I can't believe you're here!"

Zion and I break our embrace as Camila literally sprints from the door and dives headlong onto the bed landing directly on both of us. I groan in pain again.

"Uh, so sorry to interrupt, boys," Camila says with mock sincerity as she sits on top of us.

Zion admires me for a moment and shrugs. *"Twins suck sometimes,"* he signs. Hooting with glee, he pushes Camila off and then jumps on top of her. I join in as we begin to torture her with a tickle to her sides. Screaming with delight she strikes back, coming at us, mercilessly digging her strong fingers into our armpits, pinching our stomachs, and poking the creases of our necks.

Soon we're all gasping for breath, holding our aching bellies, wiping tears of laughter from our eyes, legs, and arms all jumbled together in a heap on the twin bed. For a moment we're silent and sigh contentedly and I finally feel home again.

"Wait," Camila pops up on her elbows and turns to me, "Where's Jade?"

I sign that I have no idea—that we were in The Wasteland and went to see the Librarian and a horde of Twitchers attacked and Jade rode off with the Hunters. I'm probably visibly angry at this point as Zion touches my arm after I stop signing.

I shrug. *"Whatever,"* I sign as I sit up on the bed. *"She may be an idiot, but she's still my sister and I'm still worried."*

Camila slides her eyes to Zion, then back at me. She hesitates.

I shake my hands—palm up. *"What?"*

"Sorry, Samuel. Yeah, so I heard that there was a huge Anti bonfire last night--a cleansing. Like the ones we've heard about in other places."

I don't tell Camila that I've seen those bonfires close-up. Jade and I witnessed a cleansing outside of New Orleans right after we left the Sisters last year.

"A newcomer arrived last night. Not long after Sister Lola found you. He tried to sell information in exchange for shelter. We told him we don't do that. Shelter is free for all. As we led him to his room, he started crying and said that they burned someone he knew. He also said his partner caught someone before he took off in the dark."

*"Is he still here?"* I ask.

"Yes, he might actually stay. Said he's never felt so welcomed in his life." Camila sees the concern on my face. I try to read Zion, who's still lying on the bed.

*"It's going to be fine,"* he signs to me. *"Jade knows how to protect herself."*

"Samuel," Camila adds, "Zion's right. You can't do anything for Jade at this moment. Let's get you some breakfast and we'll see if we can talk to this guy about what he knows."

*"You're here now,"* Zion signs. *"And I don't think we'll let you go this time."* He smiles and I smile back at him, he grabs the front of my loose-fitting nightshirt, pulls me into a kiss.

"Oh, my word," Camila groans, "a bunch of cheese balls." She pushes Zion and me. "C'mon, boys, it's time to eat. Then we'll see if we can find this newcomer."

A few minutes later I'm squinting into a bright morning outside. We pass the training grounds and see Santi leading five novices in Capoeira. The buzz-twang of the *berimbau* keeps time and Santi sways back in forth in a graceful *Ginga.* He stutter-steps and does an aerial cartwheel, which he's trying to teach to the novices. Santi moves lightly but with purpose. He's shirtless, of course. That's Santi. I smile and think Jade would approve.

Santi and Jade were never a thing—at least, not before we left. But it always felt like torture being around them together. The sexual tension was so thick between them that everyone joked about it behind their backs. Even Sister Lola recognized it. One time, as she was leaving a room that Jade and Santi had been filling with their pheromones, Sister Lola just started to laugh. "The Spirit is much too thick in here," she told me as she walked past me and out the door.

Santi finishes the martial arts lesson and sees me. He smiles and yells from across the yard—something about "his best student has returned." I smile back but I'm tempted to sign something with my middle finger that will need no translation. I literally hate Capoeira. Santi knows that, but he never wasted a moment in kidding me about it. I think better of the middle finger and just lift my hand in a sign of hello, all the while I'm thinking: *I'd rather dodge Twitchers for exercise, asshole.*

Honestly, it is actually good to see him—even if he does lust after my sister, which I'd prefer to know nothing about. Jade sure knows how to pick them. I'm sure if Ty and Santi ever met, they'd probably drown one another in floods of testosterone before they ever got a chance to fight over Jade. *Yeah, good luck with Jade,* I think as Santi trots across the yard, shirt still MIA, muscles glistening in the morning sun.

A faint coo slips through Camila's lips and I'm not sure if it's a resigned sigh or a groan of pain. Santi always seemed to find reasons to pop off his shirt, which of course became a running joke between Zion and me.

When Santi is still ten feet away, I make a peace sign with both hands and then touch my fingertips to my shoulders. Zion laughs and does the same. Santi always thought--and apparently still thinks it now as he starts to do the same sign back to us--that it was my special way of signing a greeting. The peace sign. It actually means "vain," but Zion and I never told him that. Poor guy. I never had the heart to tell him before, and right now doesn't seem to be the right moment, either. I drop my sign and reach out my hand. We give one another a hearty handshake.

"Samuel, I heard you were back." He looks around, while also trying *not* to look around--he's clearly looking for Jade and Camila gets the hint and decides to break the news.

"Jade's not here," she says matter-of-factly.

Santi is crestfallen, a little anyway, but doesn't miss a beat. He's an affable guy, I've got to admit. Camila fills him in on the situation. "I'm just glad you're back," he says kindly.

"We're going to try to see the newcomer, get some Intel," Camila says. Santi joins us as we walk across the yard toward the Community Table. It's a sizable meeting house, vaulted ceilings, an open design, and several long, wood tables. The Sisters use it for almost everything—common meals, meetings, social gatherings. As we approach, Sister Lola meets us at the bottom of the stairs.

"Samuel, why are you out of bed?" she chides. "You need to rest. You got a good knock on that head of yours."

"*I'm ok,*" I sign.

"You want to see the newcomer, don't you?" Sister Lola says, with a sigh. I nod and Sister Lola places her hand on my shoulder. "The newcomer is an Anti. Very hardened. But underneath, very afraid." I start to move past her and Sister Lola lets me walk up the steps as the others follow.

Inside the long tables are empty except for one solitary figure hunched over his food. I should be hungry, but I'm not. My pulse quickens as I walk to the table he's sitting at. I stop across from him. He doesn't look up. He's got long stringy hair, and the sides of his head are shaved. A broken cross of some sort is tattooed on one side of his shaved head. The word "PURITY" is etched in cursive on the other temple. He darts his eyes to the corner of the room and then down to his food again but does not meet my gaze.

"I told that nun, or whatever you call her, all I know," he says while still looking down at his plate. When I don't reply, he levels his gaze at me. I just stare at him. "Cat got your tongue, huh?" he smiles. "You speak-a dee EEngleesh boy?" he says and laughs. I visualize reaching over the table and crushing his windpipe with my fist, but Sister Lola comes up behind me and starts to lead me back toward the door. The Anti snorts a few more laughs and returns to his food.

I storm through the door and out into the yard and head toward a grove of young trees Sister Lola planted when she established the community. All the other trees she had cut down, but she said they needed to plant new ones. Trees have memory she told me once. We're teaching the new trees to remember the new world we're building.

"Samuel," Sister Lola says after we stop under the tree, "I don't know where Jade is. The newcomer wasn't able to tell us much."

I can feel my body tense and my head starts to throb again. I have to steady myself against the trunk of a tree in the grove. Zion, Camila, and Santi are all hanging around the front of the Community Table to give Sister Lola and me privacy.

"The newcomer escaped from the Anti camp last night," Sister Lola begins. She inspects the tree as she talks. "There was a cleansing last night. They burned a Twitcher along with what he described as a 'Race Traitor.'" Lola speaks evenly without emotion. She relays what she knows, not the way she feels about it. "The man said he'd been assigned to perimeter duty last night." Her voice hesitates. I motion with my hands for her to go on.

"The man had been planning to run away. He says he volunteered for perimeter duty so that he'd have a better chance of escape. After the burning, he says his partner spotted someone moving in the shadows. His partner took out his truncheon...and hit the person who had been hiding."

I start to motion with my hands. "The newcomer," Sister Lola cuts me off, "said he couldn't be sure, but he thought the person in the shadows was probably a woman. And that's when the newcomer made a break for it and escaped."

Sister Lola starts to speak again, but I can't hear her over the ringing in my ears. I walk out of the shade of the trees and head straight toward the Community Table house. I pass Camila and grab her arm and make her walk with me up the stairs and into the dining hall again. My vision tunnels. My breath quickens. I stand in front of the newcomer again. I sign quickly to Camila to ask him to describe the person in the shadows that his partner hit with his truncheon. Camila begins to speak and the man concentrates on his food.

"I already told the nun what I know."

I sign to Camila to ask him again.

"He wants to know," Camila says, "what did the person look like. Was it a man or a woman?"

"Hey, tell your silent buddy, here, I don't know shit."

"Did she have a hat? A sword?" Camila asks the man at my insistence.

"Don't know. Could be. It was darker than shit out there. I saw something on the person's back. Coulda been a weapon."

I finally lose my patience and lean over and sweep the man's plate off the table and it clatters to the floor. I turn on my heels and head to the door where Zion and Santi and Sister Lola are watching. Over my shoulder, I hear the Anti say, "Man, I don't want none of it. That's why I ran." I stop and turn back. "But you can be for fuck-all sure that whoever that person was in the shadows—she'll be next—she'll be the next one they cleanse in the goddamn fire."

I push past Zion and go outside. I breathe the humid morning into my lungs and want to scream. Anger isn't even close to what I'm feeling. I recognize instantly that this energy, this desire to do violence, is not like me. I'm the nonviolent one. Jade's the hothead. When we're all outside, Sister Lola reaches for my arm. I avoid her hand and start to run toward the dormitory room where I woke up less than an hour ago. "We don't know if it's Jade, Samuel," Sister Lola calls, but I'm halfway across the yard.

See, that's just the problem. We don't know if it's Jade and I'm tired of searching for my sister. Tired of her obsession with finding a brother who's probably already dead or, if he's not, probably like the asshole sitting at the Community Table. And I don't want to leave—not when I've just arrived. Not when I've just returned home. I'm angry at Jade and I know that's why I just wanted to tear that guy's throat out. Back in my room, I find the few things I came with then sit on the bed.

A few minutes click by and I can't think straight. It's all on a loop--Jade riding off with the Twitchers, me left standing there, and then Zion's face; finally, Zion's face. And then it's all gonna get snatched away. I think about breathing. Clearing my head. *You know what? Fuck that.* I need to be angry for a minute. It's the only thing that I get to have that's all my own.

I study my feet and I hear footsteps in hall. Zion pokes his head around the corner just like he did this morning. The memory of the morning feels like it happened to someone else. He walks to the bed and kneels on the floor in front of me. He lifts my chin. His eyes, his dark eyes, like two uncompromising offers of safe harbor to a castaway lost at sea, search mine. He leans back slightly and uses his middle finger bent at the big knuckle and with that finger's tip he moves his hand upward along his chest. He's asking what I feel inside.

"*I want to stay with you,*" I sign.

"*Who said anything about you going without me?*"

"*No. I can't let you come,*" I sign back.

"*Who said you had a choice?*" His mischievous smile returns as he signs. I sigh in relief, caress his cheek, and then fall into the safe harbor of his embrace.

After a bit, we leave the room together and find Camila and

Santi and Sister Lola are waiting outside. Camila and Santi are both wearing backpacks.

"We already packed you a bag," Camila says, handing me the small bundle. "And here's some bread for a breakfast on the go."

Zion signs to me: *"We're all coming."*

Sister Lola raises her hands over us in blessing and begins to pray under her breath.

Home. I suppose it's a moveable concept. It strikes me that it's really always been that way for me. But it sure would be nice to have a place *and* a people all at once. I say goodbye to Sister Lola. We're headed to The Wasteland to talk to the Librarian. If Jade is there, then all my anxiety is for nothing. But, if she isn't, well, it's likely we're gonna have to *rain* on a motherfucking bonfire.

# JADE

I WAKE UP. It's dark, but it's dark in a room—not outside. The air is damp with humidity. Musty and stale, like wet, forgotten laundry never hung out to dry. Light leaks around the corners of a sheet draped over a small window.

My body tenses with panic. Where am I? Shit. Shit. Shit.

I jolt upright—or, at least I try to—and pain pierces my wrist, which is handcuffed to a metal bed frame. I reflexively pull against the cuffs with my free hand. I'm lightheaded and hundreds of sparks trail in and out of my vision like fireflies and then a sharp throb at the back of my head sends me back to my thin, sweat-stained pillow.

Someone knocked me out last night. *Stupid.* I was being careless. My disastrous attempt to scout the Anti camp comes crashing in. But the pain in my head wins out over the shame I feel for getting caught. Nausea carries me up the crest of a wave, and on the way down, I'm about to be sick...

"Calm yourself," says a voice in the darkness. It's not mine but comes from the corner of the room. The voice startles me, activating some sort of reptilian brain programming, keeping the acidic stew in my stomach from boiling over. Adrenaline prepares me for a fight as I reach wildly in the sheets for my sword. Logically, I know it won't be there, but I'm operating at a loss. Before I know it, the pain in my head starts to reawaken, the world spins, and some of the acrid stomach soup again threatens to make an appearance.

The voice comes from the corner again. "Your weapon has been taken."

I peer into the corner of the room and see the outline of a seated figure. The person's face is in the shadows. The tone of voice is harsh, almost gravelly. But it sounds unnatural—like the person is trying to speak with a low gravelly voice.

"Calm down," the voice says again more pointedly. "It seems we've given you a nasty bump on your head."

The voice is definitely a *he*. I stop searching for my non-existent sword and for the first time I realize I'm only wearing my bra and underwear. My tank top is gone. *Where the hell are my pants?* A cold finger of dread courses over me and I grab the sheets again, this time to cover myself. I scoot as far back toward the headboard as I can, my body curling into a ball. My left hand sticks out, attached to the handcuffs.

"Your shirt and pants were quite bloody, actually." the voice says. "You're not in any danger. At least, as long as you cooperate."

*That's hardly reassuring,* I think. I scan my immediate surroundings for anything I can use as a weapon. "And what if I don't?" I ask the voice in the corner. "What then?" My free hand grips one of the metal rods of the headboard. Can I pry it loose?

"You're smarter than that," the voice comes back. The figure —definitely a man—rises from his chair. He wears a dark robe and a hood covers most of his face. I can't make out his face in the half-light and then realize he's wearing a beaked plague mask, which seems to glow in the darkness. He pulls back the curtain and light floods into the room. Swirls of dust dance in mid-air. I shield my eyes from the brightness, glancing quickly around the room. There's only one door and one small window in the 12 x 12 room. "Why would we bother cleaning you and putting you into a bed," the man says, "if we were intending on hurting you?"

*I can think of a few reasons, dumbshit.* "For future reference," I tell him, "taking off a gal's clothes and handcuffing her to a bed *kinda* gives the opposite impression." Great. Sarcasm. My so-not-very-helpful fear response. I mean, it helps focus my fear. It *doesn't* help me get out of sticky situations like this one. I give up trying to pry the bed frame apart and rub my throbbing head.

The robed figure picks up the chair by the window, brings it way too close to the bed, and sits down. He pulls his hood back and with the light from the window I can see that he's got one of those plague masks on--long nose and absolutely pallid. *Always with the plague masks, these guys.* "The mask really doesn't help, by the way," I say while shuffling as far from him on the bed as my handcuffs will allow.

Every movement I make on the bed lifts the smell of my body's sweat. I notice a small, irregular circle of dark, crusted blood on my pillow. Before panic has a chance to set in, I'm distracted by the robed figure reaching for his mask. I watch him and curiosity momentarily distracts me from fear and calms my breathing. Who is this sitting by my bed?

The long nose lifts up and over his head. The face of a young man, a few years younger than me, comes into view, backlit by the slanted rays of sunlight and the haze of floating dust. It's hard to make out his face clearly.

He shifts briefly forward in his chair and my father's deep-set hazel eyes look back at me. I know instantly who he is. Valerian...no. Mason. It's my little brother.

I've seen those eyes in a much younger face, one not so sad and serious. I've seen them creased with smiles and squinting in a child's giggles. I've seen them stormy with tantrums. And I've seen them wide with fear, wrenched away from me and remembered in nightmares. The features of his face—a nose grown pronounced over the last ten years, an angled chin, no more baby fat—are different. But those are the eyes of my brother Mason.

It's all I can do not to leap on him and hug him. Kiss him. But I don't. I remain still. Why? After all this time searching, he's been my mission. Finding him has been the one certain focus of my life. Now I am overwhelmed with doubt. Does he know me? And if he does...does he forgive me?

I call him by the other name, the new one. "Valerian," I say in a hoarse whisper. "You're the one they call Valerian."

It's the name given to him by the Antis. Who is the man who sits silently waiting in the chair by the bed I'm chained to? That's the truth I fear more than any other—that Mason has become Valerian and my little brother is truly gone. Not dead, but gone nevertheless.

I want some sign from him. And something I can't quite explain keeps me from forcing him to tell me that he's Mason. I'm being asked to play a game, but I don't know the rules and I don't have any idea of what needs to happen in order to win. I don't like playing games I don't know how to win. Maybe, I think, to find Mason I have to first deal with this Valerian.

He shifts his weight again and his jaw imperceptibly tightens when I say the name, *Valerian*. But whatever that grimace means, or whatever recognition it could imply, the traces of it vanish just as quickly as it appears. The dust no longer swirls in the light, just drifts silently downward.

He lowers his head toward me, fixes his two hazel eyes in my direction. "I am he. I am Valerian." He leans forward in his chair and places the mask on the floor. His fingers fold together and his forearms rest on his knees. "Would it surprise you," Valerian begins, "if I said I know who you are, too…Jade?"

He says my name and I do nothing. *Nothing.* I stare at him. *You're Mason*, I think. *You're my brother.* But the thought has no action behind it. What can I do about it? I'm alone in a room, mostly naked, with a guy who just took off a plague mask. The only real truth here is survival. My heart battles my brain and, for once, I decide to listen to my brain.

"No," I tell him matter-of-factly. "Not a whole lot surprises me." I wrap the sheet more tightly around me and Valerian stands. He walks back to the dark corner of the room and picks up a small bundle. He turns and tosses it on the foot of the bed. *Clothes.*

"You should get dressed," he says.

I tug at the handcuffs twice. *Clink, clank.* "Gonna be hard to change with these on." Valerian nods and begins to walk toward the bed. *Oh, God, I think. Please don't let my brother be a perv.* "I will unlock your hand as long as you promise to behave," Valerian says. I pull on the handcuffs again and stare at him annoyed. "You should know that outside the door are several armed guards prepared to shoot anyone who is not escorted by me."

"Guess you'll just have to trust me," I say, sizing him up and eyeing the rods on the headboard again.

Valerian takes out a small key. He bends to unlock the handcuff and the red of his birthmark flashes into view. It's otherwise hidden by his robe, but red blotches dart up and down along his neckline. Our eyes meet briefly, and I know he saw me examining it. I quickly avert my eyes as my wrist comes free and I use my other hand to rub out its stiffness. I'm sure he has a weapon under his robe, so I try not to move too quickly. Whatever my brother's strategy is, it's becoming clearer that admitting he's my brother is not part of it.

"Take the clothes," he says, moving back across the room. "Get dressed." I grab the bundle at the end of the bed. I glance back at him once I've got the clothes and notice he's staring down at his shoes. Ha. Good boy. It would be a shame to add a creepy changing situation to our list of issues. He doesn't plan to peek, it seems, but for good measure, I pull the sheet over me and squirm into a pair of jeans—definitely not a great fit, but I make it work—and a clean white tank top. Once I have those on, I throw the sheet off and swing my feet to the floor.

"Shoes?" I ask.

He just shakes his head no and I shrug and then reach for a plaid button-up shirt and put it on. It's too baggy—it could almost be a dress on me. I tie up the shirttails and make it a bit better fit. "All done," I say.

Valerian lifts his eyes and smiles wryly. It's the first time I've seen him smile since I woke up...I suppose, the first time I've seen him smile in ten years. "It's the best we could do," he says, "without measuring you while you slept."

I return his smile. "You get what you get and don't throw a fit," I say smiling back, hoping to see some flicker of recognition on his face. Our mother used to say that all the time. Nothing. His smile disappears. I cross my legs under me on the bed and hug my shoulders. I know it's probably warm outside, but the cement room feels cold.

Valerian sits again. He opens his robe and a gun tucked in his belt peeks out. I knew he had a weapon. He's trying to make that clear now that I'm not handcuffed anymore. "I'm curious," he begins to say. "What is it that you think you know about me?" Valerian leans back. His eyebrows lift in a question.

Before I have a chance to stop myself, I blurt out: "I know you by your birthmark." I search his eyes for some glimmer, some opening, anything that might tell me we can let down and stop pretending. It doesn't happen.

Valerian's mouth tightens, his eyebrows lower into a frown. "Why do you call it a birthmark?"

Is this my chance? I think. "I mean, I knew someone with a birthmark like yours." I uncross my legs and set my feet on the floor. He's close enough that I could reach over and touch him, but I hold back. "Someone I loved. Someone I still love." My voice trails off as my heart starts to beat. I say what I fear to tell him the most. "I lost him...and it was my fault."

Valerian stares blankly at me. I have no idea what he's thinking. He cocks his head to the side like he's studying me. "Heh," he smirks. "That's not what I thought you'd lead with," he says directly. "A birthmark?" He slides his hand over to rest on his gun. "Oh, no, no," he says, venom seeping into his words. "I thought surely someone from The Wasteland like you would start with me being a fanatic." Valerian turns his head to the right, focusing his gaze on some spot on the wall while he thinks. He glares back at me. "Or, maybe the term you people like to use for us—Anti...or, white supremacist." Valerian's tone turns sharp. There's an edge to it, like someone recounting old insults. "But, why would you lead with a *birthmark?*"

You're making this really hard, Mason, I think. Is it really you? I felt so sure, but perhaps I've been wrong all along? Are you this far gone, or are you just hiding?

I scoot back on the bed and draw my knees to my chest. I pushed too far. Further than he's willing to go. "Because you remind me of the person I lost," I finally say. I glance toward the floor for a moment and then catch his gaze. His eyes neither punish nor question me, and neither do they offer forgiveness.

After a long moment, he says, "Well, ease your mind." His

voice turns upbeat. His tone brightens. He stands. "I'm not that someone." He walks a few paces toward the door. His movement draws me off the bed and I stand as well. "Perhaps the disorientation of the night," he says, "has caused some...fogginess." Valerian crosses to the window and briefly scans the view. "I take no offense," he says looking back at me. "Don't worry. But it's not a birthmark. It's a scar."

"Oh," is all I can say weakly. I desperately want to drop the act--demand he admits that he knows what I know. To tell me he's my brother and that I've not searched in vain. That I can still find him after losing him. But I don't. Instead, I turn to sarcasm. "Disorientation?" I fire the word at him. "Apparently *disorientation* is what ya'll call knocking someone out cold."

Valerian laughs and waves a hand dismissively. It's off-putting. "Yes, sorry about that. We do protect ourselves from intruders." He holds out a hand beckoning me to the door. "But now, I want to show you around our camp, as my guest."

His personality change is frightening. Brooding moodiness has now morphed into some sort of buoyant tour guide persona. As I start toward the door I ask, nonchalantly, "So, how did you get the scar?"

"That's a story for another time," Valerian says as he lets me pass him. He walks behind me and when I stop at the door he knocks three times and then it opens from the outside. He turns to me and smiles: "I want to show you who we really are."

I fold my arms. "Do I have a choice?"

"Oh, it's better out there in the fresh air," he says. "And once you see who we are—who I am—we can talk about what I might know about you, Jade." He steps past me and says a few words to the guards outside the building. He wasn't lying about the armed men. He spins back toward me, almost giddy to give me a tour of what, to me, is a close approximation of hell. It's a weird day, I think. Valerian rubs his hands together—it's hard for me to tell where Valerian ends and Mason begins at this point. "You might just be surprised," he says. "You too can take part in the New Order we're building."

I take a deep breath and walk out the door into the noonday sun.

# CHAPTER 16

# JADE

THE BROTHER I lost ten years, three months, and *thirteen* days ago really is gone. I can't get him back, and the fact that I thought I could makes me so I angry I could scream. As I begin to walk out the door of my prison, I realize that Mason, the little boy I knew, is no more. He has to be. Whether Valerian *used* to be my brother doesn't matter—I'm certain he was. But time has created the man who leads me away from the cell he had me locked in. Time and loss and the twisting embrace of the Antis created someone who clearly believes giving me a tour of a white supremacist encampment is the equivalent of some sort of show-and-tell of the promised land.

I don't know if Mason can be resurrected. I hope he can, but I've little real, tangible evidence for that kind of faith. I wanted to believe that I could rescue him. As if he was a prince locked up in a tower in an iron mask—I'd unlock his chains and he'd return to Samuel and me. Instead, I climbed the tower and the prince invited me with giddy anticipation to enjoy the prison with him. *Is there any way to come back from that kind of brokenness?*

For the first time, I realize I've believed, that I've wanted, too much. Or far too little. I don't get to have the years back that I lost. I have no plan of where to go from here and it really pisses me off.

*Samuel.* Shame and dread descend on me as I think of Samuel. I broke my promise to him not to throw my lot in with Jayla again. I trust that Samuel is safe because I am almost certain he went to the Sisters. And now I'm the one that needs to be rescued. I'd laugh at that irony if it wasn't so painful. Everything I've done--in my mad search for Mason--has only served to put my life at risk and the lives of the ones I love who I know will probably come looking for me.

And now I'm caught playing some weird mind game with Valerian. *Dammit.* I should've just sat on him and made him tell me, once and for all, whether he was my brother--or whether I've gone crazy and can no longer recognize the truth. What happens if my little brother Mason really is dead and now the man Valerian is just toying with me for some other purpose? It would mean I sacrificed so much, relationships included, for nothing. That I followed a pointless quest for the last decade and hurt the people I love—Samuel, Ty, Jayla—in pursuit of an illusion. *Damn, Jayla was right.* Quijote's windmills have nothing on this...and it's really fucking with my head.

I have to hold my hand up to shade my eyes from the sun for a bit as my senses adjust to the brightness of the day. I turn back to examine the building where I was kept prisoner and realize it's one of the sports-ball structures, tennis probably, that people used to come to this park to play in The Time Before. Valerian motions impatiently for me to follow him down a path that seems to lead to the heart of the Anti camp. I track the guards over my shoulder. They stay put.

"No need for guards," Valerian says. "I want to show you what we're like. What life is truly like in our community."

I hesitate for a moment and then just decide to lean in with sarcasm. "You mean, you don't keep the womenfolk chained up *all* day? Who knew white supremacy could be so much fun!" Valerian gives me a side-eye glance. "I mean, when it comes to the end of the day, Anti women really do love to please their men, *amirite?*!" I want Valerian to know I'm not afraid of him or his people. But, honestly? I am *very* afraid of Valerian and his people; I just really don't want *him* to know that.

We're on a cracked sidewalk leading from the sports-ball buildings down to the center of camp. The outlines of a once manicured park are visible but hidden under tall grass, wild weeds, encroaching vines, and the ruins of neglect. Just as I open my mouth with another snarky comment, two young kids —buzzed hair, wiry—plow straight into Valerian's legs. I flinch and stand back expecting Valerian to get physical with them, punishing them for being careless. Valerian screws up his face in mock pain and grabs the two little boys, wrapping them in a bear hug. The kids hoot with pleasure as they try to wriggle out of Valerian's grasp.

"We found you, Val," sing-songs one of the boys.

"When are you gonna take us fishing at the swamp?" asks the other.

Valerian lets go of his bear hug on the kids. "Later, guys," he says and then glances up at me and registers my surprise. "Kids. Family," he tells me. "We're about family, here." The mention of family feels like a knife to my heart. *I* was part of his family once. Valerian turns back to the boys and explains that he has to show me around. The two little ones finally acknowledge my existence and then start to whine.

*Ok, here it is,* I think. *Probably when he says 'family' it's like a super Nazi kind of family. Take a beating for the Fatherland, little Jimmy, it's for your own good.* I brace for a show of disci-pline. But it doesn't come. Valerian just laughs at the boys, says, "Dudes, I gotta do my work, right?" and the boys relent.

"Ok, Val," the slightly older boy says in a last-ditch effort, "but you gotta promise we'll go later!"

Valerian puts up his hands as if to shield himself from their entreaties. "I make no promises," he says laughing, "and I tell no lies." He places one of his long-fingered hands over his heart, gives me a sideways smile that only serves to further destroy me. *That's a phrase Dad used to say to us when we were little. Is he messing with me? Is this all for show?* I want his kindness to be real. The hope that it's Mason's kindness, his humanity, shining through the Valerian mask almost frees me enough to play along. Almost. It's the first tangible evidence that maybe, just maybe, Mason can somehow be rescued out of Valerian's iron mask.

But then the two boys run off and leave me alone with Valerian again. He opens his arms to me, palms up. "See," he says. "We're not such monsters as you in The Wasteland make us out to be." I shrug and shake my head. I pull the knot tighter on my oversized plaid shirt and continue walking without giving him the answer I know he wants. Valerian trots to keep up with me. I finally say off-handedly, "You do remember that, like, not thirty minutes ago I was chained to a bed, right?"

Valerian echoes my earlier shrug. "Precautions," he says.

———

WE WALK into the Anti camp, and it's alive with children running after one another. Women are tending fires for the midday meal while kids play games nearby. A tired-looking mother chides a child who keeps hitting his sister. Men and boys are at work building a house. Some are shirtless and their ruddy skin glistens with sweat in the high-skyed sun. I almost forget that this is not a typical survivor's camp, it is so like the ones my family and I moved around in more than ten years ago. Except there are only white people here. And somewhere around here must be where the Twitchers I saw corralled last night are kept. I scan the grounds and don't see any signs of the makeshift cages. They probably moved them inside after the cleansing.

Smoke from a campfire blows across my face as Valerian talks with a young man around our age, possibly a little older. He's got long hair like Valerian, also shaved on the sides. Tattoos on both temples. The smoke from the cooking fire brings with it the smell of sizzling meat on an open grill.

I shift attention over to where they held the bonfire last night, where they burned alive the Twitcher and the man they accused of being a race traitor. There's almost nothing there. No smoldering pile. No ash, really. Just a dark patch on yellowing grass. The association—between the sizzling meat I smell that makes my mouth salivate and a ritual human sacrifice—horrifies me even as my stomach growls in hunger. I look around and hope that Valerian lets me have a plate of food.

The confusion and desperation I felt a few minutes ago pale in the light of a new possibility I hadn't considered. What if Mason is good at pretending? If Valerian is my brother--and I believe he is...want to believe he is--then I rationalize that he'd have to be good at pretending to fit in. To survive. He's been raised in a place and among a people who clearly have their own creepy vision of reality—one that is all white with no room for anyone else.

That idea fills me with hope—that the crazy prince is simply feigning his madness. But to what end? I can't answer that, and confusion once again rolls in like a storm cloud. Am I fooling myself again? How would I even know...?

A tap on my shoulder behind me. I spin on my heels, slightly startled, and register that it's just a girl. She's got blond pigtails and freckles. Eight or ten years old. She avoids my eyes but just nods and hands me lunch. As soon as she sets it in my outstretched palms, she sprints back to a woman standing by one of the fires.

I decide to skip the meat on my plate. The images from last night make the small piece of what might be steak on my plate powerfully unappetizing. I devour the veggies and the potatoes. Valerian finishes talking with the young man and is pleased to see me eating. Instead of walking toward me he beckons for me to follow him. "Hey, I've got someone I want you to meet," he says. I nod and keep chewing, continuing to stuff potato in my face. *It better not be Anton*, I think.

We walk over to where construction is wrapping up on a new house the Antis are building. Several tall, lean teenage boys are helping a man of about fifty move a few last boards. Clearly the Antis are not interested in restoring the old houses in the neighborhood. They probably want to build their "new order" from scratch. But it's also apparent that they have no problem scavenging lumber from the old houses for this new structure. To the side, piles of salvaged wood are stacked in various shades of green, light blue, and yellow. The wood moved by the three teenagers has been stripped, and the bleached, raw wood color contrasts sharply with the reclaimed building materials.

The older man has long, dark hair streaked with gray. Like the other men, the sides of his head are shaved. He's got a thin frame, but powerful, long arms probably formed by years of manual labor. The man's face is narrow, but his nose juts out in a sharp angle giving him a peculiar hawk-like profile. *Dammit. That's definitely Anton*. I swallow the last of my food and brace myself for the meeting.

As we approach, Valerian directs my attention to the older man. He is working alongside the boys as they move the last of the reclaimed, and now-stripped boards. Up close I notice the man's arms are traced with veins, leathery sun-dried skin pulled tight over hard sinews of muscle and bone. His hands are overgrown and his long, knobby fingers grip tightly around the board he's carrying. A long scar leads from one eye to the corner of the left side of his thin-lipped mouth.

"This is Anton," Valerian says flatly. "My father. Father, this is our...guest...Jade."

*I knew it was Anton. Of course, it's Anton.*

The man wipes his forehead with his shirt. "Good to meet you, Jade." I don't know what rattles me more—hearing Anton call me *Jade*, or Valerian calling Anton *father*. Anton spreads his arms out expansively, like some bird of prey ready to strike. "Welcome to the New Order," he says.

Anton turns to the three teenagers who've been helping him with the lumber. "Go get some grub before it's too late and all the little ones eat it all." He swats them toward the cooking fires as they run by and he laughs a sort of short, high-pitched nasal squawk. The boys are handed plates by women at a nearby campfire.

Anton saunters toward the shade of a tree, waves with his hand for Valerian and me to follow. He reaches down and picks up his water bottle at the foot of the tree, takes a long pull, wipes his mouth with the back of his hand. Valerian is standing behind me and Anton tips his open water bottle toward him. "Clean water," he says. "Mmm. That's the stuff of life. Ain't that right, Val?"

Valerian crosses behind me and stands on my left. "Yes, father, it is." He reaches for the metallic canister in Anton's hand, takes it and drinks. Anton's gaze shifts to me, appraisingly. He leans against the tree and I notice a cloud has momentarily covered the sun. Shade and shadow fill the Anti camp.

"Water cleanses," Anton muses to no one in particular.

I shift my weight uneasily. "And fire cleanses, too?" I don't put much venom behind the question, but it's clear what I'm referring to. The burnings. The terror the Antis instill.

Anton's eyebrows crease and his face goes dark. "Yes," he says, "the dross is winnowed in fire. Fire burns away impurity." His lips retract and a wide lupine grin appears, all teeth. "Water keeps the clean from impurity, while fire awaits those who refuse to stop polluting the well."

"Father," Valerian interrupts, clearly trying to head off a conflict. "I've just shown Jade our camp." Anton's smile fades and he darts his eyes toward Valerian. "We're about faith and family," Valerian continues. "This is what I want Jade to know about us."

Valerian passes the water bottle to Anton but the man waves it off. "And order," he says. "Don't forget about order." Anton directs the comment at Valerian but then turns toward me. Studies me. He moves a few feet from the tree in my direction. "Humans live best when each has his own place," Anton begins. He gestures with his leathery hands toward the camp. Women cooking for men and children. People are eating. Children playing. Some laughter. "When each knows where he belongs," Anton continues, "where he fits in the scheme of things—that's when order comes to the world."

Valerian fidgets as Anton closes the space between us. Anton stops a foot away from me. I hold his gaze, can smell the sweat hovering between us. "I read that in a book once, in The Time Before," Anton says quietly, his crystal blue eyes locked on mine. I hold my breath trying to keep still. "But what good is knowledge when it's locked up in a library, held captive by a Librarian who just doesn't know her place in the order of things?"

I exhale but don't break eyes with him. *No, he doesn't get to say that.* "What gives you the--"

Anton grabs my throat, cutting off my words. "No," he hisses. "No, I won't listen to your lying tongue." He puts a hand up to Valerian, halting him in his tracks, keeping him from intervening. Anton squeezes my neck, cocks his head slightly and re-adjusts his grip. I can barely breathe—if he squeezes any harder it will cut off the air completely. I claw instinctively with both hands trying to pry his fingers away, but I can't gain purchase as his nails dig into my skin. "What were you doing outside our camp last night?" he says in a hoarse whisper. His damp, fetid breath washes over my face. "Hmm? Jade? Daughter of The Wasteland?" he croons, mockingly.

He can't possibly expect me to answer as I fight for air. I'm barely listening as his hand pulls me up to my tiptoes, the pressure on my throat contracting and releasing over and over. Valerian's shadow moves between us. Anton lets go of my throat and I fall to my knees coughing and gulping for air. "Know your place in the New Order, Jade," he says loudly, announcing it to everyone in earshot.

I turn my head and see the activity around the campfires has stopped. The women have their eyes cast down. The men appear ready to do whatever Anton might bid at that moment. Valerian comes to my side on the ground, puts my arms around his shoulders, and helps me stand to my feet. "Well, that went well," he whispers under his breath.

Anton returns to his spot by the tree. "Jade, you too may yet find your place. But there are many things you need to unlearn first." Anton points at Valerian. "My son will help teach you. The women here will teach you." Valerian still has his arm around me, holding me up. I finally feel the air fill my lungs and the urge to cough subsides. Anton lifts his hand, waves at the camp in one grandiose motion, a signal that brings the camp back to life again. He turns away from us, leaning against the tree as if to say he's done talking.

Valerian squeezes my arms and leads me back in the opposite direction, toward my cell on the other side of camp. No children run up to Valerian this time, as the Antis go about their business. I glance at Valerian. He has let go of my shoulders and we walk side by side. His eyebrows contract in a frown and when we reach the room, he says only this: "Do not try to escape. You must be a captive a while longer."

The door slams shut, and I hear the lock turn from the outside. Muffled voices. Orders from Valerian to the guards. I fall on the bed, rubbing the welts on my neck where Anton exercised his power over me, attempting to squeeze the life out of me. Out of all of us.

I think of Valerian...or...Mason, or whoever he is. I think of my brother, so masked--so far gone--I don't even know if it's him. *Do I even want it to be him?* In that instant I realize what Samuel and Jayla have always told me, the truth I could never hear. Never believe. Mason is dead. Because if he's not dead, if Valerian truly is Mason, that's a worse fate yet. Hot tears stream down my face, and as I bury my head in the musty smelling pillow, I mourn the death of my little brother.

# VALERIAN

MY NAME IS of no consequence. Who I was. The name I was given at birth. The boy I was. All of it matters little. So, yes, my name is Valerian. It was given to me by my father, Anton, the man who raised me. But I've had so many different names, other names, like son, like heir, like Anti. And like Liar. Names mean little. What matters is what I do now. Today. Today is the most important day of my life.

---

I LEAVE Jade in the room that has become her jail. I didn't cuff her hand to the bed this time. All I said is that she should not try to escape—that her captivity would last a little longer.

I pause for a moment to listen at the door after I shut and lock it. I hear her now, crying softly. Not a sob or a wail calling out for another person's sympathy or comfort. Just tears. Tears and gasping breaths, the weight of grief pressing on your chest, squeezing your heart with an icy, tight grip. I know that sound because when I was seven years old, I made the sound Jade is making now. It's the sound of despair.

I don't linger long at the door to Jade's makeshift prison. I nod at the two guards. "Make sure she doesn't try to pry open the window," I tell them.

The larger of the two, bearded and bald Erik, nods back. "Yes, Valerian."

"I'll be back in a while," I say. I start to walk away and then remember. "Oh, and please retrieve my robe and mask from the room. Also bring the prisoner water." Erik nods again. He slings his M4 carbine over his shoulder and prepares to carry out my orders. He tells the other guard, Jon, to get some water ready.

Before I have time to make sense of Anton's violence toward Jade, his personal bodyguard walks up the path from the central camp. *Anton must want to speak with me about it.* I straighten my shoulders and meet the bodyguard, Clay, another fifty yards farther down the path.

Clay's temples are shaved after our fashion. He's got a wolf's head tattooed on one side, an Egyptian Eye of Horus on the other. It symbolizes protection, royal power. Clay has been Anton's personal guard ever since I came to live with these people, when Anton took me in. It was Clay who taught me how to use a gun; Clay who molded my fists so I wouldn't break my thumbs when throwing a punch. At 6'5 and probably three hundred pounds, Clay rarely needs to use direct force to get his way, his intimidating size is generally sufficient for making people do what he asks. Not that he never employs direct force. I once saw Clay snap the neck of a Twitcher with his bare hands, like he was getting kindling ready for the nightly campfire.

But to me Clay was always kind, even gentle, especially when I was young. I never had a mother. Anton was not married when he adopted me. His wife died during the original spread of the Twitch. Clay told me once that it was Anton who put her down. She had killed their baby after succumbing to the delirium of the Twitch and then went after Anton with a butcher knife. He ended up drowning her in their bathtub.

Unwanted flashes of what the horrible scene must have looked like come to my mind at times. Plastic boats and rubber duckies plop-plop in the water while the last bubbles of Anton's former life ascend to the surface from his drowning wife—pop...pop...pop, and she's gone. Life over for her.

Life over for Anton as well. It was as if all three of them died—the child, the mother, and Anton. But only Anton rose again from the dead, like some avenging malevolent spirit driven to make the world suffer just an inkling of the pain he himself felt. Grief so great it forces others to bleed.

Not long after, Anton started to stockpile weapons in a local church. He opened the church's kitchen for survivors—white survivors—training the mostly young men who flocked to his call. Self-defense. Rebuilding families. Mutual assistance. He blamed the virus on foreign interference from China, but also on all the non-white folks he encountered.

He had always believed in a natural order—whites on top, everyone else below—but the virus gave him a vision of the Twitch as God's second chance for white people to install that natural order once and for all on the face of the planet. It didn't take long for Anton to connect with others like himself—a network extending along the Gulf Coast from Houston to Mobile—who, as with his awakening, had come up with a very good rationale for why such bad things as the Twitch could have happened—the sin of being non-white—and a solution for putting things right again. Destruction or servitude.

Anton taught me non-whites received preferential treatment long before the Twitch. And the Twitch, he always told me, was just the latest entry on the long list of indignities white people had been made to suffer. In Louisiana, the government started immunizing inmates at Angola prison, which housed a majority Black population, in the first wave.

*"More preferential treatment,"* Anton would recount angrily to me, *"if they hadn't been wasting the vaccine on rapists and thugs, my wife and baby would still be alive."* He frequently said that *"the kindling was already laid. And the Twitch was all we needed to set the kindling aflame. The illegals, the welfare class, street thugs and drug dealers, single moms with their baby daddies--they were all spreadin' the virus through their nasty, unclean, and ungodly living. It was God who made them as they are--genetically weak. More of them got sick than us at first, after all, and more of them died. Round them up and put them in camps, let them tear each other apart! That was the only sensible thing for the government to do."*

For Anton, when the government wouldn't quarantine non-whites, it was a provocation and violence became the only option. Anton and a host of Anti groups, armed soldiers, paramilitary police forces, took matters into their own hands. Until, that is, the Twitch decimated their numbers, too.

The Antis were born out of hundreds, perhaps thousands of such personal losses and disillusionments like those suffered by Anton, which, though originally inflicted by the mute hands of Chance and Dumb Fate, were easily weaponized toward real flesh-and-blood people of color. There's nothing like hatred to keep someone going. When so much has been lost, when so much doesn't make sense, when you feel alone in the dark. Anton discovered that railing against a roll of the dice makes you feel powerless. Hating someone, well, that gives you purpose and identity. It gives you a strange kind of hope.

All I remember from the day when Anton found me was losing my parents. I remember a family I had once, but no details of what that family was really like. I remember the feeling of loss. They were gone, as if they'd evaporated. And then Anton's face filled the void. Clay's face. A woman named Elizabeth. *"We rescued you just in time,"* they always told me. That's all they said. I was inconsolable at first. Anton just held me for what seemed like days until my wailing stopped, until it was just hot tears and breathing. Then the tears dried up and my eyes were red, raw, like someone had tea-spooned salt under my eyelids while I slept. All I wanted was for the grief to end. I wanted to play with kids in the Anti camp. To outrun old memories as I chased my new friends around campfires and trees. Whatever my life had been before was over, so I forced myself to forget. I gladly answered to Valerian. I remember Elizabeth, a woman long since gone now—she caught the Twitch and got shot in the head by Anton—Elizabeth said, *"Leave your tears behind, baby."* It was a night or two after I was rescued. The nights were the roughest. *"Leave your tears behind you, baby,"* she said. *"But don't forget to make the guilty pay."*

Clay waves a greeting when he's a few steps away. His arms are like oaks, not so much sinewy muscle as they are a pair of clubs attached to his body. "Anton needs to see you," he says, slinging his AR-15 assault rifle behind his back.

I nod my head once. "I figured as much." Clay betrays no emotion with his expression. *I'm just doing as I'm told* is more or less what I'm getting. "That was not part of the plan," I say as an afterthought.

"Take it up with Anton," Clay says evenly. He points his massive arm toward the stone building that overlooks the camp. "He's down in the Twitcher pen. Wants to see you right away." Clay's tone, flat and resolute, tells me Anton is angry. It doesn't surprise me. Anton's often angry, and often angry with me. But he's the one who decided to get violent with Jade. Rage percolates in my gut, but I put a lid on it. We had talked about what was going to happen. Jade would come speak with him and we would try to get her to trust us. Apparently, Anton had other ideas.

---

THE TWITCHER HOLDING cell is essentially the basement of what used to be an art gallery in The Time Before. The structure has a spacious terrace on the second story where Anton stands to officiate at the Cleansings. Below the terrace, we installed a series of cages that lead into the basement where the Twitchers we keep can be put during the day.

There's a long row of metal bars in the basement, which creates an aisle for people to guard, feed, or provision the Twitchers while not having to be among them. On the other side of the bars the Twitchers are chained to the stone walls. It protects those who have to go inside the cell, but also serves to protect "the stock," as Anton calls them, from killing each other. Controlling and using Twitchers is part of Anton's strategy of maintaining a supply of disposable shock troops.

Clay walks with me, side-by-side, around the corner of the lower building. I'm certain Anton bawled Clay out, telling him to bring me to see him at once. The door to the outer vestibule of the cell is ajar. We go in, and a damp smell of mildew and human feces greets us. It's somewhere between the odor of a barn and the sickly-sweet stench of rotting fruit.

About three dozen Twitchers are chained to the stone walls behind the bars directly in front of us. Some are seated, rocking back and forth, while others lie motionless and moan. Still others stare blankly in the semi-darkness. All are drugged, I know. When Anton wants them active, he withholds the drugs —mostly benzodiazepines like Xanax, Valium, or Klonopin. We've collected quite a supply of downers on our raids along the southern coast. It calms the Twitchers enough for a time, at least long enough to feed them, which Anton is doing right now.

The outer cell door is open and before our eyes adjust to the darkness of the basement all I hear is the *scoop-splat* of Anton's spoon digging into a five-gallon plastic bucket we use to feed the Twitchers. He's inside busy with the daily rationing. He hears us enter but continues with his chore. I can just make out the long spoon he uses to dig into what is probably leftovers from our breakfast and lunch. Most of the Twitchers are so out of it they barely register his—and our—presence. "Slop for the pigs," Anton says gleefully, as he splats another scoop down on one of the several serving plates arranged around the room. "We gotta keep our shock troops well fed, now don't we?" The outline of his prodigious, white teeth gleam and I know he's smiling at Clay and me. He shuffles a little farther into the cell, sends his spoon into the bucket—*scoop, splat*—another plate receives today's meal of mushy gleanings.

My eyes begin to adjust. I glance at Clay, who stands at attention. "You can leave my son and me, Clay," Anton says. The burly man turns on his heels, walks back the way we came, and stands guard just outside the outer door, his AR-15 slanted at an angle in front of his chest. Anton finishes the last *scoop-splat* feeding and returns his spoon to the now empty bucket with a plastic rattle. He motions for me to join him inside the bars. "Son, sometimes you gotta do the dirty work yourself." He smiles. "'Cause, you're too late to do chores with me." I stand next to him. A Twitcher moans a little in the corner. "It's hard work. It's not always easy. But it will be worth it." Anton puts the bucket on the floor and angles his body toward me.

"Father," I begin. "I thought we had agreed—"

"That's where you're wrong," Anton says. He wipes a bit of mush from one of his hands with a quick swipe. "Jade is a problem that must be solved. She's a means to an end."

"But...?"

"But, what?" Anton turns square to me. His face catches a long, narrow beam of light from the open door. "You didn't actually think we were gonna show her the warmth of our hospitality, did you?" His face shows concern. Pity, almost.

"I thought we'd talked about seeing if she could be influenced."

Anton is about to respond when a Twitcher to my right stirs, reaches out, and grabs my foot. Anton moves in and gives the Twitcher a swift kick to the ribs. A sharp grunt and the Twitcher lets go of my foot, curling into a ball.

Anton returns his attention to me. His eyes narrow slightly. "You aren't soft on that impure girl, are you? She hasn't seduced you with her lies, I hope?"

The question hangs for a moment. "No, father." I pause, collecting my thoughts. I take a step closer to him. "The Librarian thinks she's successfully turned me against you. We may be able to use Jade as leverage to demand that the Librarian recognize our right to expand. We could use Jade to our advantage."

Anton shakes his head sharply. "There's been a change of plans, son." He shakes his head again, puts his hand to his chin, rubbing the stubble there. "No, no, no," he says pondering. "Jade will die." I try not to flinch when he passes Jade's sentence, but I know even in the shadowy basement he senses my hesitation, just slightly, my disapproval. I can see Anton begin to study me. It's the same face he gave Jade before he almost choked her out. "I'm beginning to fear your loyalty," he says sharply. He lowers his hand from his chin, steps closer to me. "Not just to me, but to our cause."

"No," I begin to protest. "How can you question...?"

He holds up his hand to silence me. "I can imagine what that Librarian might have told you about your past." Anton contemplates a Twitcher woman with long, stringy hair. He glances back at me. "The only family you have is standing right in front of you."

Instinctively, I take a step back. "I know that father."

"Do you? You remember that on the day your parents died, and I rescued you, it was the Librarian who started the killing? Right?" Anton takes a step toward me so that we're almost eye to eye. "She had started her reign of terror, flooding the city with impurity, and your family was tragically caught in the middle. It was shameful. I rescued you just in time." Anton points his finger in my face for emphasis. "The only life you have is because of us. This is your home."

It's the story I've heard all my life. I hold my ground but let my shoulders slump a bit, signaling I'm not a threat to him. "Father," I begin in a rough tone, "I am not convinced that bringing war to The Wasteland...we are not ready. We don't have enough troops."

"Well, that's where you're wrong," he points at me again and backs off a bit. "Word just came from Lafayette. The whole Anti force is on the move, converging here on The Wasteland. We'll combine forces here and flush out that Librarian from her roost."

"When?"

"Tomorrow."

"*Tomorrow?*"

"And," he continues, rubbing his hands together, "we need an inciting incident. We need to draw the Librarian out." Anton smiles wanly. "And the death of her favorite adopted daughter— well that just oughta 'bout do it." I take in the information like a sock to my gut. *Tomorrow?* Just as I open my mouth to respond, Anton reaches his arm around my neck and puts me in a choke-hold. At first it seems like playful roughhousing, but his grip tightens, and my hands convulsively shoot up to try and pry off his forearm. With the other hand he grabs the Twitcher woman's long, oily hair and shoves our faces together until they're inches apart. She starts to rouse from her drug-induced stupor, irritated by the shock of pain to her scalp. "I want to know that you are with me, son," Anton whispers in my ear. He presses his forearm tighter across my throat. "I want you to send a message to the Librarian that Jade will be sacrificed in our Cleansing tonight." I try to nod and then tap his arm three times. He releases me and I let out a sharp cough and suck in the fetid air of the cell. He uncurls his fist from the Twitcher woman's hair. "That's the kind of loyalty I require, son," he says as reaches for my shoulder and brings me into an embrace. "The kind of love I need you to have for me."

Anton pats me on the back two or three times. He pats and then he rubs my back in a circular motion. He examines the Twitcher woman coldly and kicks her until she stops making sounds. "That one was waking up too fast," he says. "You always gotta keep vigilant."

I cough once more, spit, and then straighten my shoulders. "It will be done," I tell him. "I will send the message."

Anton smiles brightly, as though nothing has happened. "Well, alright. Let's get this done, then." He reaches his hand for my shoulder, grips it with a too-tight squeeze.

I nod and Anton begins to clean up in the Twitcher holding cell. I exit quickly, without saying a word to Clay who is still posted up as a sentry outside the door. I know I have to send the message soon. I make my way around the side of the building and to the upper level. Inside is a meeting room—a makeshift office—a desk, some chairs, broken paintings fallen from the walls. I find paper to write the message that Jade will have to die.

Five minutes later I've dispatched the sealed note to a courier with instructions to get it to the Librarian. I decide to wait before returning to speak with Jade. There are details, new details, that have come to light. The Anti army from Lafayette, *tomorrow*. I have to think. To plan. But before I begin, I think about the many names I've had in my life. I've always known which one I liked the best. *Mason*. That's the name I was given at birth. It's the name I've been without for the last ten years.

Today is the most important day of my life. It's time to make the guilty pay.

# CHAPTER 18

# SAMUEL

WE DECIDE to set out west, the four of us, just after midday. As we're leaving, Sister Lola grabs me and wraps her arms around me, and we say goodbye.

"Hopefully I won't have to change my robe this time," she laughs while still holding me tight. "I only have two of them, you know, and the other is in the laundry."

I breathe in her scent: homemade lavender soap and jasmine rice. I wonder what my mother would smell like if she were alive. Her face has faded from my memory. It's been replaced by Sister Lola's black eyes, the wrinkles of her smile lines, the squished together concern of her two eyebrows.

"We should take the tracks back to The Wasteland, Samuel," Camila says. "Not the open road."

I nod and Zion and Sister Lola agree. Santi is indifferent, which isn't surprising. He thinks he can handle anything with his agile martial arts skills and devastating smile.

"Whatever you think," he says, "but it'll cost us some time."

I point out our direction and he shrugs agreement and flashes a dimpled smile.

We quickstep across the road and enter a line of trees.

Camila carries a bo staff. Zion has a satchel full of stones and a slingshot. Santi has a pair of baqueta sticks made from bamboo used for the berimbau. They double as a mean set of weapons in a pinch.

I've got nothing. No weapons. Just me. It's always been enough.

There are Twitchers in these woods. Not nearly as many as when I was a kid, but they're around. The virus hasn't disappeared. And some say that you can be immune when you're young, only to get infected when you're older. There's also a chance of direct Twitcher infection; if you don't die from a Twitcher attack, there is a good chance that the transfer of blood and spit and bodily fluids will give you the disease. Fun stuff.

Sister Lola taught us to see Twitchers as people and that embracing them--killing them--is a kind of merciful hospitality. But it was always different from the extermination campaigns in The Wasteland. The Hunters do just that—they track Twitchers down and kill them in pursuit of an idea of safety. The more Twitchers killed, the safer The Wasteland is. But it's an illusion. The virus is always with us. We have to learn to live with it, in spite of it. Sister Lola taught us to only embrace Twitchers when there was no other choice.

The forest is thick with underbrush, trees, and patches of wild bamboo. The day is bright, and the sun sends dappled shadows on the ground. It's balmy, and a few mosquitos buzz around my ears; I smack one that lands on my neck.

We stop at a cluster of trees, and I point to the tracks about two hundred yards in the distance. We decide to move forward in pairs. Two go, while the other two wait, and then we leapfrog until we near the tracks. Zion and Camila are one pair; Santi and I, the other. This way we have at least one person who speaks in each group.

Santi and I are waiting behind a tree when I hear something

off to our right. Three Twitchers crash out of the underbrush straight toward Camila and Zion. Their attention is focused ahead, and they don't see what's coming.

My insides drop as the first one--a woman with a shock of natty blonde hair--side tackles Camila. They both tumble to the ground and before I can move, the next two Twitchers--an immense bearded man and a frail woman--jump on Zion. Santi is three steps ahead of me as we sprint from cover toward our friends.

Camila manages to roll away from the blonde Twitcher. Zion throws a quick elbow to the frail woman clinging to his back. Blood spurts from her nose and mouth and she staggers and falls, dazed, to the ground. The bearded Twitcher wields a mighty branch, and just as he's about to bring it down on Zion's head, Santi delivers two quick kidney shots with his *baquetas*, dropping the Twitcher to his knees. Santi wheels and strikes the bearded man on the back of his head. He pivots and hits the frail woman until she stops moving.

Camila scrambles for her bo staff, lost in her initial scrum with the natty-haired blonde. The blonde, screaming, charges Camila, reaching her before she can get ahold of the staff.

One...two...three steps more and I jump feet first and catch the woman's face from the side before she can reengage Camila. Disoriented, the woman tries to regain her footing, but Camila has her bo staff now and she *swack-smacks* the natty blonde between the eyes and the Twitcher finally lays still on the ground.

"*You good?*" I sign to Camila.

"Fine," she pants. "I didn't see her coming."

Zion is recovering. Santi makes sure the other two Twitchers are no longer threats. None of them are dead. The frail one growls a little on the ground. The hulking bearded man is crying. The blonde's out cold, blood further matting her already matted hair.

Zion catches my eye and smiles. "*All fine*," he signs with an open right hand. I just want to hold him at this moment and, with ten feet between us, we start toward each other. My stomach finally returns to its rightful place. My sphincter unclenches, just a little, and I'm ready to let down my guard, if only for a few brief minutes. I breathe a sigh of relief. It's one thing to have to take care of myself. It's something else entirely to see the love of my life tackled by a Twitcher. I start to sign to Zion that we need to keep our eyes peeled for more threats.

And then Zion's smile freezes. His eyes go wide and some unseen force twists his body to the left. I don't hear the bullet. I'm vaguely aware that Zion has been hurt--that Zion has been shot. He drops to his knees and I run to catch him. I register that all three Twitchers are still on the ground. The gunshot didn't come from them. My feet feel like lead as I finally close the gap between Zion and me. Blood pours from his left shoulder, just above his chest. He stares at me with anguished eyes. Initial shock turns to pain and then fear clenches his face.

*It's ok. I got you. I'm here.* I say all of this with my expression because my hands are busy trying to stop the bleeding. Seconds later I hear yelling. Another gunshot rings out. I spot Camila and Santi with hands in the air. Men with plague masks—Antis —carrying guns, aimed at my friends, aimed at me, move from the trees into the clearing.

"If you touch those weapons," one of the masked men says in a hoarse snarl, "we'll keep shooting."

Out of the corner of my eye I see two Antis disarm Camila and Santi. I try to keep Zion calm. His face is ashen. Two more Antis put metal collars on the prone Twitchers, a chain attached to both like some kind of grim leash. It's no accident those Twitchers attacked us. The Antis unleashed them on us. *What the hell? The Antis are using Twitchers as weapons now?* Another pair of masks try to separate me from Zion, who's breathing hard and who I hope is not going into shock.

*Hell no. Not today.* I wheel and sweep the legs of one of the Antis and he hits the ground hard. I'm about to pounce on him when I hear the sound of guns cocking.

"Samuel, no!" Camila begs.

I stop and reluctantly put my hands up. A sharp crack on the back of my head sends me to the ground and force-feeds me a mouthful of dirt and twigs.

"He don't talk." I hear a familiar voice behind me. "Neither does that one who got shot." I can't quite place it, the voice. It's nasal, condescending, but also oddly fearful. I fix my gaze straight ahead as an Anti ties my wrists behind me, yanks me up, and forces me to kneel next to Santi, Camila, and Zion, who's still bleeding on the ground.

I catch Zion's eye and he signs *"ok"* with a bloody hand. The wound is more shoulder than chest, but his shirt is wet and dark where the bullet hit him. *What do I do? Oh, God, what do I do?* Panic is a screaming voice in my ear. *Why didn't I see this coming?* Anguish grips me. All I want to do is take Zion in my arms.

An Anti stands in front of us and slips off his mask and the same broken cross tattoo and shaved temples appear. The man with the long stringy hair we questioned at Community Table this morning.

The Newcomer. *Dammit.* My thoughts spin as I worry about what he may have done to Sister Lola. *How did he get here?* I can't follow the thought further because the Newcomer squats in front of me, gun crossed at an angle over his knees.

"Well ain't you just a sight for sore eyes. When I heard ya'll was going to the Librarian, well, I thought I'd make sure that didn't happen."

Silence from me. It's just my eyes that do violence, that bore a single white-hot beam of hatred through his forehead. *Is it just me?* I think. *Or am I really in a bloodthirsty mood today?* I could throw my body at him, tear his throat out with my teeth.

"Samuel, be calm," Camila shouts. She can read my body language, knows what I'm thinking. I sweep my eyes over to her and nod. I mouth *OK*. The bloody, and stupid, action I was about to take slips out of reach.

"What's that?" the Anti jeers with his nasal tone. "Cat got your tongue, huh?" A few of the other Antis laugh. The chained Twitchers pull against their leashes. Grunts. Moans. The blows we gave them have mostly worn off and they're beginning to mumble and hallucinate again. The natty blonde reaches toward Camila, trying to scratch at her face. The Anti holding her by the chain wrenches her backward and she clutches the dirt, writhing to get free.

The Newcomer leans closer to me. "Hey. I lied about escaping from the Anti camp. I saw it all. I helped take down that little gal who was spyin' at our bonfire." His breath is hot and smells like the eggs he ate this morning. I don't turn away. "She ain't dead yet, just like I told you." He checks over his shoulder and then back at me. "And if you tell me what I want to know—what I was sent to find—then, who knows, there's a chance she won't be the next crispy-fried vermin to go on that fire."

The Newcomer pauses and almost whispers. His attitude softens, the front he's put up for the other Antis. "If I don't come back with something, they will kill my wife and son," he whines. There's anguish in his expression behind the cunning. "That part about wanting to leave the Antis is true." He searches my face for some hint of sympathy. I don't blink.

"You know he can't tell you what you want," Camila says, "with his hands tied behind his back."

The Newcomer darts his eyes at Camila and feints a back-hand slap. Camila stares him down unfazed.

"I need to know when the attack's coming," he says standing from his squat. "That's it. Tell me that and I'll let the one who tells me go free." He says it loud enough for all of us to hear. "But we'll kill the others." He examines each of us. "Word is the Librarian and the Sisters are planning something." The Newcomer backs up a few steps. "We think ya'll know somethin' about it and you're gonna tell us before you give the intel to the Librarian."

"We're just trying to find out what happened to our friend," Santi says.

"We're not telling you shit," Camila says and spits.

The Newcomer walks over and kneels next to Zion, who lies beside me on the ground. "I'll let your boyfriend here bleed out." The Newcomer sticks his finger in the wound on Zion's shoulder. Zion grunts in pain.

"We don't know anything!" Camila pleads.

"That's a lie," the Newcomer says as he twists his finger again. The Newcomer is leaning over, not six inches from my face. "See, I think that sister of yours—Jade or whoever—was sent as a scout. Are you gonna tell me I'm wrong?" He puts more force on Zion's wound sending a fresh spurt of blood trickling out. Zion writhes and my stomach twists as I long to comfort him.

I don't doubt the Newcomer's story. That his family is in danger if he doesn't come back with valid information. But, as Zion is bleeding, screaming now in pain, I couldn't possibly care less about this guy or his family. All I care about is making Zion's pain stop. Something travels from my gut, warm energy I can't describe, and it flows up to my chest and circulates in my shoulders, arms, and tightens my neck. I pucker my lips and let out a short whistle. It startles the Newcomer and he stops and turns toward me—just three inches from my face. I rear my head back and smash my forehead into his nose with a force that sends a torrent of blood downward and he falls backward.

One of the Antis steps up and clocks me with the barrel of his rifle and I fall back on my hands.

The Newcomer's hand is clutching his broken nose as blood seeps around his fingers. "Let the Twitchers talk to 'em!" he shouts through clenched teeth. He beckons with his free hand for the Antis holding the Twitcher leashes to approach. "We coulda did this easy." The Newcomer spits. "Let that crazy blonde talk to the one we shot."

As an Anti yanks the blonde Twitcher toward Zion, a wordless growl of rage erupts from my mouth. I can do nothing to stop it as another Anti grabs my tied hands and puts his knee on my back. I can't see Zion. My face scratches against stones and the smell of earth fills my nostrils. Angry tears well in my eyes and I steel myself to endure the sounds of his agony.

But they don't come. I hear the whizzing sound of a rock slicing the air, connecting with bone. Camila inhales sharply. "What?" she says, confused. There's a brief pause, and then a thud of a body hitting the ground. An Anti swears loudly. The pressure above me releases and the Anti with his knee on my back falls forward and rolls off me. I twist my body to a sitting position, just in time to see Camila spring from the ground and knee an Anti in the gut.

And then: a flutter of cloth, the whiffle of a bo staff, and the crack of a skull as Sister Lola neutralizes the Newcomer with a single swift blow. At least a half dozen nuns materialize, seemingly out of nowhere. The Sisters of Absolute Hospitality handily subdue the remaining Antis. Another Sister whirls her slingshot and a stone whizzes past me and connects with the bearded Twitcher's head. He collapses to the ground in a heap.

With slingshots, the Sisters knocked out the natty blonde

Twitcher who was poised to attack Zion. It was their slingshots that had initially taken out the Anti on my back. Sister Lola swirls her bo in figure-eights, laying waste to the last Anti. Her robe billows, following the movement of her body, flitting and darting hummingbird quick, then her staff comes to rest and the robe flutters to her right, hovers there, and alights a split second later to its natural, resting position.

About a dozen of the Sisters surround us now. Once our hands are untied, I fly to Zion. Two Sisters are already bandaging his wound.

"He'll be fine," Sister Elena tells me. "But we've got to get him back to the hospital at the compound."

I hold up the I-L-Y signs to Zion and he weakly does the same.

"*I'll be fine*," Zion signs. "*you go.*"

I use three fingers and quickly close them. "*No.*"

Zion shifts his body and grimaces in pain. Sister Elena finishes with the initial bandages, which seem to have slowed the bleeding.

"*You have a mission*," Zion signs. "*Just come back to me.*" He gives a wan smile as I lean forward and kiss him softly. I caress his cheek. Sister Elena and another Sister I don't know quickly make a travois out of bo staffs, we carefully help Zion on it, and the Sisters begin the journey back to the cloister.

Tears well in my eyes unbidden and I hug my shoulders. It's like they're dragging away a piece of me on that makeshift sled—a lung, a kidney, a heart—an organ vital to my life, irreplaceable, but its true importance only becomes clear, and terribly so, when it's ripped away, when it's gone.

"Samuel, *lo siento, mijo*," Sister Lola says tenderly from behind me. She rests her hand on my shoulder. I turn around and she takes me into an embrace. I bite my lip in an attempt to stop crying. Now is not the time for tears.

The Twitchers are still chained. Four Sisters approach and each is embraced quickly, without a word. Prayers follow, softly, over their bodies. Silence. Peace for those suffering from the virus. It's unclear what will happen to the Antis. They all have been tied together with a rope. They'll be isolated until the community can decide what to do with them. Not everyone accepts hospitality, Sister Lola always used to say. The Newcomer's head is down. He stares at his feet, as one of the Sisters wipes the blood from his face.

Camila and Santi join me and we talk with Sister Lola.

"After you left, we realized that our friend, the Newcomer, had slipped away. He must have left while we were preparing your departure."

"So, this was all planned?" Camila asks.

"It would seem so. Various paths are converging." Sister Lola observes me as she finishes the sentence. "Samuel, there's more going on than you can know right now. Unfortunately, Jade is not our only concern."

*"Jade is my concern,"* I sign back. *"And so is Zion."* Camila translates for Lola.

"We will care for Zion. And we will do our best for Jade. But there's a more important mission."

"What mission?" Santi asks.

"It's best to know only what is necessary. Otherwise, all could be lost with a few hungry Twitchers."

Santi shifts his *baquetas* in his hands. Camila twists her grip on her bo staff.

"I need you three to make it to the Librarian and tell her this: Our Southern friends must arrive soon. It's time."

I nod but sign that I don't understand.

"The Librarian will understand. And she will advise you. We must have faith that Jade's way is being watched over by Providence."

I glance at Camila. She nods.

"I'm with you," Santi says.

"Samuel, may you be kept in the precious embrace of *Nuestra Madre Protectora.*"

Three of us leave the Sisters as they take Zion with them. We make our way quickly to the train tracks, which are overgrown with vines, much of the steel scavenged. We keep on high alert for any Twitchers or Antis who might be lurking in the woods. Traveling swiftly, we reach The Wasteland within the hour. We approach the Library and the sentries don't take our weapons.

"You are expected," the guard tells us.

*Well, here goes nothing,* I think as we take our chances with the Librarian.

# CHAPTER 19

# JAYLA

IT IS early afternoon when Tyrese comes into my office. I cross the room and sit down at my desk. "Captain Tyrese. You have news?" Tyrese nods and moves toward the front of my desk and places a folded piece of paper on the open book before me.

"We found this," Tyrese says as he moves back a step. "In the accustomed place. A message from our contact."

I start to unfold the paper. "Have you read the message, Tyrese?"

"Yes, ma'am," he says without hesitating. His jaw clenches and deep lines furrow his eyebrows. Whatever it is, it has shaken Tyrese.

I read the note and I realize it was sent from Valerian. There are only two sentences: "I AM SUSPECTED. A SACRIFICE MUST BE MADE."

I drop the note with a sinking feeling in my stomach. I wasn't expecting this. I nod at Tyrese. "Ma'am, if this is about Jade." He pauses and clears his throat. "If this is about Jade, I request permission to go find her." Tyrese puts his hand on his sword and I know he is ready to ride off after Jade at a moment's notice.

I take a deep breath and it comes out as a long sigh. I make my decision. I know what Valerian is telling me, even if no one else possibly could understand. We must get Jade, but it's risky to do it too quickly. We will have to time this just right. My decision is made. I stand from my desk. "Not yet, Tyrese." I walk around to the front of my desk and put my hand on his shoulder. "I am expecting Samuel in the next several hours. When he arrives, then you will go and rescue Jade." Tyrese flinches a bit, not wanting to wait. I can see the protest beginning on his face. I stop him before he can start. "Trust me. Nothing will happen until dark. We have a day to plan. It will be better to make your approach to the Anti camp when it is dark." He nods, reluctantly. I know he will do what I tell him, even if it takes him a bit of time to come to the same conclusion I have reached. He's a good soldier. "Prepare yourself," I tell him. "A fight is coming soon, but first we need to fortify The Wasteland and get the Hunters ready."

After Tyrese leaves, I take out the dual-band transceiver. I set it to a different frequency from the one I use to call Sister Lola. I practice a few French phrases under my breath before making the call. I hope that our Southern friends are ready.

---

"WE HAVE SPOTTED Samuel and two others," says Captain Tyrese, once more standing in front of my desk. Evening comes quickly in February, and the last rays of daylight cast long shadows in my office. We have spent the last few hours planning, going over contingencies, shoring up defenses. Captain Tyrese's fists are clenched, and I can tell Jade has been on his mind. "I am ready...Jayla, I feel like we are running out of time." His eyes are full of pleading. Agitation radiates off him and I sense his anxiety. He is not often ruffled, but at the moment, his shoulders slump uncharacteristically.

I stand and demand he straighten to attention, desperately trying to keep my own anxiety at bay. "Tyrese, we are going to get her. But we also have to do this without alerting the Antis as to our plans. Be smart." He nods and then turns quickly, on his way to meet Samuel and his companions.

From my desk, I hear the transceiver squawk to life. Static. An unclear, garbled voice. A series of beeps, then more static. I reach into the top drawer.

"*C'est Baton Rouge,*" I say in French. "*À vous.*"

"*Mission abandonee,*" the voice says in French, and then repeats. "*Mission abandonee.*"

I take the transceiver out on the balcony to see if I can get better reception. "Please repeat the message," I say, a wave of dread descending over me. The message repeats, undeniably: *Mission abort.*

My stomach turns to knots. I try to compose myself and figure out a way to bring the threads together. I feel taken off guard, out of sorts, stretched to control a situation that is increasingly uncontrollable. I stare off into the horizon, my mind spinning, searching for answers in the meandering bend of the river in the distance.

My mask of control begins to weaken and Jade's fear and loneliness envelopes me. The clear line of sight to the future is blocked by dark, menacing storm clouds I could not forecast or foresee. And then Lolita's words echo in my mind. *Faith. We must have Faith, mi amor. Jade will be the key to all of this, after all.*

# CHAPTER 20

# SAMUEL

AS WE WALK into the Library, Bea rises from her station at the old circulation desk, greets us, and then rides the elevator with us to the top floor. It's another awkward elevator ride as we all watch the numbers light up telling us we're rising through the Library's floors. The doors open and Ty is waiting. He motions us to follow. His face is drawn and tense. We're led across the long, high-ceilinged office and then out to the balcony.

The Librarian turns to greet us with an expression that I can't figure out. *Sadness? Fear?* Or, perhaps it's a mask that protects deeper emotions, deeper worlds within the Librarian-- within Jayla.

What are those worlds that I've never been allowed to see? I'm curious. Could there be more to the Librarian than I've been led to believe? She lays aside the mask for just an instant and then just as quickly replaces it. I realize that perhaps she wears the mask for those she leads, for those, like me, who she helped raise, for all those to whom she can never show uncertainty.

An early evening sky, dark blue with wisps of pipe smoke clouds, frames her resolution, despite the momentary glimpse I saw of something else. I sign for Camila to tell Jayla the message from Sister Lola. *Our Southern friends must arrive soon. It's time.* Jayla's eyes don't leave me. For a moment her expression changes as if she's growing tired of the mask she has to wear. She takes a breath, steadies herself, and closes the distance between us. She opens her hands. I take them and she squeezes.

"Jade will die tonight," she says softly, "if you don't rescue her."

I nod, registering the gravity of her statement.

"And, Samuel, I can't help you." She pauses and a tear slides down her cheek. My hands remain in hers. For the first time in years, maybe the first time ever, Jayla reaches for me unguarded, her eyes furrowed in anguished concern. All my confidence deflates as she pulls me close and wraps her arms around me. "Faith, Samuel," she whispers in my ear, "we have to have faith."

I return her embrace, confused, afraid, and with absolutely no idea of what to do next.

# PART III

*15 Years After The Event*

# CHAPTER 21

# SAMUEL

THE LAST TWENTY-FOUR hours race through my head like a really bad case of diarrhea. That's the only analogy that I can think of for my situation. First, my sister breaks her pinky-promise never to go back to her life with the Twitcher Hunters. So, I flee to the only refuge I've ever really known but before I get there, I get a friggin' concussion from some rando Twitcher who happens to be lurking about. Then, joy of joys, I actually get reunited with people I love: Camila, Sister Lola, and most importantly, Zion—people who know me and care for me and who I have not seen and missed constantly for the last eighteen months.

*Do I get, like, a moment to enjoy it?* Nope. A stupid, sleazy Anti-newcomer-guy is there to tell me that my sister—*my stupid promise-breaking sister*—has gone and gotten herself captured.

Okay, so improvise and plan her rescue, right? I nobly put my very justified resentment aside and we band together like Fellowship-of-the-Rings style Hobbits to save Jade from the evil Sauron. It's annoying and exhausting, but still okay because, hand-in-hand, Zion is with me. *It can't be that easy, right?* Uh-uh. Nah.

Remember sleazy Anti-newcomer-guy? He's got an ambush waiting, takes a potshot at Zion, and then almost feeds us to a natty-haired Twitcher. We're saved at the last moment by Sister Lola, thank God—*am I seeing a pattern to how my story goes, here?*—but the love of my life is no longer by my side. Instead, he's convalescing, hopefully, back at the convent and not getting some sort of septic blood infection from the bullet wound to his shoulder.

*Ok, so we regroup, right?* We're no closer to rescuing Jade, but now Sister Lola sends us on a detour from our quest with a cryptic message for the Librarian, Jayla, about "southern friends" that I just *have* to deliver, like, yesterday apparently.

*Did I say that Jayla is not my favorite person?* I know she took Jade and me in. I'm grateful, it's just...we've never really clicked. Jade was always her golden child anyway. Regardless, I, like the magnanimous human that I am, who cares for my sister and for humanity, in general, I pick myself up, separate myself from my wounded boo—and lead Camila and Santi to deliver the message to Jayla. BFD, *amirite!?*

We make it to Jayla's book tower, and I deliver Sister Lola's message about 'it being time' and 'to alert the southern friends.' *Ok, so can we save Jade already?* Nope. Because Jayla has finally revealed herself to be capable of human emotion, and now, I'm more or less second guessing all of my preconceived notions of Jayla, her motivations, and probably half a dozen years of my childhood in her care. She tells me that Jade is gonna die tonight unless *I* save her.

*Are you kidding me?* One last glorious sucker punch in a day made up almost entirely of sucker punches. I realize that being trauma mute is really not much of an asset in this instance.

So, yes: The last twenty-four hours have been like a bad case of the emotional runs—a bit messy, in short. And, if anyone is asking, and they don't seem to be asking—Santi, Camila, and Ty are basically ignoring me at the moment—but if they were asking, I'd tell them that all of it has given me a massive, well, tummy ache.

*Oh, man. I need to take a breath.*

I see Santi and Camila out of the corner of my eye. They appear about as glassy-eyed and gut punched as, I'm sure, I do. We've returned to the ground floor, assembled next to Galvez Plaza, trying to figure out our next move.

Ty has joined us. He said he was coming whether we liked it or not. And, honestly, at this point, I can't even with Ty because the dude has his sword out, checking its sharpness by cutting one of his fingernails with it. I mean, who checks a sword's sharpness like that? He's also wearing an M17 Sig Sauer handgun. I only know that because Santi asked what kind of gun it was, while air-twirling and swooping his *baquetas* in a show of athletic prowess.

Great. Ty and Santi: two swinging dicks, both competing to be the hero who gets to save the girl. *Whatever.*

Camila touches my arm and I flinch reflexively, hands up and fists clenched. "Woah," she says, pulling her hand back like it's burned. "Samuel, are you ok?" I need a moment. I need to center myself. I sign to Camila that I'm afraid. That I'm worried. I'm unsure of our next move.

Camila touches my arm again, squeezes it, reminding me I'm not alone. "Samuel, hey," she says. "We came to help, to save your sister, if we can." She leans in, clasps her hands behind my neck and brings her forehead to mine. "But, I am here for *you.* And, as his twin I can speak for him—Zion is here with you too." She moves both hands from my neck and place her palms firmly on my temples, forcing me to focus on her eyes as we stand forehead to forehead. "Just breathe with me." She draws air in and out. "We got this."

I close my eyes and feel the whisper of a breeze as Camila drops her hands from my temples. When I open them, I recognize the day's fading light and catch the faintest hint of musky sweetness evaporating off sugarcane bagasse drying outside the mill nearby. And then—

Ty and Santi are totally arguing about who has the better weapon. Camila rolls her eyes as we both turn to watch Ty slash his sword in the air, while Santi prepares his bamboo fighting sticks.

*Are they...? No, really? Are they getting ready to spar?*

I'm about to break them up when Camila steps in. "Children, please," she says sharply, her tone hovering somewhere between reprimand and pity. "Do ya'll even know each other?"

Ty sheaths his sword. Santi steps back and twirls the *baquetas* in a fast figure-eight and then finger-walks one of the sticks. "You must be Ty," Santi says. "Jade told me about you."

"I'm sure she did," Ty says, checking the ammo clip on his gun.

"Well, not much," Santi corrects himself. "We had so many other things to do than to talk about you."

*No, I think. Did Santi and Jade hook up?*

Camila gives me a side-eyed glance and just shakes her head. "Well, I'm Camila," she says to Ty. "And this is Santi." She motions in his direction. "We know how to fight. We know how to survive. We're here for Samuel and for Jade."

Camila plants her bo staff with a swift click on the pavement, holding Ty's gaze. Her chin is slightly raised, a hand propped on one hip, elbow akimbo, shoulders squared. I'm sort of taken aback for a minute, how badass she is in that moment— a fierceness in her eye, her afro crowning her head, her arms well-toned in a heather gray V-neck tee-shirt.

"Damn," Santi says, clearly also noticing Camila's ferociousness. He smiles at Camila and she sighs and shakes her head pityingly, as if to say *tsk-tsk-poor-child*. Camila airs out her bo staff in a long arc and then stows it on her back.

"I'm Ty. I'm the Captain of the Twitcher Hunters." He steps forward. "I'm not here to mess around." Ty finishes adjusting his belt where his gun and sword are hung. "Let's make a plan and get moving."

I nudge Camila and sign that we need to go up North Boulevard and cut over to 19th. She translates for Ty and Santi. They agree.

"We'll be approaching the Anti camp from the north side," Ty considers, rubbing his chin. "That might give us a chance to get eyes on the guards before we enter."

Camila and Santi nod. I sign *Yes* with my right fist uplifted to chest height and pivot my wrist forward twice.

*Here we go.*

WE WALK QUICKLY, but cautiously, up North Boulevard and turn on 19th. Ty and Santi are walking point, while Camila and I follow in the rear. Ty is a competent leader. He's aware of his surroundings. He quickly studies Santi, and I intuit that he's a good enough soldier to be able to set aside seeing Santi as a rival, at least for the time being.

19th Street leads straight over Government and turns into Park Avenue. That's the way we need to go. When we're two hundred yards from crossing Government Street, I remember we're close to that building—*Yvette Marie* it says on the building's side in faded paint—the place where Jade and I freed the Feral children from the scuzzy, pock-marked Older.

The last of the daylight fades quickly and the street is obscured in shadows where bushy trees—live oaks, magnolias, weedy vines, bamboo patches—overhang what were once the sidewalks that bordered the road. The cover is good, it'll keep us from being seen. If any Anti patrols venture this far from the park, then we have a chance of seeing them before they see us.

Ty and Santi shelter up ahead by an old fence, wrought iron in one part with stone pillars every ten feet apart. The iron fence gives way to wood boards and there's an overstory of thick branches and leafy vines that have grown from the fence to a series of old power lines and a slanted utility pole. Camila and I catch up to where Ty and Santi have halted, and we find them whisper shouting at one another about what route to take.

"We go around," Ty says to Santi, his voice hushed but tense.

Santi doesn't back down. "No, we go straight." He rubs his *baquetas* together.

"Why would we walk up Park Avenue without cover?" Ty's face is mostly obscured by the shadow of the overhang, but I can tell he's pissed. His jaw clenches and he puts a hand on the hilt of his sword.

Camila intervenes with a sigh. "Ya'll, let's talk about this..."

My attention snaps to a rustle and a sway in the foliage directly above us. I grab both Ty and Santi by the arm and then put my finger to my mouth signaling for them to shut up.

"What is it, Samuel?" Camila asks. She scans to her left. "Oh, perfect." Her voice trails off as she focuses on the street. The roof of branches above us rustles again, and the pitter-patter of footfalls draws nearer from the street to our left. I can't quite make out what it is. "Ferals," whispers Camila. "Stay quiet," she chides all of us.

Ty draws his sword slowly and Santi sets his feet, his *baquetas* at the ready as six Ferals step into view. They're dressed in grungy shorts, most are shoeless, and their hair is long, wild, and matted with dirt. Most look to be around the ages of five to seven years old.

"We got this," Ty says confidently.

"No," Camila tries to stop him. "Check behind you, idiot." Ty turns around and I follow suit. No less than a dozen more Ferals have snuck up on us in the dark, just ten feet away. I eyeball the street and see another pack of Ferals.

"They've cut us off," Santi says bemusedly, swinging his head around, trying to figure out which way to defend first. He curses under his breath. We turn our backs to one another, the four of us face outward, bracing for an attack.

"Don't hurt them," Camila says, her voice soft but emphatic.

"Well, what do you suggest? Ty whispers back. "There are too many of them and I don't think they want to play."

The branches jostle and creak above us and I notice just in time to see a dark shadow descending. A thick net of coarse rope falls from above. The Ferals surrounding us rush in with grunts, whoops, and screams. They knock us to the ground with the sheer force of their dozens, several dragging the corners of the net closed. Scratches leave welts on my arms. Little hands dig in my pockets and two of them pick up Ty's sword where he dropped it when the fishnet fell on us. He grasps at the sword's hilt and one of the Ferals bites Ty's finger hard. He recoils in pain and swears loudly, clutching his wounded finger. Camila just surrenders her bo staff and Santi only lets go of his fighting sticks when Camila orders him to give them what they want.

A sing-song chant begins. *An-ti...An-ti...An-ti.*

"Anti? Huh? I don't get it," Santi says confused. "Why are they saying we're Antis?"

"Maybe they're gonna give us to the Antis," Ty grumbles.

"Great," Santi scoffs and sucks his teeth, "dispatched by kindergarteners and fed to the Antis. Perfect."

"They think *we are* Antis," Camila replies. "Trust me and do what I say, and we'll be fine."

The net cinches tight and we're pressed together, flopping

around like fish caught by wild kid anglers. I would laugh if it wasn't such bad timing.

"Don't struggle," Camila says. "I can get us out of this." Camila's face is close to mine and it's nearly impossible for me to get my hands loose to sign to her. "Just follow my lead," she says.

"Great," Ty says annoyed, utterly disgusted with the situation. "Just great."

TEN MINUTES later the Ferals have managed to drag us into the junkyard outside of *Yvette Marie's*. The wood fence actually turned out to be a makeshift door they use to move dummies like us inside their interior courtyard full of the rusted out remains of The Time Before. There are piles of every bike part imaginable, but only one or two fully assembled bicycles. There are old appliances. There are washers, dryers, ovens, kitchen sinks. Mangled iron. Junked out cars. There's even an old bus that's black from a gas fire set long ago. A clapboard porch with an awning over it outlines the door into the A-frame building.

Ty and Santi bicker between themselves over who caused us to get caught. Camila stays quiet, intently studying the faces of the Feral children. "We need to wait," she says, "for the Feral leader." She strains to get a view of the porch and the front door into the old antique shop. "Just wait."

But time is not on our side, I realize, as the Ferals surround us in the makeshift junkyard-courtyard. Several Ferals, two little girls no more than six and a boy probably a year older, are laughing, playing with the weapons that were taken from us. I realize in horror that the boy is messing around with Ty's pistol. He puts his mouth on the end of the barrel, then licks it and giggles.

"Be careful," Ty says. "That's loaded." Ty bangs his head

lightly in frustration on the cement patio of the courtyard, as if to punish himself for not figuring out how to avoid this whole fiasco. The freckle-faced boy with the gun, lank red hair covering his eyes, just laughs. He has to flick his head to the side to get the hair out of his face. He waves the gun around, threatening the other children playfully.

Camila begins to grunt and several Ferals stop playing and watch her, surprised. One dashes up the staircase, onto the rickety wooden porch and disappears through the door inside. A few minutes click by and the same Feral reappears. She motions with her hand to the children. "Seerkle," she says in a sharp high-pitched voice.

The twenty or so Ferals circle around us, several jump on top of Santi and Ty and me. All except Camila. The other ten Ferals make a small gap by the opening and say *come-come-come* to Camila. Camila realizes they want her to get out of the net. The rest of us are to stay put, which we do since twenty Ferals are sitting on top of us. Camila wiggles out of the coarse net. The Feral who had been playing with Ty's gun, now holds it at Ty's head. *"Boom-Boom,"* the boy says and giggles.

Camila stands and walks into the run-down structure with the Feral who had gone in before. The wild children jump off of us, laughing and shouting in the process. The gun is still trained on Ty. A feeling of drowning hits me. Doubt. Fear. Failure. My chest grows tight and it's hard to breathe. Anxiety rises. I'm supposed to save my sister and we get caught by a band of thirty Ferals. When we left the Older to the fate of the Feral children, there weren't nearly this many. Their numbers have grown.

"What's that?" Santi asks. He's looking toward the fence. I move my head with difficulty, the net rope rubbing irritably against my face. I can just make out a dark, round shadow on an iron spike on top of the fence post. "What do you see, Samuel?" Santi asks again. I can't quite tell what it is.

Ty rolls over and scrutinizes the fence. We're all pressed against one another and the Ferals won't let us sit upright. Ty lifts his head a bit and one of the Ferals raps his forehead with Camila's bow staff. "Damn, kid." Ty grimaces. "That hurt."

Finally, we all manage to face in the same direction toward the junkyard perimeter and the fence separating us from the road outside. "Is that...a head?" Santi asks with a mixture of horror and disbelief.

Fagin. It's the Older's head, I realize, stuck on a spike jutting out of the fence post. "You gotta be kidding me," Ty says shaking his head and not having much luck because we're pressed so close to the ground.

My eyes adjust. What I mistook for a weird shadow is, I can now clearly see, the severed head of the Older who once enslaved the wild kids. I can just make out the pockmarks on the Older's face, his mouth yawning open in an eternal scream. *Well, I guess that's what happened to Fagin.* He was killed, apparently, by an avenging and spiteful Artful Dodger.

"What is Camila doing in there?" Santi asks. He tries to get a better view of the door to the house.

"Hopefully," Ty says with a snide grin, "she's making sure that your head is next on the spike."

"Pshhh," Santi replies with a burst of air through his teeth, then pauses. "You know, that's actually funny," he says with a chuckle. "But, I think they'll take yours instead since it's so big."

"Whatever, dude—" I take my finger and flick the back of Ty's head. He doesn't finish his comeback to Santi. "What, Samuel?" he says in a hoarse, annoyed whisper. I put my finger to my mouth. *Quiet.*

The porch door creaks open and closes with a bang. The Ferals guarding us move back. I strain my head to see what's happening as Camila comes into view, standing on the top step of the porch stairs. By her side is a Feral girl, thin and tall, black coils of hair frame her face. Her floral-patterned dress is too short for her and her black leggings have a jagged hole in one of the knees. A faint recognition dawns.

*It's the Feral girl who stole Jade's notebook.* Camila points toward us still ensnared in the net. "Family," Camila says to the Feral leader. She grunts and signals something with her hands that might be the ASL sign for *free.*

*An-ti, An-ti, An-ti,* the Ferals surrounding us begin their sing-song chant.

"No," the Feral leader says sharply. The chant stops. She jabbers something to the Ferals closest to us. They protest with a whine at first, but then begin to open the enclosure of the net.

"Come out slowly," Camila instructs us. "Don't do anything sudden or stupid."

"What is going on?" Ty starts to object.

Camila silences him, saying "Just come out and sit facing us. And keep quiet." An edge to her voice says *Don't screw this up.*

The Ferals stay close and the gun is still pointed at us. *"Boom-Boom,"* the ginger-haired kid says again. No giggle this time.

Slowly, we walk to where the Feral leader and Camila stand above us on the top step of the porch stairs. We sit, crossed legged, in front of the bottom step. Camila remains where she is while the leader descends to get a better view of us. She studies Ty and Santi with feline indifference, her interest in them fleeting. Her body remains still as she slowly rotates her head in my direction. She cocks her head slightly, examining me and after a moment's pause she walks the rest of the way down the steps, stopping in front of me. She sits facing me, her legs crossed like mine. She lifts both of her hands to her chest, while her eyes remain fixed on mine. One of her slender hands thuds against her chest, then the other. She begins a beat.

*Boom bah Boom Boom Boom bah.* It's the beat of "Stir it up." *She remembers.*

I start the beat on my chest, our hands move in unison. And then the Feral leader hums the melody of the song. The rest of the Ferals join, little hands beating on little chests, the melody of the chorus repeats over and over.

"What. The. Hell?" Ty shakes his head, completely confused. Ty is used to controlling his environment, commanding the situation. His tank of patience is running on empty.

Camila taps the rhythm on her chest from the top step. "Just beat along with them," she says beginning to walk down the stairs.

Santi just shrugs, starts in on the beat, hums loudly if a bit off key. I glance over my shoulder and notice the Ferals beginning to sit, some tapping out the beat on their neighbor's chest or back. The leader's eyes are closed and when she hums through a few bars of the music she peeks at me, smiles slightly, and then motions for Camila to sit with us. Camila joins us, hums along and adds a few words to the song she remembers. After a bit the beating and humming lulls and silence takes over, while the three of us—Camila, the Feral leader, and I—face one another.

The leader points at me and then puts her hands together palms up like an open book.

"*Jade?*" I finger sign.

The girl knits her brows, glances at Camila for help.

"An-ti take," Camila tells the girl.

What follows amazes me. Through a mixture of one syllable words—*Jade, chain, free*—and hand signs Camila somehow communicates to the leader that my sister is being held by the Antis, and that we've come to save her.

The Feral leader grunts a few commands at the other Ferals.

The wild children return Ty's sword and Santi's *baquetas*. The ginger kid with the gun reluctantly complies, unsmilingly. His face clouds like he's about to cry, his toy taken from him before he got to use it.

Santi fits his sticks back into his belt. He bends down and taps Camila on the shoulder. "I am in awe of you," he tells her.

Camila, still sitting by the Feral leader, her hand on the girl's back caressing her lightly, just grins. "Before Zion and I came to the Sisters we were Ferals, too." She nods her head in the leader's direction. "Her name is Bey-bey." At the sound of her name, the leader flashes a broad smile. "She was probably four or so when Zion and I left like six years ago."

"Kah-mee." Bey-bey tries to say Camila's name and laughs.

Camila glances over at me from where she sits cross-legged. Her face grows serious. "Samuel, let's go get your sister back." She communicates with Bey-bey in hand motions. The leader's eyes lighten in understanding. She makes a half-whistle to the red-haired freckled boy who had been waving Ty's gun around. Bey-bey grunts and then turns her hands into guns and makes an explosion sound with her mouth.

"What are they saying?" Ty asks, standing with his hand on his holstered gun.

Camila gets up from where she sits and I stand along with her. "We need to make a diversion," she says. "And there may be a way to do it."

The ginger Feral aims his pointer fingers at us with thumbs at right angles like guns. He giggles at Ty. "*Boom-boom,*" he says, then makes a huge explosion sound. *Boom-boom* the rest of the Feral children echo, the explosions getting bigger and bigger each time. Some fall on the ground and pretend to die in hideous, blood curdling fashion.

Bey-bey grabs Camila by the cheeks and says not two inches from her face: "Boom-boom."

Camila can't suppress a smile with the girl so close to her. "Ya'll, we have ourselves a plan," Camila says, cracking up. "Boom-boom," she says back then makes an explosion sound while Ty, Santi, and I roll our eyes at one another and hope to God Camila hasn't gone completely nuts.

# JADE

ULTIMATELY MY TEARS END, and the waiting begins. I wait on the squeaky metal-framed bed. I wait while doing push-ups. I wait while sitting in one of the two chairs in the room that has become my prison cell. Then I wait some more, both knees bobbing while sitting in the other chair. I pace and try to expend some of my nervous energy.

I clench and unclench my hands into fists as I move back and forth across the cement floor. Anger courses through my veins, tingles my fingers, pounds in my head. Anger keeps the sadness quiet, for now. Anger allows me *not* to think about how hopeless this all feels. It helps me feel like I'm still in control.

Valerian brought me back here when it was probably not long after noon. Time passes, I guess, but I have no gauge on how long it's been. Only lengthening shadows outside the one tiny window in my room confirm that the afternoon has come and will be gone soon. Last time I tried to peer through the narrow window, the butt of a rifle rapped against the glass. *Guess the guards are still keeping alert.*

Time is a cycle of sitting, standing, pacing, and doing push-ups. It lurches forward, straining for each second, heaving for the next moment. I finally get creative and do leg lifts on the bed, holding the metal frame of the headboard for leverage as I squeeze my stomach muscles until the burn turns into a knot that spasms. I lay sweating on the bed, knees to one side with my back flat, stretching the painful cramp in my side. Anything to keep thought out of my head.

And people. Definitely I don't want to think about people. Samuel. Jayla. Ty. Everyone I'm letting down. Guilt weighs on me like a pack I've been carrying full of stones that I can't put down. I've let everyone I've ever loved, who's ever loved me, down. *How do I come back from this? How do I make it right?* Those are thoughts I can't handle right now.

My hands unconsciously reach for a metal rod in the headboard, which I try to pry from its place. It focuses my attention on something other than my guilt. *Maybe I can use the rod as a weapon?*

I manage to remove one of the screws. The other one barely budges. It's useless, all of my striving, but I keep trying...it slips and my index finger scrapes a jagged shard on the rod. I put my finger to my lips, sucking the blood that tastes like metal and sweat, but then, compulsively, I'm back at it. *Loosen the screw...*

I hear a key turning in the lock. I quickly put the pillow against the headboard to hide the half-jimmied rod. I sit on the bed facing the door, which opens slowly until Valerian comes into view. He shuts it behind him and doesn't say a word, just grabs a chair and pulls it up about three feet from the bed where I sit trying not to appear guilty. I pull my knees to my chest and wait for him to speak first.

*Silence.*

We wait for what feels like an eternity. He stares at me and then studies the tops of his shoes. I wiggle my toes on my sockless and shoeless feet. Valerian's face darkens in a frown, there's a vein that rises to the surface on his left temple. His snake-eating-its-tail tattoo has grown a weird, spindly leg. It strikes me as funny at first, but then I think it definitely is not funny, especially that, if this guy really is my brother, he would have a really gnarly tattoo of a creepy-ass snake on his head.

No. Not funny. Definitely. Not.

But it is. It is, actually, really funny. I try to suppress the urge to laugh and a strange burst of air comes out my nose and I attempt to swallow whatever else might be rising from my throat. Swallow it. Think of something sad.

I glance back at the tattoo with its really weird skinny appendage that is actually Valerian's vein and I dry swallow my laugh. Valerian's eyebrows close on each other and he's looking at me like I'm totally crazy. Swallowing the laugh was not a good idea, I think, because it's coming back, angry and changed and clamoring for an exit, which I can't stop and...

*Eeerrrppp.* I let out a burp. I totally burp. Noisy air leaves my stomach and travels up and out of my mouth. I just burped and then I follow it with a hiccup. *Erp-Ehrk.* I start to lose it, my composure, and I put on a serious face. No smiling. No laughing. No more. *This is dreadful business,* I tell myself.

But, is Valerian laughing, too? Was that a laugh? Yup. He's laughing and the shock of Valerian laughing actually momentarily makes me lose the humor of it all. And then just as I think I'm about to regain composure I gigglurp again. *Erp-Ehrk.*

"Oopsie?" I say halfway between a question and an apology. I catch Valerian's eye, he's shaking up and down, he's trying to stop from laughing, and then the vein that doubles as a snake leg pops to the surface again and I just absolutely lose my shit. I let out the rest of the trapped air and start laughing hard. But, really hard. And then I start crying. Bawling. I'm laugh-crying, a massive cramp sets in, and I have to hold my stomach.

"What is happening?" I ask.

Valerian is still bobbing up and down, he can't suppress his laugh anymore, and a tear squeezes from his eye that he wipes quickly away. "Well," he says, "I came to tell you that...basically..."—he lets out a big breath, but it does nothing to stop a new round of giggles from overtaking him—"that Anton plans to burn you in the fire tonight..."

"What?" I don't really register what he's saying because I can't get my own giggles under control.

"Yeah," he says. "Woah, I don't know what is happening right now." He breathes in and out more slowly, trying to regain whatever emotional mask he's just dropped, but can't quite make himself do it. A smile spreads across his face. "But you totally messed things up, Jade." The smile is still on his face. "Don't you get it?" He pauses, an earnestness focusing his gaze. "I am Mason." Shock freezes me in place, as hope swells in my chest. "I'm your brother and we have to figure a way out of this really, really—"

He doesn't finish, can't finish, because I leap from my bed and throw myself on Mason. I absolutely tackle him and the weight of the chair teeters backward and we tumble to the floor. The metal chair smacks the floor and our heads crack together, which makes us roar with laughter again.

"Are you serious?" I whisper at him, still lying on the cement floor.

"Yes."

We're both on our sides with the upended chair between us. I reach for him, scooting the chair aside, clasping my hands around his neck, pulling him into a hug. He pushes away and shows me the red birthmark on his neck. "It's been a rough day," he says. "Probably one of the hardest of my life." A tear forms in the corner of my eye, hanging for a moment, and then descends to the tip of my nose.

"I've found you," I say. "I finally found you."

Mason sits up and I follow. "No," he says. "I found you and

Jayla found me. She contacted me six months ago." He moves the chair back farther, turns toward me and sits cross-legged. "I don't know what I want. But I don't want this." He motions with his hand around the room. "And...I have a plan..."

He doesn't have time to finish his sentence. The door opens and we both scramble to our feet before whoever it is comes in. Valerian...I mean, Mason—Mason, my brother—moves the chair into place. He sits in it and I manage to plop down on the side of the bed. We're too close to one another, I realize, and whoever comes in might find it odd. I have to wipe the smile from my face. Mason glares at me and mouths *"keep it together"* and gives me a palms-down motion with his hands.

The first thing through the door is the muzzle of a rifle, followed by the rifle's owner: A man, only slightly smaller, but no less menacing, than the Giant from *Jack and the Beanstalk.* Mason transforms back into Valerian. "Clay?" he says. "I was just interrogating the prisoner."

The behemoth of a man holds up his hand and stops Mason from saying anything further. Clay stands aside and Anton steps into the room, his presence sucking even the memory of laughter from the room.

Anton broods in the entryway for a moment and Clay starts to close the door but Anton stops him. "That won't be necessary," Anton says. Clay moves back, his rifle held across his chest at attention.

"Father," Mason starts, then sputters but Anton holds up his hand.

"Silence," Anton says as crosses the room.

He stands between me on the bed and Mason sitting in his chair. Uncomfortably close. The hand he used to stop Mason from speaking he holds up again. Long fingers curl into a fist, Anton glances at Mason, pivots and his fist crashes into the side of my face. Sound in the room muffles, then goes hollow, and then starts to ring as the force of the blow sends me to the mattress. I open my eyes and the pungent, hot, copper taste of blood fills my mouth. A small crimson streak speckles the white sheets. My hands go to my busted lip, which immediately feels three sizes too big.

"No, Father!" I hear Mason and then perceive movement out of the corner of my eye as Clay grabs my brother and pins him against the wall.

I start to sit up. "No," Anton barks at me. "You will stay there." Anton walks to my brother, who's pinned to the wall by the force of Clay's tree trunk forearms. Mason struggles, his arms flailing like twigs in the wind. Anton grabs Mason's face, forcing him to make eye contact. "Then God said," Anton begins to quote from the Bible. "Take your son to the land of Moreh and kill your son there as a sacrifice for me." Anton's voice falters, starts again. Clay's forearm repositions, this time on Mason's throat. "Your only son, the one you love." Mason tries to speak, but only sputtering breath comes out. "I didn't want to believe," Anton continues, his voice wavering between disbelief and utter rage. "After you told Clay your plan this afternoon, he came to me straightaway."

Mason's eyes flash angrily at Clay, then he closes his eyelids tight.

"You have betrayed me," Anton half-whispers. "I know you have been plotting with that bitch Librarian." Anton pulls out a massive hunting knife, one side curved, the other serrated steel teeth. Clay lets go of Mason and Anton moves in and presses the blade against Mason's throat where Clay's arm had been moments before. I start to move from the bed, but Clay pushes me back to the mattress.

"Stay down!" the big man says in a growl, like an angry bear thirsting for blood.

All I can see is the back of Anton's head as he holds the

knife to Mason's neck, his elbow pushing Mason against the wall.

"Admit it!" Anton yells. "Tell the truth."

Mason hesitates, his eyes dart in my direction. "Yes." My brother breathes the word like an exhale he's been waiting to make for years. His darkening eyes return to Anton. They play at mischief and rebellion. "My name is Mason..."

"Enough. Quiet." Anton's blade begins to draw blood on Mason's neck. A thin scratch, red and angry on his skin.

It's as if he's waiting for Mason to struggle enough so that he doesn't have to plunge the knife into his son's flesh—waiting for the sacrifice to will the knife into him. "You will burn, son," Anton says choking back a sob. "You and your so-called sister." Anton frees Mason from the wall but then leads him with the knife back to the bed and sits him down next to me. "I should've killed you ten years ago." Anton grips the knife tighter, his knuckles turning white. "Serves me right for showing mercy." He spits on the ground.

The blade returns to Anton's belt and Clay steps forward and wheels the butt of the gun around and sideswipes Mason's face with it. My brother's head whips unnaturally to the left and he collapses to the mattress. "That's enough, Clay," Anton says. His voice is breathy, almost a hiss. Clay backs off but aims the muzzle at my head. "There is no mercy for the impure," Anton adds, his rage returning to a simmering hatred. "You can't stop destiny." Anton walks to the entryway. "Enjoy your reunion," he says over his shoulder. "We've got a bonfire to make."

Anton leaves quickly and Clay follows, keeping the rifle pointed at us as he exits. The door bangs shut and the lock turns. Blood runs down my chin from the cut on my lip, and I use my fingers to trace a tender line up to my cheekbone. Mason's face is red and purple where Clay's gun hit him.

My brother turns to me, smiles, and says, "Good thing I hid

your sword under the bed." He motions for me to check. I crouch down and feel the smooth, cool metal of my saber tied to the underside of the bedframe. "And, fortunately, I gave you an oversized flannel shirt to wear, right?" I figure out how the sword attaches to the bed and leave it there for the time being. I throw my arms around him, put his head on my shoulder, and squeeze lightly. "Ouch," he grimaces. "Gently."

I found my little brother, Mason.

But I have no idea how we're gonna make it out of here alive.

THE FERALS PLAYACT exploding in hideous fashion over and over and...over. Camila eggs them on, giggling all the while. Ty folds his arms across his broad chest, looking like he's about to explode, too, but clearly in anger and impatience. Santi beams at Camila, as if he, too, has been enchanted by the same spell Camila has cast over the wild children.

"*Ngh, Ngh, Ngh!*" grunts one of the littlest Feral girls, raising a hand, bobbing up and down hoping to be next. Her hair is the color and texture of a dirty mop and a once-white T-shirt droops below her knees.

"*Boom-Boom,*" the ginger-haired Feral yells at her. Camila sneaks up behind, playfully shaking her, simulating the force of an imaginary bomb. The girl, surprised but ecstatic to have finally gotten a turn, jumps as high as she can, wheels her arms in the air, yells "BOOM" at the top of her lungs, and lands in a heap on the ground, moaning in mock death.

Ty finally explodes. "Time to wrap it up, Camila!" She freezes, her face momentarily sad that playtime is over. She leaves the circle of Ferals, who whine loudly at the loss of their new favorite playmate, and jogs back to where we're standing by the staircase to the old restaurant.

*"What are you thinking? Is there a plan?"* I sign to Camila.

"You didn't understand?" she smiles, shocked that we seem to have no clue. "The munitions storage," she says. "It's a small house on the edge of the Anti camp." She pauses for effect. "And we're gonna blow it up." She turns back to the Ferals, quickly unclenching her fists as she makes an explosion sound with her mouth. The Ferals all fall down, once again dying in agony, holding their little bellies, which ache from too much laughter.

"Oh, yeah, Camila, that's brilliant!" Ty snaps his fingers, finally catching on, but ignoring the Feral giggle-fest going on over Camila's shoulder. Camila puts a hand to her mouth, repressing a snicker, attempting to pay attention to Ty. "I forgot the Antis store all their weapons in there," Ty adds, a plan fleshing out in his mind, "I saw it during my Intel-gathering trips several months ago. Only a few guards check guns out in order to maintain order in the camp."

"Finally," Camila says putting her hands on her hips. "About time you boys caught up." Ty cocks an eyebrow skeptically, while Santi awkwardly clears his throat.

---

SO, the plan: We're totally gonna blow up the munitions house and hope that the explosion creates enough chaos and confusion to get Jade out. *Oh, God.* There's so much that can go wrong with this plan. I don't even begin to go through it all.

Santi has become Camila's shadow, repeating Camila's instructions to the Ferals, making sure the wild children gather bottles—just like Camila told them—as well as rags, and more half-full gas cans than we could possibly carry. Santi is basically smitten by Camila.

And the Ferals are smitten, too. Camila's, like, some sort of fabled Feral warrior goddess for the thirty-odd kids. She's special to me, too, always has been, but honestly, I usually gave my attention to Zion. I somehow missed this bad-ass-leader side of Camila. And probably it's here, outside the Sisters' cloistered walls, where her charisma and strength are finally getting room to breathe. She's more carefree than I've ever seen her before, and yet, driven with purpose. She reminds me of Sister Lola—caring, but tough as nails; a woman of faith, but stubborn as hell.

On the porch to the old restaurant, Ty assembles a makeshift outline of the Anti camp using a series of cinderblocks, a few empty glass bottles, and some past-date canned food. I squat on my haunches studying the model. Camila and Bey-Bey sit crossing their legs, the Feral leader leaning close to Camila. Santi stands close behind, his face squinched in thought.

*"How do we blow it up?"* I sign to Camila, who translates for our impromptu war council.

"Good, question, Samuel," Ty says with a hint of sarcasm, squatting beside me. "How *do* we blow up a munitions storage building not a hundred yards from where the Antis will be death-dancing around a bonfire?" He scans our faces. "Especially since a bunch of kids are basically our logistics specialists." Ty smiles, drolly. No one laughs.

*"Hmph, Hmph,"* Bey-Bey grunts disapproval, as Camila puts her arm around the little girl's shoulders and shushes her gently.

"I'll do it," Camila says flatly. She accepts it like someone would say yes to a household chore, with a mix of resolve and unhappy responsibility. She contemplates the model camp and begins to lightly rub Bey-Bey's back.

"I'm going, too," Santi says, sitting down beside Camila and the two share a quiet smile.

"Are you sure?" Ty asks. He points at a can of pork and

beans that represents the munitions building. "Like I said, the weapons house is approximately one hundred yards from where the Antis will hold their bonfire tonight." He glances up at Camila, resting his hands over his knees. "I scouted the camp myself about a month ago." Camila holds his gaze. Santi studies Camila's determined face, while everyone else listens to Ty. "What we need," Ty continues, looking back at the camp model, "is a clear path from the tree line here"—he points at the north end of the camp—"all the way to the building." He traces his finger from a flowerpot to the can of pork and beans.

Ty glances at Santi, who's still examining Camila's face in profile. "Santi," Ty snaps at him. "Pay attention, man."

"Oh, yes, sorry," Santi says, flashing a quick smile, slightly embarrassed.

"Ok," Ty replies. "Ya'll will need to take the guards out, so that Camila can bolt to that weapons house, throw her Molotov Cocktails, and then make it out of there before the building blows." Camila and Santi nod at one another.

"Bey-Bey go," the Feral leader grunt-speaks. "Help Kah-Mee."

"Ok, then," Ty lifts his eyebrows, shrugs. "You three need to get in and out fast. When it blows, I'm really not sure how big it's gonna be." Ty pauses, putting one knee down on the clapboard porch. "The sticky issue is that you can't light the bottles until you're at the building."

"We can premake them," Camila interjects. "One to light and one to throw, while someone stands guard."

Santi swells his chest a bit. "I'll make sure no one touches you, Camila."

"We'll do it together, Santi," Camila says, a flush creeping across her cheeks. Bey-Bey leans her head on Camila's shoulder. "I got your back, too."

Ty sighs. "Ok, but don't forget you have to break a door or a window to throw the bombs in." He shakes his head, realizing that the plan feels like a stretch. "All of that leaves you vulnerable."

I snap my fingers. Camila turns toward me. I sign that we have to wait until all the attention is on Anton and that will give time for them to blow the munitions building.

"Good idea," Camila says.

"Translation?" Ty says, annoyed. Camila fills him in. "Ok, fine. Now the hard part." Ty puts his hand on my shoulder.

I sign with two fingers like a claw hitting my other hand molded into a fist. *The hard part?* Camila relays it to Ty.

"*Our part*, Samuel," Ty tells me. "I can't even believe I'm suggesting this." Ty shakes his head. Bey-Bey giggles. I take in a breath and don't let it out. We all listen as Ty lays out how we get Jade before she burns to death in the Anti bonfire.

---

THE MOON HANGS like a half-lidded eye above us as we move silently toward the Anti camp. The night is heavy with humidity and although it's not hot, anxious sweat pools in my armpits and a single rivulet traces the length of my torso to my waist. My skin dapples in goosebumps and I shiver. *Are we gonna be able to pull this off?* I shake doubt from my mind and focus on the moment. The droopy-eyed moon barely gives off enough light to signal we're a quarter mile from the camp. Ty and I whisper a quick goodbye to Camila, Santi, Bey-Bey and the rest of the Ferals.

Yeah...*the rest of the Ferals*...we'll see what happens with them. I think we managed to communicate the plan but it's anyone's guess if this is gonna work. Ty gave his gun to the Feral who had been pointing it at us—Boom-Boom, we started to call him, mostly because every time we tried asking his name that's all he would say. *Boom-Boom.*

So, Boom-Boom has Ty's pistol, and that leaves Ty with a sword and me with nothing by my wits and, apparently, a death wish. Darkness swallows Camila and Santi and the rest as they head off to blow the munitions storage building. Hopefully, they don't get killed in the process.

*The timing will have to be near perfect...*

I catch myself spiraling again. I'm really trying to keep it positive, but it's getting increasingly difficult to manage my thoughts.

We shelter near one of the old neighborhood houses. Scavengers have picked most of these houses clean of wood, glass, and roofing materials. Now they sit like carcasses exposed to the hunger of carnivorous birds. I scale a mound of unusable trash and dirt in front of the desiccated house in order to view the Anti camp. A bonfire grows higher, hooded figures circling the flames. *Bum-bah-Bum-Bum, Bum-bah-Bum-Bum.* The drums start a driving, quick beat and I return to where Ty is crouching by the base of the trash mound.

"Let's get closer," Ty whispers. I nod and we cross the road and enter the park, taking cover under a live oak. Two guards stand silhouetted against the bonfire, about fifty yards from where the Antis are assembling. The *thrum-thrum* of the deep bass reverberates in the hollow of my chest as we move to a tree just ten yards or so from the two guards.

We have the benefit of darkness, as well as the noise from the drums and the crowd. The Antis around the bonfire seem to be singing or chanting something, it's unclear what, but whatever it is it will hopefully cover any noise from what we're about to do to the guards.

Ty circles around to the right flank of the guards, leapfrogging from tree to tree. The guards are posted up at the point where the treeline separates clumps of live oaks and magnolias from a grassy expanse. I pick up a few acorns and several small rocks and put them in my pocket before jumping upward to reach a branch not far above me. I clasp my hands on both sides of the tree limb, dangle for a moment, then lift my legs around it, clambering to the topside of the branch. It sways a bit under my weight, but it's sturdy enough and I edge my way toward the trunk. I lean my back against the tree, my feet poised under me, and throw two rocks and all the acorns over the shoulders of the guards.

They wheel around confused, looking intently into the deep shadows. One has a rifle and the other carries some sort of club, which is hard to make out in the extra darkness of the tree cover. They strain to see, scanning their surroundings, but never looking up into the trees, hunching their shoulders a bit as they unknowingly walk straight toward my position. They stop directly under the branch I'm crouched on, whispering to one another. Both wear robes, but their masks are attached to belts slung around their hips.

"I know there's somebody out here," the first Anti says. He pulls the cowl off his completely bald head in order to see better.

"Man, it's probably just some damn animal," the other replies, also lifting the cowl off his head, revealing long hair tied back in a bun.

I slowly reach into my pocket for a rock, slide it out, and then let it drop on the head of the bald Anti with the gun.

"Wha—?" the Anti starts to say, instinctively looking up, immediately followed by the full force of my weight descending on his head, neck, and shoulders, which turns his word into a smothered grunt of pain.

Ty appears from behind the other guard, grabbing his bun of hair and slashing the Anti's throat, the man's words catch in a silenced choke, followed by a gurgle of blood. I'm on top of the bald guard, who thrashes wildly in an attempt to throw my weight off his back. Ty intervenes. I roll off the bald man and Ty sticks his blade in the Anti's neck.

I grab the club dropped by the hair-bun guard who's clasping his neck with both hands in a futile attempt to pinch off the hose of blood coming from his carotid artery. Ty removes his sword from the bald Anti's neck, and I step forward with the club—one swipe to his head stills his thrashing legs. With the bald guard dead, Ty walks over to the other guard, the one with the hair bun—he's dead, too.

My stomach turns to knots and my hands shake with adrenaline. The club slides from my loosening grip to the ground next to the now-dead guards. My face burns hot with shame as I think about two more deaths added to my account.

*How many more will I need to kill tonight?* I flinch at the compromises I've had to make to get my sister out and try to remember a prayer Sister Lola taught me, something to center myself, but nothing comes. It's like a name that hangs on the tip of my tongue, I've used it countless times—for years, even—but I just can't seem to recall it when it matters most.

I bend down on my haunches beside Ty as he strips the bald Anti of his robe. "Hope it fits," he whisper-shouts to me, the drums covering the volume of his voice. I don't respond but move to where the other guard lays crumpled in a heap and start removing his robe as well. We slide into the heavy black material and untie the plague masks, which the guards had strung from a short rope on their belts. The acrid smell of old sweat hits me when I secure the mask in place.

I examine Ty, who returns my gaze with a long-nosed bird grin. "That's freaky," he says and adjusts his mask a bit. He checks the rifle and swears under his breath. "There's only one bullet in the chamber." He bends down and pats the dead Anti looking for more ammunition. "Dammit. Nothing." Ty stands and manages to hide the gun under his robe. "Guess we gotta make this work," he says through the plague mask.

The barrel is pointed down and it's pressed against his leg. The robe is baggy enough to hide Ty's sword, too. We took precautions, and Ty takes out a pair of gloves we found at the Ferals' hideout. Between the darkness of the night, the gloves, and the robe, Ty's dark brown skin is sufficiently covered so as not to be a dead giveaway.

The chants from the bonfire grow louder. The Antis are disorganized at the moment. Some dance, twirling in circles. Other grasp one another by the shoulders and sway. I glance at Ty and he nods. We begin to walk slowly from the treeline toward the fire, hoping if anyone spots us we'll be mistaken for the guards. No one appears to notice. A loose semi-circle of four or five people deep begins to form. Ty makes sure his cowl covers most of his face.

*What a nightmare,* I think. Courage is something I've recognized in Ty, something I've always chalked up to bravado, but the guy has balls to be here with me. We're doing this for my sister, and basically have to walk through hell to do it. The Antis are exultant, like demons waiting for the newest damned soul on which to feast.

We station ourselves in the back of the crowd closest to the balcony where Ty told me Anton will appear to make a speech. The different chants all begin to coalesce around his name: *An-ton. An-ton. An-ton.*

The semi-circle tightens and then the side closest to the main stone building stretches out with people who rearrange to form an aisle. It's a gauntlet, I realize, for Jade to walk through on her way to the bonfire. We move closer to where the human handle meets the human frying pan that circles the flames.

Ty nudges me. My eyes are the size of saucers, which thankfully are mostly obscured behind the hideous beaked mask I'm wearing. Ty winks at me. Takes a breath. Invites me to do the same. *Damn, Ty,* I think. *You are as cool as a cucumber in a pinch.*

The chants of *An-ton, An-ton, An-ton* grow clearer, more defiant. Near where the human gauntlet stops, the Antis are erecting a wide metal box connected to a door. It's some sort of makeshift caging; Twitchers are being led out of the door into the metal holding pen. One or two of them begin to howl; another screams. A bearded and hairy Twitcher crouches on all fours and grunts. I try to count them and lose track at around twenty.

All along the crowd torches are handed out. Flames spread along the line starting at the bonfire. The Anti next to me hands me a torch without looking at me. I hand mine to Ty and then take another. The flickering glow dances on the white plague masks and my stomach begins to tighten.

*Please,* I think, *don't blow up the munitions building until they bring Jade out.* Contemplating the timing on this—the mechanics of exploding a weapons cache, somehow freeing Jade and not, like, friggin' dying in the process—sends blood pumping harder through my hands, feet, and head.

When the torches are all lit the drums stop and the last *An-ton* chant recedes from the lips of the revelers, the man himself appears, as if on perfect cue, from the terrace above the crowd.

A loud cry begins to come from the crowd, like a primal groan of ecstasy. I scan the scene and realize that everyone in robes and bearing torches—they all seem to be men. I can't be sure, but their builds and the few hands I can see all appear male. *Where are the women and children?* Hopefully hiding elsewhere...

The man atop the terrace comes to the stone balustrade. He lifts his hand and the cries from the crowd crescendo. The Anti next to me glances in my direction and I immediately open my mouth pretending to yell along with them. Anton's hand drops and the noise from the torch-bearing, freaky crowd ceases until the only sounds are moans, growls, and hyena-like laughter from the Twitcher cage. Feedback squeals from a portable microphone. I hear the oil-driven buzz of a generator in the background. At Anton's side is a tall, hulking bodyguard carrying an assault rifle.

Anton speaks, the microphone poised under the beak of his mask. "Brothers," he says with a high-pitched nasal tone. "We've come once again to purify our numbers." Cheers from the crowd. "But I take no joy, no solace, from tonight's sacrifice. It's the sacrifice of a father." Anton's voice falters. He starts again. "Bring out the race traitors."

Drums again start their forceful beat, *bum-bah-bum-bum, bum-bah-bum-bum*, which turns my legs to rubber. A slight breeze shifts the smoke my way and stings my eyes. Sparks crack and pop off the bonfire like fireflies. Burning wood and the strong smell of lighter fluid creep their way up the long nostril slits of my mask.

Jade comes around the corner of the stone building, her hands bound in front of her with rope. A guard leads her by her upper arm. *But who is the other?* A young man, long hair, shaved temples, walks next to Jade. He also is bound like Jade. His face is expressionless except for the deep crease between his eyes. *Who is that? Valerian?*

The two prisoners stop at the entrance to the torch-lined gauntlet. They are made to face toward the flames and from where Ty and I stand we can see Jade's face. She gazes down at her feet, which are bare, and then she lifts her head, her eyes sparkling in firelight.

From above and behind my captive sister comes Anton's nasal falsetto. "Behold, the race traitors." He motions with his long fingers. "One is unknown to you, my brothers, but she is not unknown to me." Anton pauses for effect and the crowd begins to roar again. "The girl is a spy from the so-called Librarian. She is an impure vessel of the race she inherited at birth." Cries of hate come from crowd—*daughter of a whore*, one voice yells; *dirty bitch*, yells another—and the slurs go on for some time. Ty fidgets beside me, and I let my free hand graze his wrist and let him know it's not yet time for us to make our move.

Anton silences the crowd. "The other," he begins slowly, "is my son Valerian. My only son." The crowd erupts differently, a few yell *No!* but others lower their masked faces and seem to begin to pray. *Oh, Lord no* and *So Be It* come from their bowed faces, whispers almost, in the dark. "The Lord God Almighty has commanded me to make this sacrifice." Anton lowers the microphone for a moment, then raise it to his mouth again. "But the boy is not innocent. He is the brother of the girl, Jade."

Loud shouts again from the crowd. My mind whirls, spins on Anton's phrase: *the brother of the girl, Jade. Is it true? Mason...?*

"My son, Valerian, is dead," Anton continues. "The young man you see has betrayed me and will die tonight for his sins."

Someone in the crowd throws a piece of rotten fruit at Valerian. Another throws a small stone. Valerian, or Mason, lifts his tied hands to shield his face from any further flying objects. Anton's voice thunders now: "Chain them in front of the fire!"

The two guards lead Jade and Valerian—*or is it Mason?*—toward the fire. Both sides of the gauntlet scream obscenities at the two prisoners. Someone masked but without a torch, steps in front of them and backhands Jade. She falls to her knees, shaken, but stands. Neither Jade nor Mason struggles with the guards. They appear resigned to what's next. Several Antis throw more wood on the bonfire and the flames roar higher as the exultant mood of the robed figures grows to a frenzy.

My heart thuds in my rib cage. *Now would be an excellent*

*time to blow the weapons.* Jade and Mason are almost through the gauntlet and they're only ten feet from Ty and me. *Blow the weapons,* I think. It becomes a mantra in my head, willing it to happen. Ty readies the rifle under his robe. One bullet. One shot. I tighten my grip on the torch.

*Blow it. Blow it. Blow it.*

Jade and Mason are five feet from us, and several guards bring chains in order to bind them together when they're thrown into the bonfire. Now is our chance.

*Blow. The. Weapons.*

Above us Anton is murmuring a prayer into his microphone. All I hear is a faint chant from the balcony: *God and the Father and the Holy Ghost and the Sacrifice.* The drums beat. And through the din of prayers, chants, and drums Ty's voice pierces everything, like a knife slicing through the cocoon of sound, freeing me to hear him and him alone.

"NOOOWWW!" Ty screams and adrenaline soaks my body, pushes me forward, past the Antis directly in front of us. In an instant, Ty wheels his rifle upward, levels it and shoots the guard to Jade's left. I send an elbow to the Anti to my right and step into the aisle between the two rows of people.

Jade and Mason and the other guard behold me in horror—they see a masked, robed figure with a torch above his head about to strike. Just as the arc of the torch connects with the guard's face, the munitions building, barely one hundred yards away, finally blows up.

Everyone is knocked to the ground and all sound is silenced in the roar of a massive explosion.

# CHAPTER 24

# JADE

**THE RINGING** in my ears passes from left to right as I try to lift my face out of the dirt.

*What just happened?* Some sort of explosion. Everyone hit the ground. I use my tied hands to push up on all fours and then struggle to kneel. I shake my head several times, my left ear feels muffled, like water sloshing in my head after a swim. But there's no more incessant beating--the drums must have stopped. Smoke billows in my direction as the wind changes and I start to cough.

*The Anti.* There was an Anti who came out of the crowd and shot a guard, while another one used his torch to whack the guard holding my arm. *Oh, God I thought he was gonna hit me.* But he didn't. I shake my head again and everything spins.

I bring my clasped, bound hands to the center of my forehead, close my eyes, and take a deep breath but cough again from the smoke. When I open them, I see an Anti crawling toward me and another standing above someone on the ground. He brings his torch down on the person, again and again, until the guy on the ground stops moving.

I scan for Mason who's getting to his knees. He opens his

mouth, seems to be yelling at me, but I can't hear the words he's saying. The ringing in my ears fades and his soundless voice finally goes stereo. "We have to move!" he shouts.

The Anti with the torch for a weapon rushes toward me, while the Anti crawling for me finally reaches out and grabs my shirt. I pull away, wildly kicking my legs at him to get away. The two Antis lift their masks and—

"Samuel?" I say out loud—or what I think is out loud but I'm not quite sure—"Ty? Is that Ty?" His eyes are set in determination. Concern. He asks if I'm ok. "Yes," I manage weakly.

"Jade. Jade. JADE!" Mason's voice finally breaks through my stupor. Reality rushes in. Antis are still on the ground, disoriented like me. *We need to move.* I remember our plan, the one Mason and I made. I prop myself up on my knees and Mason steps behind me. He takes his hands, still bound by rope, and reaches into the collar of my shirt, pulls out my sword, which we hid beneath my baggy plaid shirt.

"Lift your hands, Jade," he yells in my ear. I thrust them upward and feel cold metal against my wrists--the rope binding my hands tugs and then gives way.

The faces of Ty and Samuel look on in confusion and horror as Mason—Valerian to them—holds the sword over my head. I shake out of the remaining fogginess dogging me like a bad hangover.

"It's ok," I shout, as I spin on my knees to face Mason, he drops the sabre handle in my now free hands.

With blade upright I twist my wrist so the business edge faces me, threading the space between Mason's hands and the ropes, cutting upward. In one motion I spring upward and release Mason's hands, and the momentum carries me in the other direction putting me face to face with Samuel.

"Yeah, I know," I tell him in a hurried voice, "we planned this." Before Samuel can register my words, I wheel my sword and cut an Anti down before he jumps on top of him. "Can't talk now, but we found Mason." I flash a smile at Samuel and he just stares dumbfounded. He turns to Mason, who just gives him a quick nod and prepares for attack. I watch the crowd for more Antis coming our way. Samuel, still holding his torch, spins around. We stand side by side, while Ty and Mason do likewise with their backs to us.

"This is a surprise," Ty says flatly, jabbing his sword in the gut of an Anti charging at him.

"Any ideas?" I ask, glancing at Samuel who shrugs, then quickly swings his torch at an Anti to our right.

"Nope," Ty says. "We definitely gotta get outta here, though."

The disorientation of the blast has worn off on most of the Antis. Several spot us. "They're getting away," an Anti yells, pointing in our direction.

"Honestly wasn't sure we'd get this far," Ty comments over his shoulder. "But, it sure is good to see you."

I smile boldly as two Antis with torches rush us. "This is no time for sentiment, Captain." I parry the blow of the first and Ty steps up beside me with a quick thrust-stab of his sword. Samuel head-swipes the other Anti and Mason kicks the robed figure to ground. I finish him with a downward jab which pierces the Anti's right eye and his body goes limp.

Withdrawing my sword, I prepare for more. I catch Samuel's eye after he torch-thwacks an Anti who's already on the ground. "Where are the rest?" I say, exchanging bewildered looks with Ty. No more Antis run at us and it quickly becomes apparent why.

Ferals. Lots of Ferals.

On the South side of the bonfire I can hear a clamor of little yips and screams and chants. An Anti runs half in and half out of his robe while two Ferals ride on his back, biting and scratching at his back, ears, and face. Three other Ferals sit on top of a prone Anti, while a fourth—a little dark-haired girl with fingernails like claws—rips off the man's bird-beaked mask and promptly uses it to gouge out the eyes of her screaming victim. At least ten Ferals link hands and run at a group of Antis standing by the bonfire. Surprised, the Antis venture too near the flames and their black robes catch fire, which sends the human torches shrieking into the darkness.

A Twitcher ambles past us, and I do a double-take. "Shit, where'd he come from?" I say, scanning the chaos around us. I survey the makeshift cage for the Twitchers and realize it's now empty. "Watch your back," I yell at Samuel. "Twitchers are loose."

Samuel shoves Ty's shoulder and grins. "Boom-Boom did it," Ty says with what seems like boyish glee.

"Who?" I ask, having no idea what he's talking about.

Twitchers attack the Antis closer to the stone building. Several Ferals run to our little fighting circle. One lifts a pistol and says, "Boom-Boom." I guess that explains who Ty was talking about.

"Good work," Ty tells the red-headed kid, who smiles ear-to-ear, completely deranged. He scampers off toward an Anti being chased by a Twitcher, levels his pistol and shoots the Anti dead.

"We have to move soon," Mason says sharply. "Now." Ty motions toward the north side of the camp. "Anton and Clay will be down soon, if they aren't already," Mason says. "They'll be coming for me."

Boom-Boom, or whatever the gun-toting Feral is named, has about ten kid fighters with him now. "Let's get to the rendezvous point," Ty shouts at the wild children. The Ferals contemplate him blankly. "To the trees," he snaps, annoyed. "Let's get to the trees." Another Feral runs up, the poof of her black hair bobbing up and down as she arrives. *It's her.* The girl from the house. *She's here?* She smiles at me, her eyes like two half-moons.

"Kah-mee," she says. "Ouch." She points in the direction of the explosion. Samuel grabs her shoulder and starts to sign too quickly for anyone to understand.

"Is she Ok?" Ty asks directly, concern spreading across his face.

"Yes." She points again. She swings her arms like she has sticks. "With her. Ouch."

Ty furrows his brow, asks: "Santi is with Camila?" The girl nods her head. "Ok, we need to go right now."

But the Feral girl doesn't move. She stands in front of me, puts her hand to my chest. "Yes, I remember." My voice is a ragged whisper.

"Bey-bey," she points to herself, her other hand still resting over my heart.

"I'm Jade," I say, placing my hand on top of hers, bending down so our eyes are on the same level. I take her hand from my chest, twining our fingers together, and say softly, "We need to go." It's just a moment between us and then it ends. Mason stutter steps backward and I look up. The firelight illuminates a nightmarish giant-of-a-man standing thirty or forty feet from us, near the Twitcher cage. He levels his assault rifle in our direction—at me—and Mason screams.

"Clay! No!" Mason pleads.

Bey-bey pushes me backward. I trip over my feet and lose my balance as I hear the report of the rifle—*Rat-tat, Rat-tat*—and I fall. Bey-bey pitches backwards with me and I hear a sickening *thrump-thrump* of bullets hitting the small girl in the abdomen. I reach for her and she lands on top of me. I brace for more rounds to hit us.

Mason yells in anger and runs at Clay but, before Mason can reach him, three shadows descend on the lumbering Anti, tackling him. Clay disappears from sight in the semi-shadow and fire flicker of the night. The Twitchers' moans and screams are joined by Clay's agonized and enraged howls.

Bey-bey lays on top of my chest, and I roll her off onto her back. Blood comes from her mouth in sputters, in coughs, and in her eyes, I glimpse confusion, pain, and fear before they turn to glass. Ty's hands reach down and fold Bey-bey into his arms. Mason, Samuel, and Ty run toward the north side of camp. I get to my feet. Somehow I wasn't hurt. I'm running with them and I see just three steps in front of me, Bey-bey's vacant face bobbing against Ty as he cradles her against his shoulder.

A yell comes from the shadows in front of us as we run. "Valerian, stop!" the voice demands. Anton steps out of the darkness, blocking our way, his hunting knife ready in his hand. "Boy, you ain't leavin'," Anton says.

Sword in my hand, I brace for attack, while Ty and Samuel continue running to safety and the Ferals follow behind them. Boom-boom and one or two others lag behind and stop. Mason grabs my arm, pulls me back. "No, Jade! Stop," Mason says.

"What are you doing?" I wheel toward him, fear overcoming my surprise.

Mason doesn't respond but takes a step toward Anton. The Anti leader's arm lifts upward prepared to strike, his face a mask of steely determination, intent on carrying out the hellish deed commanded by his spiteful God.

"Father," Mason says in an even voice. "Here's your chance." Mason takes a step toward Anton. His palms held up, empty. "Your only son is ready for the sacrifice."

Anton hesitates. It's hard to see in the dark, but his eyes seem to narrow and he edges forward toward Mason as Mason bows his head. Anton wavers, lowers the blade, but then raises his knife again—*he's going to do it*—and my feet feel frozen in place. It's like I'm watching helpless in a dream, a nightmare, where I can't scream, can't move. Anton is two feet away and the blade catches the firelight from the bonfire.

Before the blade can start its arc downward, a gunshot tears through the night.

"Mason!" I hear myself yell, but my voice sounds detached, far away.

But it's not Mason who's hurt. My brother's eyes go wide in surprise. Anton drops to the ground and then begins to crawl backward. I check to my right and three steps behind me a Cheshire cat's floating smile appears from the night's gloom. It's the smiling face of a red-headed Feral with a pistol aimed at the spot where Anton had just been standing moments before.

"Boom-boom," the Feral cries in delight and lets loose a high-pitched laugh. The imp takes aim again to finish Anton off. From the ground, Anton bellows in anger, and pain, and hatred.

Mason grabs the barrel of the gun. "No," he tells the Feral. "It's enough."

I snatch Mason's arm and yell at Boom-Boom and the other Ferals with him to run, to follow us out of the Anti camp. In my peripheral vision I can see Anton struggling to get to his feet. When we're fifty yards away I tell Mason that Anton isn't dead.

"I know," is all he says, without looking at me.

AFTER RUNNING in the dark for a few minutes—or is it seconds? or hours?—I hear the whinny of a horse up ahead.

"Jade." It's Ty's voice. "Over here." We find ourselves on the outside of the old City Park. Six horses trot out from the shadows cast by several houses. Ty is mounted on one of them. He holds the limp body of Bey-bey. The flowers on her dress, too short for her lanky arms and legs, are stained red. Boom-boom and the other Ferals walk to where their young leader lays across Ty's lap. Several small hands reach upward to touch her.

"Is she...?" I ask Ty. I can't finish the question. He just nods. Ty gently takes his hand and closes her eyelids, then wipes the blood from her mouth and cheek. A sob rises in my chest, but I quickly bring a hand to my breast, gripping sorrow tightly before it escapes. I lock it away for another time, adding it to all the other precious griefs I keep hidden, like bittersweet charms safeguarded within a little girl's music box. *We have a job to do. Grief must wait.*

On the horse next to Ty rides Santi with Camila in front of him. Santi's soot-blackened arms hold her upright in the saddle. Camila leans back, her eyes shut in a grimace of pain. Her arm and shoulder were badly burned in the explosion. Charred skin peels off in patches, a clear liquid oozing from her red, raw flesh. Her arm hangs motionless against her side, her forearm limply resting in her lap. Samuel walks his horse into view, he holds the reins of an empty mount beside him.

A final rider approaches, leading a riderless horse. "Jayla?" I say, in disbelief. A sheathed katana sword juts out from behind her right shoulder. She looks down at me from her horse, her eyes full of concern.

"Jade and Valerian..." she begins. I shoot a quick glance at Mason. Jayla reviews both of our muted reactions. "Or, should I say Mason?" She nudges her horse's flanks and hands the reins to Mason. "Whatever your name is," she continues, "we need to retreat." I mount the horse next to Samuel and take up a position beside Mason. "The Antis won't be far behind," Jayla says. She tells the Ferals they can follow on foot.

We ride back to The Wasteland, my two brothers behind me. I can barely resist the urge to steal a glance back over my shoulder, hoping this is all not just a dream, that after riding to hell and back they'll both be with me still.

# CHAPTER 25

# VALERIAN

THIS IS THE END. As I ride behind my sister, my brother to my right, I know this is the end. *It should be the beginning, right?* Riding off with my family. Leaving behind the man who kidnapped me and then lied to me all my life. Making the guilty pay...

But, somehow I don't want to lose Valerian. *Why is that?* He's been with me, he's *been me*, for the last ten years, that's why. He's who I've known. He was the face I knew how to put on. He gave me strength, protected me, when Mason was just a seven-year-old boy who couldn't stop crying. Mason or Valerian? Who survives in the end? *Do I contradict myself?*

What I *do* know is this: Anton is not dead. I heard his voice in the dark as we ran off. And what I realize is there is so little time. The night is already half over, and the Lafayette Antis will arrive in the morning.

A fight is coming, and it's coming hard. I am going to have to fight the people I've lived with for the last ten years. I'm ok with that. But it feels like the guilty are not the only ones who will pay before the next twenty-four hours are over. Everyone pays a price.

WE APPROACH The Wasteland and our horses slow from a canter to a trot. I look over at Samuel. He keeps glancing at me. How strange to see him. Stranger still, I'm sure, for him to see me. Samuel motions something with his hands.

Jade told me he doesn't speak. She said he just quit after our mother and father were killed, after I was kidnapped. I want to say something to him, but I'm not sure how or what. He rides up close to me. He's not frustrated that I can't understand. We slow our horses to a walk. He reaches out his hand and puts it on my shoulder, squeezes it. He mouths to me. He says *I'm sorry*, and I can see his eyes are wet with tears. I release the reins with one hand and place it on his shoulder.

"Samuel," I say my voice catching. "It's not your fault." He shakes his head, releases my shoulder, and puts distance between our horses.

Jade's horse slows in front of us when she realizes we're no longer directly behind her. The Library stands illuminated down the street, a hazy halo outlining it against a dark sky. The wounded girl, Camila I think she's called, is being taken straight to the Library. The Black man, Ty, carries the limp Feral in his arms. He hands her to a waiting guard, dismounts, and then takes the small girl once again. His expression is blank. He stares straight ahead in numb exhaustion.

Jade circles back to Samuel and me. The three of us are still on our horses, not far from the entrance to the Library. Jayla's still mounted on her horse, too, but confers with several guards not far from the entrance to the Library. She glances back at us.

It is just the three of us here. Samuel places his hand on my shoulder again. His eyes are fixed ahead, studying his horse's mane. Jade brings her horse to the other side of me. Her hand reaches for my shoulder as well.

"Mason," she says. "I'm sorry." She pauses trying to find words to put to ten years of separation. "We...searched for you."

I know this should be our moment, the siblings reunited. But it's not. All I feel is a gnawing in my gut. It feels like anger. "Don't be," I say, a slight edge to my voice. I raise my eyes to meet hers. "There are no *sorrys* big enough." I shrug their hands from my shoulders.

Light from the Library streaks Jade's face, just enough so I can see her expression...fear?...rejection? I'm not sure. "Hey," I tell her, my breath uneven with pent-up emotion. "I can't do this now, all of this has to wait." Jade starts to reach her hand toward me again, thinks better of it, places it on the horn of her saddle.

"Mason is right," Jayla says. I didn't notice her coming back from the Library but she must've overheard our conversation. I wince a little when she says the name *Mason*. We all turn in her direction as she joins us. I push down the emotions that are trying to surface. All the Mason versus Valerian crap. I focus. Jayla doesn't say anything about my name, just studies me a moment and continues: "The Antis will be here by dawn."

"And there's a force arriving from Lafayette as well," I add. Jayla's face narrows at that news. "Anton told me yesterday that they would be here soon. To make an assault on the Library."

"That's not great news," Jayla says, adjusting the reins in her hands. Her horse paws at the ground a little. "What can we expect?"

"Around 150 from our camp," I reply, "and another 200 probably from Lafayette. Women and children will be left behind"

"How will we stake up against that?" Jade interjects. "How many fighters do we have in The Wasteland?" She directs her question to Jayla.

"Not nearly enough." Jayla thinks a moment. "With Hunters

and others, we have approximately two-thirds of that number." She turns to face me. "Weapons?"

"Well, with the explosion, we could have a chance. Most of our guns are not heavily stocked with ammunition. The assault rifles have an extra clip, but not much more than that. We kept a dozen crates of grenades and several RPGs with extra rockets in that weapons storage which, thanks to tonight's fireworks, won't be an issue. Depending on what Lafayette brings—and I'm really unsure on that front—it's probably not much. Anton was talking to Clay about counting all of our conventional weapons —clubs, knives, chains, some swords, axes—to outfit the Anti force." I take a deep breath, let it out. "We might get lucky."

"Hand to hand," Jade says.

"It's certainly not lucky," Jayla corrects. "But it does mean a better chance at winning." Jayla glances over her shoulder and looks back at us. "It will be a very bloody victory, though."

Samuel snaps his fingers, trying to get our attention. He holds his hands together, palms touching like a prayer. He points at himself.

Jayla nods. "Yes, Samuel." Her lips tighten, considering. "Go to the Sisters and ask for Lola's help. Maybe we're in dire enough straits for some help in this instance."

With that, our planning session ends and the four of us trot to the plaza that spreads out in front of the Library. Jade dismounts and walks to where Ty has just put the Feral girl on the cement ground. He covers her with a jacket. Ty stands and Jade embraces him. "Oh, God," Jade says. "That girl saved me..."

Ty gently rubs her back with an open hand. "Her name was Bey-Bey."

"Yes, Bey-Bey..."

People begin to assemble on the Library's patio. Some give me strange looks--my shaved temples and tattoos no doubt tell them who or what I am. Jayla barks orders at several individuals.

She tells Samuel to ride to the Sisters' convent. He nods. Before he leaves, he walks his horse over to me. He puts his hand over his chest, where his heart is. He nods his head three times. "Thank you," I say in a voice that's thin and weak. I look away and Samuel turns his horse and rides off into the night.

A few guards, or probably they're just people from the community, pick up the dead Feral girl while Jade and Ty look on. A contingent of about fifteen to twenty Ferals arrive and surround the people carrying her. Some touch her face. Others begin to cry. I dismount my horse.

Through the window of the Library's ground floor I can see the woman, Camila, getting a bandage on her shoulder. The guy who rode with her strokes her forehead. She smiles at him confidently, but as the crowd carrying the Feral passes by the window, her face clouds. A tear streaks her face. She wipes it away quickly, but just as quickly, more tears fall. She turns back to the person attending her burns, and to the man reaching to comfort her. She straightens her shoulders, takes a deep breath, and speaks words to them I can't hear.

Ty and Jade stand hand in hand, watching the Feral children mourn their leader. Ty releases her hand and hugs his shoulders, like someone trying to warm himself from the cold. Jade slides her hand around his lower back, pulls him close, and Ty relaxes, laying an arm across my sister's shoulders. Jayla is busy talking to a few people, probably other leaders. Their conversation is intense, but she's obviously in control.

I survey it all. See it all. The dead Feral carried off. Camila bandaged. Jayla organizing. My brother Samuel, mute these ten years, a brother I hardly know, just rode off to get help from the Sisters. And Jade. She turns to Ty, a good foot taller than her, she gazes up in his face. Their lips meet. It's tender. Intimate. He says something to her I can't quite make out, but then they both hurry to join Jayla.

Jade glances in my direction, and then turns back to the conversation. She tucks a strand of hair behind her ear and says something to Ty. She breaks off from the group and walks toward me. She stops, facing me, holds out her hand.

"Come on, *Valerian*," she says. A smile plays at her lips. "We've got work to do."

I give her my hand, she squeezes, begins to pull me toward her. I take a step forward, then another, until I'm walking with her in the direction of Jayla's planning circle. Jayla glances up at me when I arrive, asks me about the Antis. I tell them everything, truthfully.

The guilty will pay, surely. But it's not them I'm worried about anymore. It's the innocent. *Do I contradict myself?*

I contain multitudes.

# CHAPTER 26

# JAYLA

*THE BEST LAID PLANS.* That's the phrase that keeps rolling through my brain like some sort of God-awful sample loop played by one of the DJs in Galvez Plaza.

I have laid my plans and I do not accept defeat. Not now. Not yet. Not when there are so many possibilities left hanging like unanswered questions.

I sit at my desk. The Librarian's office. My office and *my* Library. Ty and Jade just left. They will mobilize the Hunters and also start to arm civilians. Guns have been scarce for some time. All our plowshares will have to work as swords for now. It'll be old-fashioned warfare, close, eye-to-eye; the kind where you smell the breakfast on your enemy's breath before you kill him.

Camila has improved. Lolita told me about that one. She'll make a very good Mother Superior one day. Santi is a good fighter, too, and he seems to follow Camila's every direction completely. We'll need them both to lead the civilians who volunteer to fight, and by volunteer, I mean everyone who *can* fight *will* fight.

Defenses are being erected. Cars are, at this moment, being

moved to provide a barricade around the Library's perimeter. The entrance to Third Street will be blocked with broken-down automobiles as well. We've had our war council and the dawn is on its way. We'll make our stand.

That leaves only Valerian, or Mason, sitting in a leather-backed chair on the other side of my desk, watching me watching him.

"Have you decided?" I finally ask. I sit back in my chair, leaning my elbow against the armrest.

He shoots the question back after a long pause. "Decided, what?" He glances behind me out the window over my shoulder. No doubt light is rising in the predawn sky.

"We are people of action," I say, "lies do not become us." I allow myself to smile and give in to a little chuckle. Valerian raises his eyebrows, confused. I lean forward, putting my fore-arms on the desk. "I'll tell you a secret." I lower my voice to a whisper. "That's from a movie. It's not a literary reference."

The young man on the other side of my desk shifts in his chair. "I'm not sure what you mean."

"Let me help you," I say. "I told you in this office not long ago who you really are. That Jade is your sister and Samuel is your brother." I push myself back from the desk and stand. "And *you* told me that you wanted nothing to do with Anton. What was the phrase you used? *Make the guilty pay*. Yes, well it seems you've started down that path, but you also wanted nothing to do with Jade or Samuel." I circle around to the front of my desk and move to the chair beside his, I sit and straighten my pants after crossing my legs. "So, who are you? Have you decided? Valerian...or...Mason?"

He closes his eyes for a moment, opens them. "I've always been Mason," he says finally. "But..." His voice falters. He turns his head and meets my eyes. "Valerian allowed me to survive, to find a home, some peace. Not everyone, or even most, of the

Antis are evil. They're just people, like me, clinging to something and someone who helps them make sense of the world's cruelty. And in exchange, they too learn to be cruel. Valerian allowed me to survive, but he also killed every ounce of the Mason I once was." He thinks, shakes his head slowly. "I'm afraid." He pauses, his voice catching in his throat. "I'm afraid that there are too many that will have to suffer for the guilty."

I nod. "I didn't want this war. Not yet, anyway. But it is here. It is coming to our door." I motion with my hand toward the window. He looks away, back toward the window and the new streaks of pink that paint wispy clouds on the horizon. "Children can spend their whole lives dealing with the consequences of their parents' unresolved issues." I lean a little closer to him. He looks at me. "I'll tell you another secret. That's not a quote from a book, either." I pause, letting him wait. "It's a phrase I remember your father said to me once."

"My father?" He narrows his eyes.

"Not that one. The other one. Your real father who died a decade ago."

He leans forward, arms hugging his knees, curling into a ball and rocking gently back and forth for a moment. His whole body shudders and he sits upright. "Call me Mason," he says with determination. "I've decided to be Mason."

"Alright, Mason," I say softly. I reach out with my feelings and can sense his internal turmoil. He's like an addict detoxing from ten years of shooting up.

Mason stands and paces for a moment, stops, and then sits again. "Anton and the force coming with him probably won't bring women and children." He turns to face me. "We have to think about those people, too. The non-fighters—mothers, sisters, daughters, sons. They are the ones I care about. It won't be easy."

"I understand." I stand up from the chair and lean on the

edge of the desk facing him. "A new world means growing pains." I reach down and take his hand. He looks up. "Fight with us and I will not forget the innocent."

Mason lets go of my hand, searches my face, trying to see the future. "We must win." He glances down at his feet and then stands. "Will we have help?"

"I hope so." I go around to the other side of my desk, open the drawer and take out a small handheld transceiver. "I need to rally the troops outside, Mason. And I need you to stay here for now."

He nods. "I know. The fighters in the plaza may not be ready to trust me." He clasps his hands behind his back.

I cross to the front of my desk. "Stay here for now and keep calling on the channel this is switched to." I hand him the hand-held and walk to a cabinet near one of my bookshelves. It's finished oak, an antique with brass handles. "But, I also want you to be ready when the fighting starts." I unlock the cabinet and motion Mason to join me. Inside are two swords—twin katanas, one set above the other on a wood stand. I give him one and take the other, using the loop tied to the sheath to sling it on my back. Mason takes his sword and follows suit. "When the fighting starts, I want you by my side."

Mason finishes adjusting the sword. "I'm not sure the people here will accept me."

"They accept blood. They accept sacrifice." I close the cabinet doors and Mason returns to my desk.

*The best laid plans*, I think as I exit my office and prepare to speak to my people, many of whom probably won't survive the day.

THE ELEVATOR DOORS slide open and I exit quickly. To my left, Bea sits at the circulation counter. She takes off her glasses, lets them hang from the chain around her neck, and stands. She pulls out one of the few guns we keep in the Library—a sawed-off shotgun—and pumps it once.

"Ma'am," Bea says with a small nod of her head. Light from the floor to ceiling windows illuminates her face. She's done her cat-eye makeup this morning. *War paint*, I think.

"Good luck, Bea," I tell her as I walk toward the exit.

An old F-150 pickup, several Hondas, and many other cars too mangled or burned out to discern the make and model have been pushed into the plaza as a barricade around the Library.

Ty greets me at the exit. "We're here. All of us." He turns and Jade walks up with a contingent of Ferals. Probably two dozen wild kids with clubs, sticks, anything they could get their hands on, mill about impatiently. A red-headed Feral called Boom-boom snaps orders at his troops. He's taken over as the new leader of the pack. He waves his pistol at the kids trying to get them to obey his commands.

The Hunters are mounted, their horses paw the ground and snort in place. At least two hundred men and women, civilians with axes, shovels, swords, and chains fix their eyes on me, waiting for me to speak.

Ty leans in next to me. "We've used the Watermark and the old Governor's Mansion for the too young and others who can't fight. Caregivers are with them."

"Good," I say.

"Ma'am," Jade interjects. She wears a black jacket and jeans and calf-high boots laced tight. Her blade is on her back. "A scout reported five minutes ago that the Anti force is on the move on North Boulevard. We don't have much time." She turns and says something to Ty I can't make out, then barks an order at a Feral to take up positions along the car-lined perimeter.

Camila and Santi arrange the civilian force on our left flank, protecting Third Street and the entrance from the River Road.

I walk out to the center of the patio that stretches from the Library to North Boulevard. The morning has almost fully arrived. There's no chill to the air, but it's cool and as the sun rises, fog begins to settle, limiting visibility beyond the barricade. "People of Baton Rouge," I say. My heart begins to beat faster. "People of The Wasteland." Ferals sit down ready to hear an Older speak. A young man puts an axe on his shoulder. It's silent. The muted sun, a yellow orb behind a cotton sky, glows above the corner of a building across the street. "This is our time. Today. We didn't choose this fight...but we will not run away from it."

"We are with you!" says a tall man, a teacher in the community. Others second him, but weakly. *I need to give them more.*

"I am Jayla, your Librarian." I scan the audience, my shoulders straight, thrown back in pride and strength. "A virus took our fathers and mothers. Our friends and lovers. But we defied the odds. We rebuilt. We turned the lights on."

"That's right, but *we* did the work!" shouts one of the refinery engineers. The crowd erupts in laughter, pent-up emotion escaping in fits and starts.

"That's right!" I shoot back, not missing a beat. "*You* did it. We all lean on everyone who has survived, and we have remade families, adopted children, and loved whomever we please." Two men not far from the barricade clasp hands. "But an enemy still remains out there who wants to destroy what we've built, who *will* destroy us if we don't fight back. What we've built will last." I unsheathe the sword from my back; a slight grinding accompanies its path and then it's free. "It must last." I take a few steps forward, turning to face all sides of our fighting troops. "There's a new world coming. Are you ready to see it?"

"Yes!" someone yells. Applause starts. The Ferals start to clap and chant in their sing-song: *Jay-la, Jay-la, Jay-la.*

"I am with you!" Jade yells. Ty begins to pump his fist.

"For our world to begin...the old world must end!"

*Yes! Yes! Yes!* The crowd begins to beat their weapons. Against the cars. Against the cement ground. The Ferals continue to chant in their wild language, something I can't make out.

I hold up my sword, blade upright, held above my head. Steel glints in the sun. Jade lifts her sword. Ty and the mounted Hunters as well. I let out a scream from deep inside. "FIGGGHHHT!"

"FIGGGHHHT!" the crowd yells back in unison.

And then, as if in reply, drums, Anti drums, begin to beat in the distance.

"Go!" I tell Ty and Jade. "Take up your positions." Ty mounts his horse, while Jade takes the Ferals and separates them into different squads. Camila and Santi form civilians with axes, shovels, and lead pipes into two skirmish lines behind the car barricade. The drums grow louder, but not from North Boulevard. They come from Third Street, which dead ends into North. *They might be coming from two directions?*

"They're approaching from Third Street," Ty yells from his horse. He tells the Hunters to divide into two groups, one on each side of the street. Horses weave around people who quickly reposition. Over the hoods of the car-lined perimeter, the Antis come into view, making their way toward the Library from Third Street.

Anton is out in front—apparently not dead—but directing his forces to create a battle line from which to make their assault on our position. *But, is this all their troops?* It appears to be a force about our size, weapons similar to our own. The masked and hooded figures clang together their steel and iron, their chains and pipes, their swords and knives.

The Antis have stopped advancing, but the drums are still beating. The sound of a motor, hardly noticeable at first over the thudding of drums, begins to cut through the beating and the twang of the clashing metal.

"It's a jeep," someone yells from our right flank.

All heads turn toward the sound of the motor, coming up North Boulevard. I catch Jade's eye and gesture for her to meet me at the North Boulevard perimeter. Before I can move a sickening *thwump-thwump...thwump-thwump-thwump* of machine gun fire begins to shred car plastic and aluminum to pieces—flesh and bone, too. The fighters taking up the North Boulevard position crumple to the ground, some cut in half. The man who yelled, who spotted the jeep, disappears as the machine gun starts a new barrage of bullets, laying waste to our defenses.

".50 cal. It's a .50 cal," one of the Hunters yells from across the plaza trying to find some cover.

Another barrage of bullets whizz like steel hornets through our lines. I drop to my knees and see Jade run for cover. The firing continues and behind Jade I look in horror as the first line of Antis advance, making their way to the car barricade on the Third Street side.

Manacled Twitchers are led to our perimeter and released. Above me, a voice yells. Up on the balcony, Mason is holding the handheld transceiver up. He yells my name but the .50 caliber *thwump-thwumps* again and Mason's voice is drowned out amidst the bullets shredding apart our forces and the cries of Twitchers overrunning our perimeter.

# CHAPTER 27

# SAMUEL

SISTER LOLA LEADS a dozen nuns armed with bo staffs toward downtown Baton Rouge. A dozen more acolytes are with us, each with their chosen weapon, slingshot, bo staff, or bamboo sticks. Zion walks beside me. He told me he had to come. He wouldn't take no for an answer. He tied his injured arm to his chest and signed that he only needed one hand for his slingshot.

*"Lucky you got shot in your left arm,"* I signed to him.

He took one stone out of his leather pouch tied to his belt and playfully tapped it against my forehead. I took a step back so I could see his smile. Leaning forward, I kissed him and hugged his neck. We will join this fight together.

* * *

I ARRIVED AT THE SISTERS' cloister on horseback in the middle of the night. Sister Lola, always with her sixth sense, was up and waiting for me. Said she knew something vital was happening. I signed that the Antis were coming, and there was an impending battle at the Library. Her usual open and bright countenance became drawn, worried. She went to wake the Sisters and the acolytes. An assembly met shortly after at Community Table.

"All of you must make a choice," she said, the musicality of her accent beautiful even when speaking gravely. "War is coming to The Wasteland and our way of life faces a dire threat."

I couldn't believe what I was hearing. Sister Lola always taught that violence had no role in the Way of Absolute Hospitality. Zion, standing beside me, looked as confused as I did.

"I confess to you all," Sister Lola continued, "that I have a personal stake in this fight for which I am prepared to sacrifice all." Her voice trembled. "I have a commitment to Jayla, the Librarian, even unto death, that I must, that I shall keep." A low murmur moved through the meeting hall. "I shall spare you theological justifications, there will be death and there will be killing. Only know that it is love I follow down this path and, perhaps, your love for me shall compel you to join me." The murmurs in the hall ceased. Silence hung in the room like the incense of prayer. "I leave it to each of you to search your conscience for the decision you must make. I have made mine. We leave within the hour." When we left the cloister, nearly all of Sisters and acolytes had decided to join us, come what may.

The memory of her words flash through my mind as Zion and I, along with Sister Lola, the nuns and the acolytes walk quickly through the area once called Beauregard Town to the East of downtown Baton Rouge. We had to double time it to get here, hoping we wouldn't be too late to reinforce Jayla's fighters. We thread through the neighborhood, weaving through side yards and backyards, across rubble-strewn roads, stopping at ruined cars and twisted trees.

The Anti drums begin to beat. I glance at Zion and he gives me an expression of disgust. Sister Lola has sheltered on the east side of what was once the city's stone courthouse building. Most of it was burnt out years ago and the stonework is crumbling at the top. The Anti drums are louder now and we hear cheers and shouts coming from the Library just a block or so away.

Sister Lola motions for me to join her across the street. I hop over an uneven pothole in the street and then skirt around a mangled BMW, it's flayed and flattened tires make it look like some sort of squashed insect. I crouch walk the rest of the way and put my back against the stone wall. Lola leans close. "We have the element of surprise, Samuel." I nod. "The Antis will think our forces are confined to the Library." She signals to the Sisters on her right and they head farther up the street to the north. Another series of signals are given to the Sisters on Lola's left and they head south.

Sister Lola opens her mouth to speak, but machine gun fire stops her and makes us all flinch. The base-metallic staccato of the gun drowns out the drums. I sign to Zion across the street to hurry and he quickly joins me next to Sister Lola.

"We need to move," Sister Lola says. The machine gun stops for a moment, then starts again. "Come with me."

We skirt the perimeter of the courthouse and turn west once we have a view of North Boulevard. We crawl the last half-block toward the street. The machine gun fires again and as we near the street we see two Antis standing in the back of a green jeep with a faded blue star on its side. The gun shaft sticks out over the passenger side of the vehicle. I sign *two men* with my fingers to Lola.

"We must take out the gun, Samuel, now." Lola's whisper is quiet but harsh. It has to be now and she wants me to go with her. There's a break in the firing and we hear the shouts of the injured, those fighting, and those dying.

Zion grabs my arm. *"Let me go,"* he signs. I shake my head.

There's another register of screams, wild ravings, like

animals, coming from the Library. *They must be using Twitchers again.* We crouch walk the last bit of the block through a yard of a house that fronts North Boulevard. Zion winces as he snags his arm on the branch of a bush that sticks out far enough from the porch to make our way difficult.

We finally reach the edge of the yard and scan to our left and right flanks. The Antis don't seem to have guards directly next to the jeep with the machine gun. Their forces are clustered on the far side of North Boulevard. I glance at Lola and know what she's thinking. There might be enough time to take out the gun before the Antis are able to make it across the street. Sister Lola was right, the Antis did believe all the forces would be at the Library. Bad assumption.

All along the hedgerow that makes up the boundary between the yards of houses and the street, I can see the red and white habits of the Sisters of Absolute Hospitality. Lola lifts her hand in a fist. And then extends an index finger. The signal is passed to the left and the right of us. It's the signal that no one is to move until she gives the command.

"Zion," Lola whispers. "Let the stones fly at those two on the jeep." She points at the two Antis. "We'll follow after." Sister Lola gives me a wink. Zion nods, going into his satchel and producing five smooth stones. Despite his wounded arm, he manages to put one projectile in the leather thong of the sling and holds the rest of the stones in the palm of his hand. He gets to his knees and twirls it above his head.

The *wiffle-sizzle* of the rock leaving the leather holder is our cue: Lola and I run for the two guards. The first stone hits the Anti working the trigger on the gun. Seconds later the next stone hits the Anti working the ammunition. Both stones make direct hits to the heads of the men, knocking their masks off.

With five yards remaining between us and the jeep, Sister Lola twirls her bo staff. I'm carrying nothing and mold my hands into fists. The men receive two more stone hits, which don't immobilize them but disorient the Antis enough for Lola to vault into the bed of the jeep with her bo staff. Lola lands behind the trigger man, who turns and is greeted by the crack of hard wood against his skull. He trips backward off the jeep and lands on the concrete of the street with a loud thud. I jump in the driver's side as the ammunition Anti watches his comrade hitting the ground.

From behind, I wrap my arm around his neck and squeeze off his windpipe. Lights out in ten seconds. I know he'll come to rather quickly, so I take one of the half empty ammo boxes and crash it down on his head. I roll his limp body over the side of the jeep and he joins his companion on the road.

Zion slips out of cover and Sister Lola gives the signal for advance. The Antis congregated on the other side of the street don't notice, as their attention is focused on breaching the barricade around the Library. The Sisters and acolytes move noiselessly toward the jeep.

"We need a driver and someone to work the gun," Sister Lola snaps in a hushed tone. "We need to take out the rear flank of the Antis." Sister Lupe, husky, and a force to be reckoned with, jumps in the driver's seat and two other sisters take up the machine gun post in the back. The jeep roars to life and across the boulevard we see Twitchers drawn to the sound. Sister Lola orders the jeep to move, and it's off, firing at the Antis and Twitchers across the road.

Lola smiles at me. "It seems *Diosito* wanted a special job for us," she yells over the report of the gun. She pats my shoulder and heads off across the boulevard and crosses the grassy median between the divided road. The Sisters and the acolytes follow after her. The machine gun barrages our enemies, quickly scattering those that are not already dying in the street.

Zion heaves a big sigh of relief seeing that I made it through safe. As we turn to start following Sister Lola and the others, the machine gun clicks. Jammed. Sister Lupe curses loudly, stops the jeep, and turns to help the nuns working the gun in the back of the vehicle.

Beyond Sister Lola, a masked figure levels an assault rifle in our direction. The click-click of the machine gun's trigger jamming must've drawn the Anti out of cover. Sister Lola gives orders to several acolytes, her back facing the man with the gun.

Everything moves in slow motion. I wave my hands in Lola's direction who, seeing the expression of horror on my face, turns toward the man with the assault rifle on the other side of the street. The report of the rifle cracks the air, cracks again and Sister Lola crumples to the ground.

Zion crouches, grabs a stone, loads it and, with a cry of rage, slings it at the masked shooter. It knocks the rifle askew, saving us from being shot next. Two Sisters fly to the man's position, disarming and immobilizing him with their bo staffs. Two bo staffs beat the man with the rifle again and again. The machine gun finally fires, unleashing hell on several Twitchers who appear from around the corner of a building.

*Lola. Lola, no.* My feet slog forward as if weighted by concrete as I run to her. I roll her to her side and my hands are wet with blood. Lola's eyelids flutter as she takes a rattling breath. Two crimson holes stain her white robe, the blood covering her stomach and chest. Lola draws a gurgling breath, as though she is drowning.

"Sam..." Lola tries to speak.

I can't. I don't reply. I have to find her eyes. Zion kneels beside me. He's taking off the cloth wrapped around his shoulder and arm. Something for the blood. There's so much blood.

"No," Lola says. "Finished....it's..."

I shake my head as a deep groan escapes my mouth. Sister

Lola's eyes open and then close. She struggles to breathe, using me as leverage to break the surface of her drowning, to pull her out. The rattle in her chest grows louder. She grabs my shirt, pulls me to her, her hand comes to my cheek. "Protect...Jayla..."

Her body seizes in pain, then relaxes. *"Te amo,"* she tells me and then: *"Diosito...Diosito..."* Her hand flexes once, twice, and then goes limp and her eyes, fixed on me for that long moment, widen and then she sees nothing. My head goes to her chest, and the Jasmine in her robe embraces me for the last time and I begin to sob.

Zion's hand lays heavy on my shoulder. The machine gun starts again and from the direction of the Library an explosion sends us sprawling for cover. The smell of burning metal and rubber descends over me, the scent of Jasmine disappears, and one of the Sisters yells that the Library is on fire.

# CHAPTER 28

# JADE

I HIT the pavement when the shooting starts. Seconds later, the windows of the library crash apart sending a spray of glass shards across the patio like water from a partially plugged up garden hose. There's a ricochet of bullets and the smell of gasoline leaking out of one of the perimeter cars. I crawl away from the gasoline and make it to a crumpled, red car.

"Jade! Over here." It's Jayla. She screams at me from the other side of the car. "Keep your head down!"

*Yeah, no need to tell me twice...*

I crawl toward her. Jayla's eyes go wide, then they narrow sparking with a kind of hatred I've never seen before. "Down!" she yells at me. I duck, and she uses her katana to slice apart a Twitcher just before it took a bite out of my neck. Jayla frees her blade, as I grip my sword and make sure no other threats are on top of us. "We're being overrun," she says. Jayla turns her attention up to the balcony and I follow her line of sight. Mason is on the balcony, crouched down behind the balustrade, waving a transceiver in his hand. "We've got to get back to my office, Jade."

"Now?"

Another burst of machine-gun fire and then it stops. Jayla and I peer over the crumpled, red car and the most beautiful sight in the history of the world appears. A flutter of robes. The disappearance of the Antis on top of the jeep with the machine gun. Sister Lola standing tall with bo staff in hand.

A dozen Sisters fan out to take control of the Jeep and I glance behind me, making sure there's not another Twitcher on my six. The Hunters have formed a skirmish line and our foot soldiers are holding off the Antis at the perimeter. A few Twitchers managed to overrun us like Jayla said, but Ty seems to have eliminated most of those who made it through.

"It's Lola," Jayla says. I turn back around toward where she's watching the action unfold on North Boulevard. A line of several cars block our way, but our view is unimpeded. Samuel and Zion run to catch up with Sister Lola. A pair of Sisters are firing the .50 caliber at the Twitchers on the other side of the road, bullets cutting them down like paper dolls.

Out of nowhere it seems, Sister Lola falls to the ground. "Oh, Jesus, no!" Jayla yells, her words catch in her throat. I follow the imaginary line from where Lola was standing to the other side of the street. An Anti. A gun. Sisters descend on the man. Samuel and Zion go to Sister Lola.

A voice comes from the balcony. "Jayla!!" Mason bellows at her to come.

"Jayla, we have to go."

"No," she suppresses a cry. She drops her sword, holds both fists to her temples, yells at the cement. She turns her back to the car and grasps her sword again.

"We have to go," I say again. "Mason is calling for you." Jayla studies me, her eyes full of anguish. "Samuel is with Lola."

Jayla glances back at the scene of Samuel holding Sister Lola, but then grits her teeth, forcing herself to focus on my words. "The transceiver. It's our reinforcements," she says. It's as if she turns off whatever flow of emotion that motivated her just moments before. She grabs my shoulder as the .50 caliber begins to work again on the Antis and Twitchers up North Boulevard. We run on a diagonal course back to the front of the Library.

When we're halfway across, we see to our horror, a force of Antis advancing from the River, up the hill and toward the Library. A long flat-bed truck pulls dozens of Anti fighters. Troops hop off, they light torches and then use the torches to light Molotov cocktails. *They're gonna set the Library on fire.* Two Antis sprint with lighted bombs in hand toward the Library entrance. We spring from our position to intercept them.

We surprise the first two Antis before they reach the Library. I go high and Jayla goes low and the pair slump to the cement patio of the Library--one without legs and the other headless. But six more are in pursuit as we make it through the entrance and duck in front of the circulation counter.

Bea comes up from the other side, shotgun blazing. The front line of Antis is blown backwards, which knocks the Molotov cocktails from their hands, blanketing the first-floor entrance in fire. Bea shoots again, pumps the shell free, but comes up empty. *Click.* Two Antis lunge at her and we manage to roll away just in time.

We stand to our feet and run toward the back stairway. A dreadful smack reverberates over our shoulders as we reach the door to the stairs and hope Bea can fend them off for a few seconds to give us a head start. The door is locked, but Jayla brings out the keys and we manage to make it inside before any Antis reach us.

"That should hold them briefly," Jayla says. "I made sure to switch the elevator off. This might buy us some time." We take the stairs two at a time. Jayla stumbles once and I help her up. "Oh, Lolita," she says under her breath.

"Samuel and Zion are with her." I try to comfort Jayla, but she just stares at me through grief-stricken eyes and shakes her head. We continue our ascent and burst through the door at the top of the utility stairs. We reach Jayla's office and Mason meets us at the door.

Mason holds out the transceiver and Jayla takes it from him without stopping and quickly goes to her desk. "It's something about final approval," Mason says. "I couldn't give it. They needed *your* approval." Jayla depresses the call button and speaks in French. She releases her thumb. Static. Jayla says something again. Static.

The transceiver comes alive. "*Oui, affirmatif.*" And then in English: "Troops landing."

Jayla's face lifts with hope. She turns to Mason and me. "Go through the tunnel. It will bring you out near the river."

"What's going on?" I ask.

Jayla puts the transceiver down. Her gaze smolders. "The Haitian Army. They're almost here." I stand in stunned silence as Jayla strides across the office toward her private quarters. She emerges a few moments later with a long black and green steel RPG. She loads the shoulder-held missile launcher on her desk. "We've got to hold off the Antis until they arrive." Jayla's face is a hard mask of determination. "Go!" she yells at us and turns toward her terrace with the RPG.

Mason and I run for the exit passage located behind the bookshelves and I hear the *whistle-whoosh* of an explosive projectile being fired down Third Street from the Librarian's balcony.

THREE MINUTES LATER, Mason and I are sprinting through a subterranean tunnel that runs under the Library to the Mississippi. The corridor is dark and narrow, weak fluorescents light the hall and it smells musky with mold. What looks like black living vegetation creeps out of multiple sections of the wall and the floor is wet with slick viscous liquid. It's as if we're running up the esophagus of some primordial monster, hoping it doesn't swallow.

"Keep running," I shout at Mason beside me.

"Yup." He eyes the floor, jumping over a slippery patch.

We make it to a pair of double doors and pray they're not locked. We slam into them and the doors open mercifully. A flight of utility stairs winds upward and then finally another set of double doors greet us. They don't budge at first. I give Mason a quick glance and he reads my mind. We backup to the top of the stairs and run together toward the doors. A quick, sharp pain flows through my shoulder but it's enough: we tumble through the doors and breathe fresh air.

We find ourselves on a raised concrete platform. We both grab our swords and try to get our bearings. One side has an outdoor staircase that leads down to the street. The other side is a bridge leading to the levee and the river.

On the surface of the water I glimpse a magnificent sight. Three long, flat barges glide on the river. They blow their foghorns. There's also a steel gray battleship with several long guns. A flag flies above the ship, enormous and waving in the early morning breeze coming off the river. It's bi-color, red and blue, with a crest in the middle that looks like a palm tree.

Boots on the pavement of the street below send us reeling to find a way to peer down. Streaming up the road toward the Library are soldiers in green fatigues. The same crest from the flag is worn by each as a patch on the shoulder of their uniforms. They carry semi-automatic weapons and march double-time up the hill. From our vantage point, we watch as the soldiers engage the Antis. There are shouts and then the *pop-pop-pop* of gunfire.

We fly as fast as we can down the staircase to the street. Haitian troops file by but take no notice of us at first. Then, a Black man wearing a beret who I assume is one of the commanding officers yells at us to halt. He levels his pistol at us.

I drop my sword and Mason does likewise. I lift my hands. "Librarian!" I yell trying to remember some of the French Jayla taught me. *"Bibliothécaire,"* I shout. He approaches warily. "I'm Jade." I hope Jayla remembered to tell them we were coming.

He drops his aim and summons a nearby soldier with a gesture of his free hand. He gives the subordinate a message and then turns back to us. "Let's go," he nods at us. "Pick up your swords," he says in accented English. "You'll need them."

We run with the commanding officer up the hill and stretched out before us is Galvez Plaza in full battle. The Sisters have joined the fight, their bo staffs twirling, robes whipping, beating back Antis and Twitchers as they overtop the western barricade. Mounted Hunters chase dozens of Antis down Third Street, the Antis turn toward the river in an attempt to escape but are met on the hill by the Haitians who mow them down with a hail of bullets.

The killing is quick and terrible. The fire in the Library grows bigger, burns hotter. Black smoke billows from the line of first-floor windows. A riderless horse streaks by Mason and me, its nostrils flared in fear and rage. Civilian fighters from The Wasteland hack at black-robed Antis like farmers breaking up fallow ground. Ty rides his horse lighting fast across the plaza, two Hunters following close behind. They wrestle with a fire-hose attached to the lower basement in a desperate attempt to put out the blaze.

As we move farther onto the plaza, Camila and Santi come

into view. They're fighting hand to hand with a group of six or seven Antis. Camila swings her staff with one arm, the other one injured, and held close to her body. Santi parries the attack of one Anti who swings a club at Camila's weak side. Santi's move saves Camila just in time, she pivots and her staff meets the face of the Anti, who falls to the ground.

But Santi's parry leaves him open to an attacker from behind whom he doesn't spot until it's too late. The Anti thrusts a sword through Santi's leg, he falls and a Twitcher runs up and clamps its jaws on the wound. Several Haitian soldiers intervene and kill the Antis and the Twitcher in a quick succession of gun blasts.

But it's too late.

Camila screams and then runs to Santi, who roars in agony. Camila calls for help. Several Haitians hold Santi down as he thrashes in anguish. *The Twitcher bit Santi's wounded leg.*

Camila wastes no time, understanding the terrible decision she has to make in order to save his life. She barks an order at one of the soldiers, then ties a tourniquet around Santi's thigh, and moments later a sword is brought to her. Camila's blade is swift, cutting Santi's leg off just above the knee, desperately hoping that the viral infection has not yet spread to his brain.

Santi lets out a pitiful yelp and passes out quickly from the pain. Camila and the soldiers immediately staunch the bleeding stump, tightening the tourniquet as fast as they can. A Haitian medic takes over and Camila holds Santi's bloodied hand.

"Hold on, Santi." Camila sobs. Several more soldiers arrive with a stretcher.

As I struggle to wrap my mind around the sight of Camila holding Santi in a pool of blood, Mason grabs my shoulder. "Jade," he says flatly, "It's Anton." I have to stop myself from helping Camila and Santi. I whip my head around toward where Mason is pointing. Samuel and Zion are carrying Sister

Lola, coming from the direction of North Boulevard, almost at the Library entrance.

In the foreground, Anton slinks into view. It's as if time stops. He strides toward the Library's entrance silhouetted in flame. I'm caught in a moment. It's a moment I've fantasized about—to face down the man who ruined my family. Turns out, it's a moment I never want to remember, but always will.

From behind Anton, Samuel sees Mason and me. He stops walking and Zion immediately takes Sister Lola wholly in his arms. Samuel pivots and runs toward the Library entrance; Mason and I follow suit, rushing toward the same point of convergence—Anton.

Anton doesn't check over his shoulder, doesn't see Samuel running toward him from behind. Anton fixes his gaze on Mason, only on Mason—the boy who he kidnapped, the boy who he loved as his own, the boy who he must now destroy. Mason is just ten feet away, a lamb rushing toward a ravenous wolf; in the end, nature and habit gain the upper hand. Anton pulls out his knife, and I know what he will do. My knees wobble slightly, but I can't stop, whatever happens. The serrated teeth of Anton's knife glint in the sun and with a grunt, Anton hurls it at Mason, the annihilation of the past borne on the point of a knife.

He drops. Mason. My brother falls to the ground. I don't have time to scream or think or hesitate. I inhale sharply, smoke burning my lungs, pain awakening me to my purpose. Revenge. *Kill Anton*, I think. *Kill him, now!*

Two yards behind Anton, Samuel slides on the pavement and kicks the black robed figure's legs out from under him and Anton lands hard on his back. He never saw Samuel coming. I unsheathe my sword; rage propels me forward. I wheel the saber once, lunge upward and land beside Anton, the blade pierces the middle of his chest. Anton's head and feet bow upward for an instant from the impact of the sword in his abdomen, then he lays flat.

His eyes go wide with fear and pain and confusion. "That's for my little brother you sonuvabitch." I twist the blade with both hands, Anton screams—half in pain, half in exaltation.

He bleeds.

And then he dies.

ANTON IS DEAD.

I watched life drain from his face, saw his black eyes dilate and then get that faraway look. The last thing he registered was me, my face alive, staring down at him. No remorse or pity or forgiveness for him. He said nothing. No last words.

It is done.

But there's no pleasure in it. My anger, the mask I wear like a second skin, sloughed off and exposed raw, red sadness. When his life was gone, his last breath exhaled into the void, there was nothing. There is nothing. No feeling for the living. For me. The living.

I used to think about finding Mason, avenging my parents, making it right. Hell, I used to dream about it. Then there would be an end to grief, some bit of peace. Something, I guess. But all I'm left with is another corpse. It's as if the last ten years have really not been about finding Mason, but about delaying the grief, avoiding the feeling I have right now. Loss and...

"Jade." A voice speaks my name from far away, like an echo down a long hallway, hollow and faint. I snap my vision up and Samuel's face hangs before me like a mirror. There's pain in his face, a reflection of my own. He reaches for me, puts his hand on my shoulders. *Was it Samuel who spoke?* A frown of confusion forms on my face.

"Jade." The voice comes again. It's not Samuel. Samuel motions behind me. I turn my head and against the wall of the Library, Mason sits with his back against stone, his hands are on his stomach. A bloody knife lays beside him. "Jade," Mason calls my name again. Smoke, gray and black, wafts over us from the entrance to the Library. The breeze from the river brings black billows and heat in thick patches and then it clears. I leave my sword lodged in Anton's chest, a burial marker for my life over the last ten years.

Mason coughs raggedly, wincing in pain as his body moves involuntarily, shaking slightly. Samuel and I rush over, kneeling on either side of him. "I'm ok," he says.

"Mason, oh shit." Someone has to help us. "We have to get some bandages." I yell for help. Samuel takes off his jacket and shirt, ripping a piece of cloth to use as a dressing.

"No, Jade. I'm ok," Mason says again. He coughs. "The wound's not so bad." He lifts his hand and a long, ugly gash in his side comes into view, but the blade only grazed him, only cut his flesh, no vital organs. Samuel ties a wide strip of cloth around Mason and cinches it tight. He winces but then takes a deep breath.

I check the bandage. It looks good. "Once we stop the bleeding," I say. "It'll heal." I try to lighten the moment. "It'll be sore as hell, but the Sisters can take care of that." I manage a wan smile.

Samuel swivels around searching the plaza for Zion, who is sitting with the body of Sister Lola across his lap. Zion studies her with love and sadness as if what is most beautiful in life can also be most brutal. It immediately reminds me of a sculpture I saw once in an art book at the Sisters' cloister: Jesus dead in the arms of Mary, his mother.

The image of Ty holding Bey-Bey, Camila holding Santi, and Zion holding Sister Lola all merge in my mind's eye and I see myself, small, a child held tenderly by my own mother. But the face I recognize is not Sarah's—not my birth mother. It's someone else. The mother who raised me from the time I was thirteen.

From the direction of the river, Jayla's voice reaches me. She speaks in French to the officer wearing the beret. She must've left the Library through the tunnels, too. The fire cut off any other exit from the first floor.

Jayla spots Zion holding Sister Lola. "Oh, God, no. No!" She runs to Zion and drops to her knees, laying over Lola's body. Jayla sits up, pulls Lola across her own lap and deep sobs roll over and through her.

"Jade." Mason's voice calls me again. I turn away from Jayla's grief and catch my brother's attention. He shakes his head. "It's time for me to go."

Samuel uses both palms of his hand to sign, "*What?*"

"What do you mean?" I ask Mason. I search his face. I don't understand what he's trying to say. Or, I don't want to understand.

Mason shifts his weight and I can tell his side hurts, but the bleeding seems to have stopped. "I have to go back to the camp," he says. "I already talked it over with Jayla."

"No," I say sharply. "You can't."

"Yes, Jade." He starts to nod his head. "I have to."

"I won't let you."

Mason smiles at that.

Samuel let's out a sigh, he turns to watch Jayla and Zion weeping over the body of Sister Lola. Samuel glances back at Mason. He takes Mason by the chin to get his attention. "*I love you,*" Samuel signs with the I-L-Y arrangement of his hand. "*But, I understand.*"

"Samuel," I translate for Mason, "says he understands. But I don't. We just found you. You helped us..."

Mason cuts me off. "That's why I have to help the ones left in the camp." Mason gestures at the plaza. "Look around you, Jade. All the older Antis are dead. Take off the masks of many of these Antis and you'll find kids. Some twelve or thirteen years old." The thought of dead teenagers turns my stomach. The bodies on the patio of the Library are being carried like rag dolls by green-fatigued soldiers. They're stacked one on top of the other. "There are women and children and kids back at the camp," Mason continues. "Kids like me. Like I was." Mason shakes his head again. "I can't abandon them, and we can't live here. Not yet, anyway. Too much hatred. Too much bad blood."

Samuel nods. He nudges me. "*We have to let go,*" he signs.

Mason turns his head to face Samuel. "Go on," Mason says. "You need to go to Jayla and Zion." Samuel nods *OK,* he leans his forehead against Mason's forehead, pauses for a long moment, and then backs away. Samuel stands and then turns and sprints toward Zion and Jayla. Sister Lola's body is covered with a robe, several nuns pray over her, and Samuel embraces Zion.

I turn my attention back to Mason and he starts to lift himself up the wall, his back pressed against the stone for support. I grab his arm and help him to his feet. He steadies himself. "Jade," he says. "Give us time." He runs his fingers through his long hair. The snake tattoo on his temple eats its tail. "You need to go, too." Mason motions behind me.

I turn around and see Ty standing there, relief in his face. He holds the reins of his horse and starts to speak but before he can get a word out, I barrel into him, wrapping my arms around his waist, burrowing my head into his chest.

I'm dimly aware that Ty's horse trots away, but he just holds me in silence, unconcerned. I breathe him into me, taking in his life, his strength. I pull away, locking eyes with him, our fingers braided together. *I need to talk to Mason.* I turn back to my brother and—

He's gone. The wall where my brother was a moment before is empty. A few smudges of dark red remain, the only evidence that he'd been there.

"Should we go after him?" Ty asks. The question hangs there with the weight of years. It feels like someone asking whether I'm going to keep carrying a backpack filled with stones, or whether it's finally time, whether I'm ready, now, to leave the stones behind. To walk on without them.

A memory of my dad flashes in my mind. I remember once, while training, he had me spar with him while carrying rocks on my back. He kept adding more and more to my bag until I finally couldn't stand up. I remember I started to cry. He bent down, lifted the bag off my back, and started emptying the rocks. *"When the stones are too big to carry, it's time to build an altar."* I didn't understand what he meant back then; I was only twelve. But now...

"No," I say and turn back to Ty. "No, we're not going after him." I put my arm around his waist. Ty lays his arm across my shoulders. We walk, together, toward Samuel and Jayla and Zion. The Sisters are already preparing Lola's body for transport back to the convent. We pass Anton and I stop, reach for my sword, pull it from the dead man's chest, and drop it with a clatter to the pavement. Ty leads me by the hand the rest of the way as we join the others, mourning for those we've lost in The Wasteland.

# CHAPTER 30

# JADE

SISTER LOLA WAS BURIED under the spreading branches of one of the live oaks she had planted on the grounds of the convent she called home. Jayla shaved off her locs in mourning. She said nothing during the ceremony, just held my hand tightly. I started to ask about her relationship to Lola—I had never guessed at their connection—and she just shook her head.

"I can't," she said. "Not yet." The words began to catch in her throat and she just squeezed my hand tighter.

Samuel, Camila, Santi, and Zion helped lower her cypress coffin into the ground. The Haitian colonel attended but the Sisters made him surrender his weapons in order to enter the convent grounds.

Samuel has decided to stay with Zion and help Camila, who seems poised to one day take over for Sister Lola when she's ready. For now, Sister Lupe will be caretaker of the community. Santi's leg is healing. He's shown no signs of the Twitch. But since the Battle of the Library, he's changed. It's as if the light he once radiated has been snuffed out. His relationship with Camila has all but ended before it had time to really begin. He blames her for taking his leg. I overheard a tense conversation between them.

"I'd rather have died on that plaza," he told her, "than live without a leg."

"I'm so, so sorry, Santi..." She reached out to comfort him, but he just brushed past her on his crutches.

I don't think they've spoken since. Camila is strong and resilient, but lines of concern crease her face, the cares of the community pulling her down. Every day for the last two weeks that I've been at the cloister, I see her returning from prayer at Sister Lola's shrine. She feels a weight of responsibility for Santi, but also for the community itself. She's searching for something and I hope she finds it. I empathize with her. I spent ten years on a mission running from grief. I have a suspicion it won't take Camila nearly that long.

It doesn't surprise me that Samuel wanted to stay, but, God, I'm not ready to leave the Sisters without him. I've decided to just take off without saying goodbye. It's better this way. Ty has our horses saddled and ready to head back to The Wasteland. I slip out to meet him. As I'm placing my foot in the stirrup of the horse, I feel a hard tap on my shoulder.

"No, Samuel," I say without even turning around. I know it's him. "I'm gonna see you soon." I proceed to mount my horse. Once done, I look down at him and he just smiles at me.

He signs, *"Well, who knows?"*

"You better come visit me." I take my foot out of the stirrup and shove him playfully backward with a little kick.

*"Hey, watch it,"* he signs, his exaggerated grimace quickly melting back into a smile. He holds up his pinky and winks at me. *"I promise,"* he signs.

Instead of grabbing his pinky, I lean down and grab his neck instead. "I don't know what I'm gonna do without you," I whisper. He pats me kindly on the back and starts to squeeze, almost knocking me off the horse. "Samuel!" I yell at him and then we both start to laugh. *Better to laugh than cry*, I think. He steadies me and helps push me back upright on my saddle. I hold out my pinky and he wraps his around mine. "You promise?" I point at him. He nods. "Remember, it's forever."

Ty says goodbye and Samuel holds up the I-L-Y sign to us, then turns his hand toward Ty replacing the sign for *I love you* with a solitary middle finger. He starts to crack up and Ty just shakes his head, letting his frown turn into a smile, while Samuel waves goodbye.

I spin my horse to follow Ty and then shout over my shoulder: "You pinky promised, Samuel. Don't forget!"

***

SIX WEEKS LATER, my days are full. We had casualties in The Wasteland. We buried Bea, who died at her post at the circulation desk protecting the Library. The Haitian soldiers help remove debris, bury the dead, and start the process of cleaning out the burned first floor of the Library. The Haitians, I learn, are actually part of the United Caribbean States, which has been growing in strength and influence over the last five years.

They're here to stay, it seems. It was part of Jayla's plan to simultaneously establish The Wasteland as a northern port city of the UCS and also wipe out Anti power in the gulf south.

"Oil," Jayla says about the UCS. "They want our oil." Then she scowls at me. "But if they want our oil, they will have to listen to me, too." She smiles and chuckles to herself. Jayla and the Colonel often butt heads. And they often end their conversations, always in French, yelling at one another. "It took long enough," I heard Jayla say recently to the Colonel. "Just two hundred years!" The Colonel rolled his eyes and Jayla left the meeting in a huff.

What comes next? It remains to be seen. Ty and the Hunters are still needed, and I go out with them from time to time. The Twitch still plagues us. The older you get, the greater chance you have to develop the disease. There's never been a cure. And Ty has mentioned strange behavior from Twitchers on recent encounters—as if their behavior is not strange enough...

But there's hope.

No word from Mason. The Anti camp in City Park is gone. Mason is gone. The Colonel says he heard word of a group moving West, which was made up of mainly women and children. But no robes. No plague masks. It's just a group of survivors, the Colonel tells me.

I miss my brothers. I believe I'll meet Mason again. When he's ready. When we're all ready.

---

TY CLEARS his voice behind me, and I turn. He holds out a small daisy. I'm finishing my daily rounds, overseeing a lot of the reconstruction work.

"*Pour moi?*" I ask, smiling coyly and placing a hand on my chest.

"Well, Jayla asked me to come get you and, well, I saw it growing up between a crack in the cement as I walked over here."

"Well, thank you, Captain," I drawl, batting my eyelashes at him, playing the damsel for a moment. I cross to him and, standing on my tiptoes, kiss him lightly on the lips. He leans in for a deeper kiss and I push him away, playfully. I grasp his face with both hands. "But, next time I want a Wild Aster." *Then,* I let him kiss me.

Ty pulls back, squinting at me. "It's always something with you."

"How about we get a drink after I go speak with Jayla?" I suggest through a doe-eyed smile. He nods, smitten, and then I let him kiss me again.

---

FIVE MINUTES later I'm climbing the utility stairs of the Library toward Jayla's office. The elevator's still offline and the Library still reeks of stale water and old smoke. I reach the top floor and stop briefly at the door to Jayla's office. I peer in and see Jayla with a book in front of her on her mahogany desk. She glances up, motions me to come in, and then returns her attention to the page. I open the door and walk along the crimson carpet running from the entrance to her desk.

"Ty said you wanted to see me."

She puts up a finger while she reads. "Hold on."

I cross my arms over my chest and wait. Around Jayla's neck is a small cross necklace; the bead that used to be woven into her locs is now strung next to it. She reaches up and absentmindedly tangles her fingers in the chain, holding the bead and the cross lightly.

Jayla finishes reading and glances up at me. I raise my eyebrows, giving her a slightly annoyed expression.

"Walk with me out on the balcony," she says.

I follow her to the terrace. Late afternoon is turning into evening and below us the construction work is finishing up. It's dinnertime. People are returning to their homes, their loves, their nightly routines. To life.

"Let's just wait a moment," Jayla tells me. She puts her hand on the balcony railing and I do likewise. "What will you do now, Jade?" She pauses a moment, then studies me. "A lot of the work is almost finished." I turn and catch her gaze. "More windmills to chase?" Her eyebrows lift in a question.

I turn back toward our view of the city. "No," I say. "The Librarian is rebuilding her Library." My eyes flash in her direction. I hold out my hand. She puts hers on mine. "And I hear she needs help from her daughter to do it."

"Ah, yes," Jayla nods. "That would be perfect." A light smile plays about her lips. "Just so long as my daughter hasn't lost her taste in good literature."

I start to reply, something snarky, then bite my lip. I think better of it and say instead: "I'd love to hear *all* the Librarian's suggestions."

Hand in hand we gaze together at the deep reds and purples of a darkening sky, watching over *our* city, plotting its future, as twilight rolls across the horizon.

I remember it was in the chaotic days—the panic-stricken days—of March 2020. My wife and I were in bed. We'd put the kids down. Finally. A moment to rest. To breathe.

But we were busily reading the latest news about the novel Covid-19 virus. It wasn't, in other words, very relaxing. New cases of the sickness had appeared everywhere. China had over 80,000 cases. Italy was on lockdown. Every country in the EU. Then-President Trump halted air travel from Europe. Colleges and universities were putting instruction online. Students with little means, and international students, were kicked out of dorms. Officials dawdled and conferred. Little action was taken. Presumptive positives went from one to four—then from six to sixteen, virtually overnight.

"What if this is the way the world ends?" my wife said to me while looking at her smartphone.

"I've been thinking the same thing."

We both continued to doom-scroll. To click. To read. It seemed a real possibility in those days. My mind began to spiral.

The book you just read was the result. Now, with hindsight, we can look to the past pandemic as an era of tireless heroic action by our frontline health professionals. The real heroes. And there are the vaccines, the masks, the social distancing. Humanity is both more robust and more tenacious in its will to thrive in the midst of adversity than I have perhaps expressed in these pages. But, like a child standing before an old shut up wardrobe in an empty room, unaware of what it contains, we still fear the world we might access in the coming days, months, and years. This book was my song of hope, a prayer I could repeat, a whisper in the dark. *Go ahead, step through, it will all turn out ok, in the end.*

Many thanks are due to those brave souls who traveled on the book journey with me. Line by line, the writer Noelle Allison edited the manuscript. She reminded me what characters should've said in the manuscript, which I hadn't yet figured out. She provided suggestions on how to make dull prose pop. With painstaking love and attention, she corrected grammar and style. It's a debt I'm sure I can't pay, but I promise to do likewise when given the chance. Jesse Allison offered encouragement and the always troubling question that made me realize an oversight. Jason Glaspey ignored our decades-long friendship, which might have made him spare my ego, and provided the honest feedback that I needed. James Wilkey believed I could write a novel before I believed it. Deranged Doctor Design made an amazing cover. Stacey Glemboski copyedited the manuscript. Jared Chapman of Apotheosis Press inspired me to revise. Any mistakes that remain are my own. Thank you to all my beta readers. As always, Sarilyn has my heart.

~ Stephen J. C. Andes

**Thank you for reading my book!**

I sincerely hope that you enjoyed the first book in my *Jade, Daughter of the Wasteland* Universe, as much as I enjoyed writing it. I've been a story-teller for as long as I can remember, always writing stories that I want to read and creating worlds that I want to see. My hope is that you will like them as much as I do.

I truly appreciate getting feedback on my work. Please consider leaving me an honest review on Amazon, as word-of-mouth is the best way people can learn about new and wonderful books to read.

If you see any issues (typographical, grammatical, or otherwise) or have questions, concerns, criticisms, please feel free to email me:

steveandes@gmail.com

*Amethyst's Secret*

Book II in the Daughters of The Wasteland

Amethyst has a secret she can't tell her mother, Jade. Twitchers have been speaking to her and what they have to say has the power to change everything.

The end of the world was only the beginning.

———

For updates you can sign up for my email list:

https://zorrosghost.com/stephen-andes/

Stephen J. C. Andes is the author of *Zorro's Shadow: How a Mexican Legend Became America's First Superhero*. A native of Portland, Oregon, he lives in Louisiana with his wife and three kids.

www.zorrosghost.com